THE PROPOSITION

He was sitting in his car behind a dumpster outside a blues bar being lifted on its foundation with the sounds of a saxophone and the smell of hashish. Monty yawned, closed his eyes. The SIG model 228 was now snug over the car's sun visor, inches from his reach. The baby Browning was monitoring his pulse from a strap around his wrist. The music lulled him. He nodded off.

Something opened his eyes. Not a sound, not a touch, not even a shadow. The blues music had stopped. Nobody mingled under the single glare of the parking lot light just beyond him. Something smelled strangely clean and sweet.

She said only, "Hi," from behind him, and then a plume of blue-gray smoke shot over his shoulder.

He whipped around, the Browning straight between her brows like a flaming arrow.

They were speechless an eternal thirty seconds. From the bar someone screeched a jazzy version of "Betcha, By Golly Wow."

"I was wondering," she said, and her red shiny lips made firefly patterns in the neon blinks, "if you would kill me, please."

Killer Gorgeous

Jane Holleman

POCKET BOOKS
New York London Toronto Sydney Tokyo Singapore

This book is a work of fiction. Names, characters, places and incidents are products of the author's imagination or are used fictitiously. Any resemblance to actual events or locales or persons, living or dead, is entirely coincidental.

An *Original* Publication of POCKET BOOKS

POCKET BOOKS, a division of Simon & Schuster Inc.
1230 Avenue of the Americas, New York, NY 10020

ISBN: 1-4165-0188-6

This Pocket Books paperback printing May 2004

10 9 8 7 6 5 4 3 2 1

POCKET and colophon are registered trademarks of Simon & Schuster Inc.

Cover photo by Alexa Garbarino/Photonica

Printed in the U.S.A.

The unyielding faith that went into making this novel is respectfully dedicated to my children, Sarah, John and Blythe. No matter what else I may accomplish in my life, they will be the best thing I'm ever wise and lucky enough to create.

Killer Gorgeous

1

Maybe a razor blade. No, too painful. How would a girl who couldn't stand a finger prick at the doctor's office expect to slash her own wrists?

Pills. She sighed. Sipped the vodka with some tonic water accidentally spilled in it. Pills would make her vomit. No beautiful, elegant society babe like Allison Robbins would be found dead with puke dried in her golden hair. Her golden hair. She picked up a piece of it ladled over her slender salon-tanned shoulder and twirled a tress. She saw it through a growing haze of intoxication. A throaty laugh belched from her that could just as easily have been a bleat of pain.

Like a tough broad who'd just climbed off a Harley-Davidson, she clinched the cigarette between her teeth and untangled parts of the tress from a delicate chain that lay against her milk-white cleavage. If the chain broke, then the paperweight of a diamond the chain might fall into the hand-dyed marshmal of a carpet in the Chippendale prison of her em historical landmark of a house. The smoke from cigarette curled into her Garbo brown eyes. The came free. The chain held. The diamond plunked back snugly into the crack between her perfect, luscious, augmented breasts. She swigged vodka again, lost a foot on the bar stool where she sat at her living room's art deco bar of inlaid Italian tile.

Fuck, she muttered. Not about the slipping foot or the high-heeled shoe that dropped off her pedicured pinkies or the music she'd put on that blared so loudly the G. Harvey originals vibrated on the walls. She muttered "fuck" because she had thought of running her car full speed into a wall. Then she realized she could chicken out and not do the full deal, and then she'd end up only paralyzed or something.

She perked up, had a moment of bleary optimism. A gun. That no good son of a bitch hotshot lawyer husband of mine has a fucking arsenal in that walk-in safe. She slumped again. The strapless red leather Valentino minidress made a crinkling sound like someone hoisting onto a saddle.

Shooting yourself is so pedestrian, she thought warily. Past presidents of the Junior League do not kill themselves the same way women in trailer homes kill themselves. She spoke to her lovely and petite if somewhat haggard reflection in the mirrors behind the bar where she sat. And with these damned acrylic talons of mine, she mused while Joni Mitchell crooned at painful decibels, how could I even get a grip on the trigger?

She sloshed Absolut into Waterford. Fuck the tonic. Fuck women in trailer homes. Fuck that nanny up there with my children, making them laugh like that, like a congo line of Casper ghosts dancing down the spiraled staircase. She stared a moment at the mountainous stained glass that lined the stairs. She could go [illegible] there and fire the bitch, point a bloodred claw at [illegible] door, plunk out some of the hundred-dollar bills [illegible]er Gucci jeweled evening bag, send that sorry [illegible]ny with the stiff collar packing.

[illegible]e looked away from the spangles of colors that

seeped through the stained glass from the setting blob of sunlight. The Waterford was cool when she pressed it against her forehead. The Caspers twisted at her muscled calves and thin ankles like cats that wanted just a touch. Her children.

The first hot tears squirted out but not down, because she wiped quickly with a linen embroidered napkin so as not to mess up her eye makeup.

Hang herself? She didn't know how to tie a noose. Drink herself to death? She actually laughed, having already tried to do that slowly now for thirteen rotten years of marriage. Electrocution? Drop a radio in the bathtub? No. Hell, no. The no-good son of a bitch hotshot lawyer had everything in the house built in, stereos that slid out of walls, TVs flush with cabinets. She'd have to go buy a damn jam box at a mall. She applied lipstick onto the Playboy centerfold likeness of herself in the mirror.

Jody came every morning to do her hair and nails. Maybe she could get him to accidentally leave a blow-dryer or curling iron. She could get drunk, make a big bubble bath, sit down naked, and . . . clunk . . . sizzle in her own soup.

Here? In the caverns of the master suite that she shared with the master motherfucker? In that spa he'd designed that made most common bathrooms look like gas station urinals? In a bathroom with a whirlpool and a sauna and a steam room and cable TV and multilines on the telephone by the toilet and a wet bar and a shower with four nozzles? No. It would be like dying on a movie set.

Four nozzles. Yeah. Like without money, like with just his charm and wit he could get three chimps to play sex games in the shower, much less three women. Or even one wife.

The Waterford stem broke when she set the glass down too hard. She chucked it into the trash under the scrolled and sculpted cabinets, carelessly plucked another one.

Poison? She brushed her hair, lifted it, and then let it flop down her curvy, defined back muscles now bared by the nasty little red dress. When was the last time someone had dragged a sensual finger along the tones and nuances of muscle definition she worked so hard to get every day?

Oh, yeah. Last summer at her high school reunion. She went alone, the cutest, sexiest, skinniest, friendliest forty-year-old nobody in the room. That idiot boy she'd dated in high school took her home with him. Even with his cock buried in her, lavishing her with compliments about her perfect body, she had only been in it for the rocking motion.

Cock or not, being rocked back and forth felt good.

Poison? She slapped on a lynx fur, started out the beveled glass bay doors down the long circle of a drive. Then she halted. A thought hit her like the blip of lightning that kicked its toe at the darkening horizon.

She had a million dollars in life insurance. It's not like her kids would ever need money—their goddamned bastard of a lying daddy would see to that—but maybe if she was worth something to them in death, then he wouldn't be completely able to convince them she was a zero in life.

Fuck self-pity. The Jaguar moaned to a start and in total civil disobedience, she set the sloshing Waterford right on top of the heap of a lynx in the seat beside her.

A cowboy in a mammoth truck on the highway almost crashed trying to get a look at the blonde vision in the exquisite car. She barely touched the accelerator and the cowboy was a blown-away leaf.

She played a tape. Loud. Rock and roll. To drown out the echoes of her precious children laughing without her.

2

Monty Ray Jones pulled the trigger, and a sweaty fat white boy's head exploded as if Monty had done nothing more than blow on a dandelion. The splatter of brains and bone went all backward, onto the peeling wallpaper of the sleazy apartment. Not a drop on Monty Ray.

That's what he liked about his sawed-off double-barreled shotgun with the self-cocking hammer, which he loaded almost reverently with buckshot before he made a kill.

The boy had soiled his pants just after Monty put him on his knees and made him suck on the cold black double barrels. It had distorted the boy's face. Before the kid was decapitated at Monty's steady black hands, the kid had appeared to be puffing like a blowfish, a blowfish with snot running down onto his lips, and pupils like pinholes.

Then there was the smell, the defecation, the body's last fearful surrender when all other hope of living was gone. Monty had smiled. He practiced smiling like Dracula, lifting his top lip in a sort of scowl and narrowing his eyes like Clint Eastwood. When he did it, Monty himself looked to be straining mightily to defecate, but he was working to make the whole effect more scary. The trigger almost pulled itself when the smell came.

Monty imitated Darth Vader, still trying to look like Dracula and Clint Eastwood, when he growled, "You did what I told you not to do, boy. It ain't like I heard it or thought I saw it or fell for no bad information. I seen you, boy, with my own eyes, doing what I told you not to do."

The boy wept. With the gun barrels in his mouth he could only shoot mucus out his nose. His hands were tied behind his back. He wet himself first. Monty heard it and then felt the warmth spill near his Belgian suede loafers, stepped back. Then the shit came, and Monty felt so sorry for the kid's fear that he just pumped. One shot. Simple as swatting a fly.

He abandoned Darth Vader and went for the Isaac Hayes effect as he stood over the body. As Super Fly, Monty breathed out, "Don't nobody sell none of Mojo's blow to junior high school kids. I told you that when you bought my shit."

He had touched nothing in the stupid male whore's dilapidated slum of a government apartment. Down the dark stairs he stepped over one crumpled human and on his way out of the broken glass door held it open for an old woman carrying a bicycle tire as if it was a trophy she had won.

In two minutes he was back in his Coupe de Ville, double barrel under the front seat. He straightened his tie, checked his gold cuff links, dug an orange Tic Tac out of the breast pocket of his Armani suit, popped it into his mouth, crunched, started his car, and adjusted the rearview mirror.

Nobodies. Refugees. They dared not notice him. Two whores congregated under a streetlight, passing a joint, having given up long ago on hitting on Monty when he passed through the ghetto neighborhood. A white guy with his pants on backward and his baseball cap on backward and his dumbass gaze straightforward waited for his dealer and pretended not to have seen Monty or heard the shot. Some old black men malingered outside a barbecue joint that had long ago stopped smoking anything but cheap dope in the cooker. They were drunk, skinny, and toothless and didn't give a shit about anything but getting drunker. The Coupe made no sound when Monty started it and drove away.

The lights of the makeshift downtown hit the hood of his car like a bouquet just beginning to die out in the wet air.

Pawnshops. Dry cleaners. Fried chicken joints. A florist. A black lawyer's office. An oriental grocery store. A coffee shop. A twenty-four-hour adult movie theater. A second-hand furniture shop. An Army Navy store. A big bank as black inside as if it had sunk under murky water. Some restaurants that all had Home Cooking signs in the windows. Bars named after numbers. The 2400 Club. The 512 Club. The 50-50 Tavern.

They were strung together like stinky fish left to rot on a forgotten trot line. Every window on every storefront was as thick with bars as if there were prisoners inside. Fact was, Monty knew, the proprietors wanted to keep out the ex-cons and criminals that lurked outside.

The Platters syncopated on the radio. Monty cranked the volume. "Only you . . ."

At the drive-through window the grotesque white woman with skin like an alligator and hair like a yard weed slipped him some chicken wings in a drawer that popped out so she was safe behind the glass. He set his money down in a stain of grease and fried chicken skin bits. His change was grimy when the drawer popped back out. He would've thanked her but she ducked when he held up a hand just to ask for an extra jalapeno pepper. She screamed at the mere lift of his hand. He drove away slowly, shaking his head as he munched a wing.

Up the lazy river of human slime he went. Through

prisms of neon light and dope smoke and distant gunfire. A cop in a cruiser beside him at a light gave Monty a so-called icy stare. The cop seemed to be imitating Stallone, so Monty imitated Jack Benny. A shrug, a hand in the air, a chicken wing clamped in greasy lips. The cop hit the lights and siren and fishtailed away. Monty hit the windshield wipers and laughed.

"Smoke gets in your eyes." The Platters again. From the briefcase that held his Sig model 228, which could shoot thirteen rounds of ammo as fast as Monty could pull the trigger, which was about eight times a second, and which was loaded with federal hydra-shock ammo, from this briefcase he pulled a moistened Handy Wipe to clean the chicken grease off his hands.

He was sitting in his car behind a Dumpster outside a blues bar being lifted on its foundation with the sounds of a saxophone and the smell of hashish. Monty yawned, closed his eyes. The cocaine was beside him on the seat. The money for it would be outside at the band's first break in just over fifteen minutes. The 228 was now snug over the car's sun visor, seconds from Monty's reach. The baby Browning was monitoring his pulse from a strap around his wrist. The music lulled him. He nodded off.

Something opened his eyes. Not a sound, not a touch, not even a shadow. The blues music had stopped. Nobody mingled under the single glare of the parking lot light just beyond him. For one vacuum of a moment, Monty felt alone on the planet. Something smelled strangely clean and sweet.

His voice sounded hollow. "What?"

She said only, "Hi," from behind him, and then a plume of blue-gray smoke shot over his shoulder.

He whipped around, the Browning straight between her brows like a flaming arrow.

They were speechless an eternal thirty seconds.

From the bar someone screeched a jazzy version of "Betcha, by golly wow."

"I was wondering," she said, her red shiny lips making firefly patterns in the neon blinks, "if you would kill me, please."

"How'd you get in here? How'd you get in my fucking car?"

She pressed her dainty forehead against the gun to lean forward and put out her cigarette in his backseat ashtray. "I opened the door, you moron. You were passed out drunk."

"I do not drink," he said, feeling insane. He cocked the gun. She moved around as if it wasn't following her skull, making a circle on her ice white skin. "Sit still, bitch."

"Okay, just give me a light."

She couldn't hurt him. Jesus H. She didn't weigh much more than a hundred pounds, and in that tight red dress she couldn't jump him anyway. They stared each other off, he with the Browning now starting to waver as the length of her crossed legs gelled in his sight. The dress was no longer than a minute.

She cocked the cigarette between her pouty lips. Her voice was someone walking on gravel. With her teeth—expensive teeth, Monty noted to himself—she wiggled the cigarette up and down.

"A light, please?"

"Say what?" He was waiting for the other shoe to drop, for the cops to jump from the bushes and ambush him for kidnaping a rich white girl, for her to whip out some goddamned rocket launcher and blow his ass sky-high. But she only brought one willow of a hand up to the cigarette and batted black lace eyelashes at him.

"Before you kill me, I'd like you to light this cigarette."

He laughed, a mixture of Eddie Murphy and Rock Hudson. "Bitch, get outta my car." He lowered the

Browning, wiped sweat off his eyebrows and his upper lip. She was still there when he stopped rubbing his eyes.

She dropped a high heel and hit the backseat lighter with her stockinged toes. It flamed when she touched her smoke with it. "You're a negro, aren't you? You're in a bad part of town. You have a gun. So. Kill me and rape me. Please."

"In that order, you say?"

She leaned her head back on the seat. Her throat flowered like a white daisy. "Preferably."

"I don't fuck white girls," Monty tried.

She closed her eyes. "Rape isn't fucking."

"And I don't fuck drunks. You're drunk."

"So don't fuck me. Just murder me. You people do it all the time."

"Us people?"

"Black men. Like you."

He found himself whining. "You know, lady, I mostly like to kill people who are begging me not to. I don't usually murder somebody because she just out and out orders me to fucking do it. Have I been sucked up onto a spaceship? Who are you?"

She let out a sigh. He watched her pretty breasts heave and then fall. "I want to die."

"Then open your eyes. And I'll kill your fucking ass right here."

She sat upright. The breasts heaved again. He could smell their perfume. Her eyes were empty, not dope-empty or crazy-empty. He'd seen all that plenty. Her eyes were human but had no soul.

"Do it," she whispered.

Her diamonds glinted like spears of fire in the neon flashes. The one between her breasts, the nuggets on her fingers, the flashes dangling from her gentle ear-lobes, the fire blue rings on her tiny wrists. Monty wasn't impressed with diamonds. He'd stolen some of the best in the city and then turned them into nothing but a junkie's white dust hours later. But her diamonds meant something more than the addled bullshit of some common cat burglar snorting in an alley as Monty counted the cash. Her diamonds meant a man.

"Now?" he asked, letting the Sig 228 come from its menacing perch and dangle between them.

"Yeah. Now." She pushed blond hair back off her shoulders and straightened herself as if posing for a yearbook photo. With her eyes closed, she handed him the smoking butt. He took it, looked at it, thought about it, smashed it in the ashtray, lowered the 9mm from between them.

"Get the fuck outta my car. I ain't in the mood for this shit, you fucking cop. I oughta kill your sorry ass. Ain't you motherfuckers got nothing more on me than to set up this fucking attempted murder shit? I been out of prison almost fourteen months and you ain't got shit on me. Like I'm dumb enough to sit here and say 'Yessuh, miss massah, I'll be blowing your brains out now causin' you said I should,' and the fucking SWAT team drops down like fucking Spiderman. Shit. You sick sons of bitches. Oh, Mojo tried to take down a white woman cop. Fuck that!" He threw the gun onto the dash. "Fucking cops, think because I'm black I'm ignorant! Go on home. Go bust some fat white conventioneers down at the big hotels."

She stared at him. The saxophone carried on the misty night air like someone weeping for joy. With her fingers she raked hair like he'd never touched back from skin he had never seen so close up. He saw a sheen of tears.

Then she was crying, and he was ten minutes from making twenty-five thousand dollars if nothing went wrong, and already something was very, very wrong.

3

"Don't yell at me," she whimpered.

His globes of eyes swelled out of his chocolate visage and he made squeaking sounds. "You want me to kill you, but I'm not supposed to holler at you?" Her logic was so broken that he thought he heard his brain snap.

He faced front. Whores and dealers appeared in garish costumes beyond them, churning like hurdy-gurdy barkers with handguns and dime bags. He scratched his head with the Browning barrel.

Allison knew she should have felt afraid. But she only felt numb. She had driven straight to the worst part of the city, an enclave where cops were required to ride with a partner and carry rifles on their persons. She walked through the teeming danger witlessly, hoping a shot might ring out and she'd crumple to the ground while a black circle widened over her vision until it closed on her completely. Suicide by proxy. She grinned dimly to herself. The black man glaring at her in the mirror rolled his eyes, checked his watch.

"Look, lady," Monty said urgently, "you got to go away now. You're fucked up, and when you get outta my car you're going to get killed for almost sure. So let me take you back to wherever you parked. I'll give you an armed escort back to the war-zone lines, and you can go home to your rich neighborhood where the police don't draw their weapons before they even step out of their cars."

Allison felt the ringed impression of the gun barrel on her forehead. Her fingers were cold and tingling. Her throat ached with the muscle strain of holding back tears. "I need to die. I can't kill myself. I'm too chicken. I walked along down here and nobody shot me like I thought they would. So I get into your car and now you're giving me shit about how you'll protect me till I get in my car. You're black. You have guns. I'm white. I have diamonds and am responsible for all the oppression of your race and your life. So shoot me, okay?"

The big black man's shoulders sank. His suit was impeccable. He handed her a handkerchief without looking back at her. She blew her nose.

He rumbled, "I kill for business, not for pleasure. I ain't got no business with you. And I might mention that I resent you saying that all black men are killers. Most of us love our mothers and eat with utensils and go into stores for reasons other than robbery."

She sniffled again. He rolled down his window. Slanting ribbons of mist tangled in the autumn air. Through the open window they fell in onto him, but he didn't care. He needed to breathe something besides her delicious perfume that smelled like sex in clean sheets and shampoo on soft hair. He needed to breathe the familiar neighborhood scent of gunpowder and burned grease.

"Great," she snapped. "I found the only black man in this whole dumpy side of town who doesn't hate white people. If you don't kill people, what are all these fucking guns for?"

"I didn't say I don't hate white people. I do hate white people. Unfortunately it's still against the law to pick them off with rifles like buzzards on a fence, and as long as poaching white folks carries a prison term, I will restrain myself. Unless you fuck me on a dope deal." He deflated, stunned to be actually conversing with a beautiful white woman in a fifteen-thousand-dollar lynx coat, who was obviously as crazy as she was rich.

"And my guns are my tools of the trade. Your old man probably carries a calculator and a Mont Blanc pen to do his job. I carry firearms and kilos of cocaine and heroin." He slapped his hands over his face. "Lady, please, please get the fuck away from me. Let me take you to your car."

Something about him, she thought. The mist was making a damp shadow on his left shoulder, wetting his white collar. He was so beautifully groomed, like a funeral parlor director almost. What is it about him? From the music club a clarinet played lugubriously, and the notes fell into the car like beads of chilly rain.

She announced without passion, "My car is gone. Someone stole it, drove it right past me while I was walking around trying to get killed."

He groaned, punched a button to roll up the window after he started the car. "You're pissing me off."

"So shoot me."

He groaned again, near tears of frustration, and then very loudly he yelled, "I cannot kill you, lady. Your fucking hair and fingerprints are all over my car, which is nothing compared to the tissue and bones that they'd find after I blew your screwy brains out of your pretty face! Don't you see? Normally when I shoot someone I try not to get caught—though my prison record might possibly reflect otherwise—and I promise I'd be a suspect after they found your dead ass in my trunk. Do you see?"

He was pleading with her. She felt a goofy grin and couldn't suppress it. A case was beside her. She took hold of it. "Fine, then I'll take this gun here and threaten to shoot you and you'll have no choice."

He pondered, glanced at the metal case suspended in her manicured hands. "You're going to shoot me unless I shoot you? Fine. Open it and blast away."

Allison opened the case and gasped. Monty gave a low chuckle. She said, amazed, "It's a flute! To kill me I picked a man who plays the flute? I wanted a murderer and I got a sensitive artiste who kills only bad guys?"

He couldn't stop laughing, didn't even try. She tossed away the case onto the floor. "Where the hell did you learn to play the flute? Jesus. I want a martini."

"I was first chair in the chamber orchestra at the University of Texas at Huntsville. Cell block D. If you learned an instrument you got to go on Sunday to play at little old lady clubs. The punch always tasted funny because the blue hairs spiked it, which was good, and sometimes one of the old bags wouldn't look so bad to sit and talk with, which was when you knew you'd been away too long."

She was drifting on the sinewy distant music as if it were a magic carpet carrying her deeper into melancholy. "I should call the police about my car," she said aimlessly.

"Oh, use my car phone, would you?"

"Could I?"

He screamed spit onto her. "No, you couldn't! It was a joke! The last time I called a policeman it was to turn myself in for attempted homicide because my lawyer said if I did I'd get only ten years instead of life!"

He grabbed a lock of her hair and pulled her up to his face. His teeth were gritted. "This ain't funny, bitch. Now get out of my car and walk away or—" He stopped.

"Or you'll kill me." She sighed it with satisfaction.

Monty let go. She smoothed her hair and sat back. A door back of the club opened. Monty stiffened, took up the Sig 228, and positioned the Browning back on the band around his immense wrist. He turned to her, and she saw the killer.

"You sit right here in the dark and don't make one sound, you understand? Your little sick fucking joke to get your husband's attention will come true if these two motherfuckers see you in here watching us. They'll kill you . . ." He backed away, and she felt that a moment of something like sentiment had played in his mind. ". . . But before they kill you they'll tie you up and take you to hell. Quiet, girl. No movement, no cigarette light, no coughing."

Her chest sank under the weight of ancient grief. "I came here to die. Let them do it if you won't."

He lifted the collar of his cashmere overcoat up around his neck and fixed the interior light so it wouldn't come on when the door opened. He sighed heavily. "What the fuck is your name?"

"Allison Robbins." She said it and wished she could look down and believe it, believe that the dainty hands were hers and the bashful brown eyes were hers, wished she could believe that she was anybody at all.

Monty stared at her. The dark strangers behind the building passed a glowing joint, shuffled heavily under coats stashed with deadly metal. "Allison Robbins, I'm Montgomery Jones. If you'll be quiet until this dope deal is done, I'll kill you tonight like you want. My way, though. Quick. No torture. No hot-dogging. Just a clean kill. See, these bad men over here, honey, will cart you off so they can have hours of good old boy fun raping you with knives and their fists. But first they'll gun me down like a dog. So I'm not asking you to shut the fuck up for your safety. We're talking about my black ass, and I do not, unlike you, wish to die tonight."

A morsel of fear touched her tongue. "Before you shoot me, will you buy me a martini?"

"I reckon it's the least I can do. Now duck down and stay there." He left the car, mingled under a dull light laced with thugs and thickening raindrops.

Allison huddled on the floor, resting her head on Monty's well-worn silver flute. Listening to Monty Jones had given her an odd rush. She was having a feeling, a sprout of weak, tenuous emotion cracking her numbness like a baby chick's first peck from its dark world.

Allison Robbins wasn't afraid. Death would be welcome. But before she died she would remember that at the end she did what she thought she could never do again . . . she had felt a flicker of life's long-lost excitement.

Outside the car she heard men's muddled laughter. Monty's feet crunching toward her on the gravel parking lot. The rapid spittle of gunfire was gone before it even had time to echo on the night air. Allison made one reflexive little yelp and crouched harder against the car's carpet.

She sat upright as Monty calmly pulled into the squeeze of low-riders and pimpmobiles crowding the slushy street.

"You shot those men dead?"

He tooled the steering wheel easily with one finger,

popping a Tic Tac into his mouth with the other hand. The windshield wipers pushed aside a gritty coating of raindrops. Monty twisted his head with his hands sideways until the cracking sound made Allison flinch.

"Shut up," he commanded, looking left to right continuously, nervously. "Do you go to your husband's office and sit around asking what he's doing while he works? This is my work."

Allison pouted. "You can kill them but not me?"

Smokey serenaded while Monty ignored her. The street scene had a Renoir quality about it; seen through the oily sheen of sooty mist on the windows, everything was obscured and twisted. Allison could only make out clumps but not definite shapes of the moving mass of people.

She lighted a cigarette, lowered the backseat window an inch. "What if I pay you money, like a hit man, only the hit's on me?"

They rolled silently past a corner melee where two cops stood, their helmets bobbing as they beat two scuffling men into submission against a wall. Monty didn't gawk at the scuffle, but Allison did.

He maneuvered through the snarl of slow-moving cars. "I got plenty of money already. Shit. I'm going to one of my car washes and launder me some dirty money."

Allison drank from a sterling silver flask that she took out of her purse. The instant warmth and lightheadedness felt supremely good and normal. She exhaled twenty-year-old Scotch.

Monty commanded, "And when we get to my car wash you're calling a friend of yours to come get your ass."

"Why'd you kill them?" she asked, the words smoky white from the cigarette.

She was exhilarated somehow, not frightened. In her pedigree world the most exhilarating thing that had happened in years was when her water broke two weeks past due in the buffet line at the country club brunch one Sunday morning. All the debutantes and docents spotting the tables in sporty hats had swooned with the excitement of someone's body fluid escaping. Oh, what a scandal it had been. Something unsterile and unarranged.

"I ain't saying I did kill them, but if I did it was because they were four thousand dollars short on the money for the coke, and to make up the difference they offered me movies of themselves fucking little black boys. Want a Tic Tac?"

She swilled Scotch deeply, ignored the offer until Monty took his outstretched arm away. She told him morosely, "I never go to my husband's office. Everyone there hates me."

He stopped at a red light. An ambulance careened past them, the red and blue lights splintering through the prisms of leaking rain on the windows.

"Maybe they hate you because you stand around asking them to kill you."

"I do not."

The car lurched forward. Allison set her feet over the seat, almost touching Monty's cheeks.

She sounded purposefully pitiful. "They hate me because I hate them. I'm not good with people. People misunderstand me. I try to be funny and it's not funny. So, to answer your question. No, I never go to my husband's office. They look at me like I have cancer and they're trying to pretend they don't know. I'm nice to them, though, I really am, but they hate me."

Two screaming cop cars hurled by. Monty drove slowly forward, stopping when the traffic collapsed while a boy bought a girl. He ceremoniously pulled a long fat cigar from his pocket, bit off the end, and held up a gold lighter until the tip of the cigar erupted into reams of smoke.

With the cigar clamped in his teeth he asked, "Now,

why would you go and be nice to people who hate you?"

"What, I should just shoot them like you would?"

"I don't shoot people who hate me. I shoot people who need killing."

The second belt of Scotch hit her brain and the world slowed, became a kinder, clearer place.

"Well," Allison breathed, "that's one way to handle it, I suppose. But they didn't teach us that in charm school. They taught us that before you sit down in a chair you never look back at the chair, you merely feel the chair with the back of your leg and then you sit. You never smoke or chew gum in public. When you stand or sit, hold your hands cupped together at your waist, elbows bent just so. Look people in the eye. Introduce the older person first by name. And if anyone acts unkindly, pretend you didn't hear and simply move on in the crowd."

"It's easier to shoot them," Monty declared. The car in front of him, into which a black hooker wearing a leather crop top and a bikini bottom had just climbed, was long ahead, but Monty hadn't moved on. He was busy looking mystified at Allison over the seat, his head cocked like a confused puppy.

"I'm really nice to people," she confessed.

"Yeah, well, people are really fucking nice to me, Allison Robbins, and I like it better that way. I figure if anybody in the room is getting what they want and I ain't getting what I want, then something's wrong and I better handle it."

She rode in silence, watching a human shipwreck outside slip further toward the bottom of decency. But she was more interested than alarmed. She felt safe in Monty's barge of a Cadillac.

"Montgomery," she said as if he were the limo driver instead of her chosen form of suicide, "do people really fuck small boys and make movies of it to sell?"

"Two less of 'em do now," he muttered.

"I'm glad you killed them, then. I kill small children, too, you know, but first I torture them; I make them drink their own urine and look at pictures of me when I was going through my first face-lift."

He gnawed the log of a cigar and didn't look back at her. "Nice try. I ain't shooting you."

"You said you would."

"Honey, all killers lie. You're going to get out of my car at this car wash of mine and get you a ride home."

"You said you'd buy me a martini. You've got oodles of money in that bag you took from those dead hoodlums. You said it was the least you could do. I don't have any friends to call. I don't have any friends."

"How about those rich broads you sit around drinking lunch with after charm school?"

"Oh. They're not my friends, really. We just hang out because we share the same hairdresser and our nannies like each other. They don't even know my middle name or anything. You know, there wouldn't be any evidence if you put my body in your trunk and drove your car into a lake."

Monty pulled into the parking lot of one of his car washes. It was ablaze with lights, but in the rainy film he could see that no cars were rolling on the huge conveyor. The joint could've closed except that nightly he took money there to get it laundered, and Andy the night manager knew not to close until Monty had brought the night's deposits.

Monty turned at her quickly. "Run my car into a lake? My car? Bitch, you are crazy. First I thought you were just weird, you know, hopped up and all wacko 'cause your old man don't give you the garlic enough to keep you calm. But now, now you tell me that after I kill you I should ruin my car, the only thing besides women and a royal flush that gives me a hard-on—my car? I don't think so. I do not think so. Did they not tell you in charm school that you don't ask a man to kill you and put your body in his trunk and then drive his automobile into a lake? Did they not say to you that you should not ask a man to do this?"

He lay his head against the headrest, feeling immensely weary. "I cannot kill you. I cannot let you live and go tell what I've done. I cannot drive you home or let somebody see me put you in a cab. I cannot call a cop or push you out on the hospital psychiatric ward ramp. I cannot believe this. I cannot pretend I didn't hear any of this shit and move on through the crowd. What can I do?"

She snuggled into her fur coat. Drunkenness was reassuring. "Kill me."

"I'd like to. But I am now wearing your fucking DNA like a cheap suit, woman. Some hotshot somewhere is going to be looking for your sorry ass in the morning, not because he loves you but because he wants to know who to thank. And them fucking cops will find you dead, then they'll find my happy ass alive."

Allison whined, "Well, you killed those two men back there just like that and it didn't bother you."

Monty grimaced. "Woman, ain't nobody caring about those two dead drug dealers. Their charm school teachers ain't likely to be calling a press conference in the morning, if you get what I mean. But you—they won't know whether to shit or go blind when you turn up murdered."

"They won't catch you. There's nothing to connect us."

He slapped at the steering wheel. "Goddamn it, I got to make a living. I got to get money and move around town. And those cops, they ain't got one fucking thing else to do but look for who killed the socialite babe. They don't look for my ass in their spare time, you see. They'll look for me all the fucking time, while I look away and do something else, like try to get on with living. Shit. Look at you, all diamonds and curves. You are somebody's property, honey, and he may not like you but he puts some bucks into making it look like he likes you. Strapping my ass into an electric chair makes some motherfucker a hero for sure, you get it?"

Her voice was a dying moth. "Montgomery, you kill people all the time. This is no big deal. Just shoot me. It'll look like the people who stole my car did it."

"Yeah, sure, except they won't never find your car, 'cause it's in pieces by now in a chop shop. No, they'll be down here asking did anybody see you, and sure enough some motherfucker saw you waltzing your little ass down that street back there, trolling for an assassin, and saw you open my car door, and to make a deal-off on a two-bit drug rap he'll drop my ass in the grease like a french fry, and there'll be your goddamned fibers flying around my car like parade floats. Uh-uh, no. I cannot let you kill yourself until somebody sees me leave you somewhere alone, alive. Now I'm going in here to clean up this dirty money, and you sit your ass right here. We're going somewhere public, and I'm going to walk off and leave you in front of four hundred witnesses while you're still at ninety-eight-point-six degrees so there's no fucking questions about time of death. Goddamn it."

He darted into the rain, into the bath of car-wash lights beyond his headlight beams. His hair glistened when he returned and slammed the car into drive.

"Montgomery," she said dully, "there are two women in that alley giving head to a white man dressed like a priest."

"Father Gates. He's here every Friday night. His name is Percival. He likes his dick sucked by women, which is not what most of the priests want when they come to this side of town. Most of 'em want boys or retarded men to draw the poison out of them."

Allison, who hadn't seen anything really gory or giddy or even mildly shameful in real life since she once saw her doubles tennis partner Madilyn Peterson blow her nose on a country club towel, was enervated by the sight of life's real freak show.

"Father Percival Gates," she mused aloud.

Monty chuckled. "His nickname down here is Pearly Gates. Though I don't suppose he's likely to get through them any quicker than them angels he pays to make him feel like a god for a few minutes every Friday night."

She laughed. Montgomery put on loud music and revived his cigar with great blobs of smoke around his head in the front seat. She put one stockinged toe against his cheek, then took down her feet dutifully.

"Hey, Montgomery, my middle name is Elizabeth."

"How charming," he answered. "Now shut the fuck up."

5

Detective Mike Shiller lowered his head, not to look at the two cocoons of dead bodies behind the 512 Club, but to wince at the rain damage being done to his new 'gator-skin cowboy boots. Water poured off the brim of his giant black Stetson hat as if he was a tea kettle tipping.

"What?" he growled at the young uniformed cop who called his name.

In a thick Middle-Eastern clip, his face peering from the hood of his yellow slicker, the officer said, "The paramedics say these men are dead."

"Well, who knew?" Shiller bitched. "I thought this here was trick photography." He angrily took off his Stetson and slung water from it against his duster coat, which was quickly becoming soaked. "Officer Hadeesh, either move those drunk hookers and junkies back from this scene or collect a cover charge from them. Can you do that?"

Hadeesh's eyes were stark white against his bronze, wet forehead. "Yes. And then what?"

Shiller clamped the hat back into the groove it had impressed around his unruly black hair. He had left a blonde bent over a chair, giggling and shaking her tits upside down, to slosh into the common spectacle of another killing. He thought her name was Rhonda, and he hoped she didn't lift anything from his tidy white frame farmhouse while he was gone, most especially her ass from that chair.

"Hadeesh, what time today did you finish the police academy? Haven't you ever seen a television cop show, son? First you put up a mess of that yellow crime-scene tape, which ought to circle around this whole cesspool of a city, then you pick up some stuff around those bodies with tweezers and put it into a baggy."

"Ah, yes, evidence."

Shiller flicked away a lit cigarette that sizzled into a puddle in the gravel. His Texas drawl was as thick as his black moustache. "Evidence. There you go. Body parts and bullets. I guess back home where you're from in Iraq they'd call it dinner."

The young cop's yellow slicker glistened as rain streaked it. "Sir, I am from Iran. Now I am an American citizen, proud to protect and serve."

Shiller wanted a beer badly. "Then protect me from blue balls tonight, Officer, and make this quick so I can go home and serve myself up to a nasty cowgirl who doesn't wear panties."

Hadeesh seemed to beam a moment. "Already I have found this, Detective. This is important?"

Shiller reached, glancing his gaze away from the now blank slot on his finger where his wedding ring had sat for twenty years. "This would be what, Sherlock?"

"A cigar band," Hadeesh said.

Shiller's flashlight beam spotted the ring of paper. "You found it on the ground? Why ain't it wet?"

"It was under the taller man's body, there, under the awning where they were shot."

"Either of these losers got a stogie on him?"

Red and blue cruiser lights sliced Hadeesh's shadow, which towered over the short, stocky Shiller. The younger cop sounded grateful to have been solicited by a legend like Shiller, who was not a hero but more of a famous despot.

"No, sir," he replied crisply. "But this band was near the spent casings, as if when the perpetrator pulled out his weapon, the cigar ring fell. It's a clue, isn't it?"

Shiller was easily amused by everything in life; it was a flaw of his that he never took anything seriously. "A clue? Like Colonel Mustard did it in the kitchen with a rope? Yeah, Hadeesh, it's a clue. Imagine right here behind a bar discovering that someone has been smoking a cigar."

A whore in a blond wig, with breasts as big as barn doors, yelled at him from the crowd, "Yo, Shiller, shot any more fourteen-year-old boys lately?"

He rolled his eyes. Hadeesh said quietly, "You had no choice, sir. We all knew that."

The rainwater ran off Shiller's Stetson like silver confetti when he bent his face to the ground. "That fucking district attorney almost died trying to have me put up for murder."

Hadeesh demurred. "Well, it's not murder to shoot a person pointing a gun at you, no matter his age."

"What would they do to that crowd over there yelling that shit at me if we was over in Iraq?"

"I don't know. I'm from Iran. And in Iran hurling epithets at a police officer carries a death sentence. Shall I go and torture their children and then kill them?" He smiled.

Shiller grinned wryly. "You're gonna make it here, kid. Now, this here cigar, I don't think it means much, but bag it anyhow."

With the hush of a conspirator, Hadeesh whispered, "This is not just any cigar, Detective. It's a Hoya de Monterrey. Almost seventy dollars for a box. Not likely on the menu of the usual clientele here at the 512 Club. I believe it is a clue. A rich man in the parking lot with a gun."

Not much caught Mike Shiller's interest anymore unless it was something he saw through the bottom of a Budweiser bottle and would stay after she drove him home. And in sixteen years of working homicide, he knew that not many people cared about two black guys shot dead in a pile of homemade kiddie fuck films, which the wet tapes now stacked in his front seat promised to be if they weren't snuff films of begging, crying women being gagged and stabbed. But maybe this time the point of interest wouldn't be the losers that were killed as much as the big daddy who did the killing.

Hadeesh was comically serious. "I could find out which regular around here smokes this expensive brand. We would have something of a suspect then, yes?"

Shiller laughed, wondering if he'd ever cared about anything at all. "Okay, Hadeesh, except these native savages around here aren't known for their devotion to civic duty. They don't talk much, and if they do, then they don't live long."

The bodies were stowed in a silent ambulance, blood seeping through soggy white sheets. The crime-scene cops loaded stuff into the open doors of an unmarked police van. The unruly crowd wandered back inside to resume dancing to blues music as if the whole thing had been nothing more than a commercial break.

Shiller's boots would need a polishing tomorrow. If the blonde was gone when he got home, his ego would be equally tarnished. The rain stopped. Shiller wiped his face with a kerchief from his duster pocket.

"You work it," he instructed, and wanted to chuckle at the boy's rapt face. "Go get you some snitches who hang around here, and do like they do on TV. Put them under bright lights, beat them about the head and face. You be the bad guy, all snarly and anxious to kill them, then I'll come in and be the good guy so they'll feel relieved and talk to me. It'll be fun, like real-life prime time. If they won't talk, pistol whip 'em."

Hadeesh had been bending to hear. He straightened indignantly when he realized he was being joshed.

He frowned at Shiller and said, "Perhaps I'll just find a few people around here and ask who smokes this cigar."

"Yeah." Shiller sighed, using his hat brim to shield his cigarette lighter from the damp wind so he could get a flame.

The blonde would be gone, Shiller thought as he drove miserably through a settling nighttime fog. But Othel Middleton would be waiting as always, like a fire that caught Shiller's bedroom curtains and choked him in deadly smoke. He said aloud, flat as a wet newspaper, not noticing the city sludge droning in the streets beyond him, "You little jerk, pointing a toy gun at me. I said, put it down. I said it twice."

As always for the last year, Shiller blamed the sudden tears on the cigarette smoke that curled up and blistered his raw eyeballs.

"But you didn't drop the gun, did you, Othel? No. You were playing a game. Bang, Copper, you're dead. Fucking television shows. Fucking district attorney."

He had left Hadeesh enthusiastically if woodenly doing his best to imitate interrogation on the mean streets that hid a cigar-smoking killer. Mike Shiller expected never to hear another thing about any of it.

6

He watched one minute of one unmarked videotape and then turned it off. He wanted to throw something, but anything he threw would break and everything in the place was important to him. The remote control, the beer mugs, the portable phone.

Instead he threw himself into an hour's worth of weight lifting in the second bedroom. It was strewn with his bench and his barbells. No bed. No bureau. No signs of life.

Trisha took the furniture from that room when she went. She left everything else, and he bought her all new stuff for her new tract home in a new suburb. He planted his feet and stood firm—not when Trisha had left, but now as he curled the free weights repetitively and broke a sweat. When Trish had left he had cried like a baby and begged. People can cry like babies and beg only when they're really proud, he had told himself, when they're too proud anymore to be vain or arrogant. It takes a giant of a man to feel hurt.

The kiddie fuck film rattled into his head over and over like a drifting bad smell. In the first moments that he had glimpsed, two black men and a white woman were passing back and forth in front of the camera, talking in chemically altered slurs, moving in shadows around the filthy, cluttered room of bare lightbulbs and dope smoke. A small black boy who appeared prepubescent by his small build, a boy about ten or eleven, lay naked on a bed. His skin was smooth like shined mahogany. He was not restrained but was obviously drugged. Shiller killed the picture when the fat, naked white woman crouched on the bed and began to fondle the boy's flaccid penis. The men oohing and aahing in the background were the two men who were found dead behind the 512 only an hour ago. That was the only thing that made Shiller feel better.

He had come home to find the blonde vacated. She had taken the wine they had bought at the liquor store on the way to his house, but she'd left the beer. He showered, put on sweatpants, and flopped into a recliner with a beer bottle jutting up in his lap where an erection would've been if anybody had asked him for one. He turned on CNN without the sound, sinking the room in washes of blue and yellow. His hair dripped over his shoulders onto his chest. The rain fell outside, a cold biting rain that sounded just like the shower he'd stood in for almost a half hour. The property of his farm was deserted outside.

He reached, dialed, hung up, reached, got one ring, hung up, jammed the phone under the recliner cushion, took it out, dialed, hung up, swigged beer, changed the channel to Nick at Nite, smoked, watched Rob and Laura sing with Buddy and Sally, dialed, and this time didn't hang up.

The hello was as good as the day's first sip of coffee.

"Trisha? How you doing?"

You couldn't hear the rain falling on her house. You could hear only kids chattering, Clint Black singing, and smells wafting like warm waves of opera through her happy kitchen. Shiller felt like a corpse.

"Well, there's a nail in the garbage disposal so it sounds like an airplane crash when you run it. It's almost winter, and Hannah is having a tantrum because she wants to wear her bathing suit to preschool tomorrow."

He wanted his arms around her. "Where's David? It's almost seven o'clock."

He hoped for undertones of bitterness, but got only pleasant conviction. "He's on his way home. He got a promotion today so we're having champagne in bed tonight."

In the recliner in the dark room, in the synthetic hue of loneliness cast from the television, Shiller shot his middle finger into the air. Rob and Laura tap danced together in their living room beyond him.

"You doing okay, Mike?" She asked the way she probably asked the grocery checker. She mentioned their youngest son. "Corey got his baseball letter jacket today. He's so proud. All those hours you spent showing those boys how to throw a baseball are paying off." And their eldest boy. "Little Mike topped ninety speed in practice today. The whole coaching staff at TCU is terrified he'll quit and go on to the minor leagues. I'm begging him not to; he really needs to finish his education."

"I told him if he gets an offer, Trish, he should go pro. No use risking a bad shoulder or arm injury in college."

There was an inaudible frown from her end, as if by parenting his son he had invaded her territory. Then his youngest boy took the phone, and Shiller felt like standing up in honor of something noble.

"Hey, boy, the only freshman on high school varsity. I'm real proud."

"Dad, can I get a hardship driver's license?"

"Shit, no. What does your mom say?"

"She says shit no."

Shiller almost smiled. "You sorry you're not playing football this year?"

"Oh, yeah, Dad. I wish my shoulder was dislocated or my knees wrecked like all my pals. How about a motorcycle?"

"I believe we've discussed that."

The kid was funny. "Yeah, except the last time I asked I couldn't hear your answer because your hands were clamped so tight around my throat."

Shiller felt tired. The boy needed nothing from him except quick answers and slow anger. From his cute little mother he got hugs and shoes and chores and cheers on the mound. From his father he got ten-dollar bills and idiotic, apologetic winks.

Trisha was back. She asked, "You through with law school yet?"

He had told her a hundred times that he had one more year. She wasn't forgetful, she just didn't care about his answers anymore. "I got one more year."

"I don't see how you do that, law school part-time and work full-time," she said more disgusted than sympathetic.

"It keeps my mind off things," he groused.

She swerved as always, knowing that asking what was on his mind would be like it used to be when what was on his mind was never happy. "David's home!" she squealed, and Shiller thought goddamned balloons floated up from the stadium.

"Trish?"

"Yeah?"

A pan lid clattered. She was cooking. Her husband was bounding through the door with happy news, something Shiller had never brought her. Since they had married when he was twenty and she barely eighteen, he had only lumbered in at night to tell her horror cop stories. Tonight's chilled champagne said it all. Trisha had wanted occasionally to celebrate. Shiller had thought it was heroic to mourn.

"I got to go."

"Okay, Mike. We'll bring little Mike this weekend. Make sure he spends some of it with you and not every minute with Melanie."

"Melanie?"

She opened a pan lid, and caution lilted like the steam through her voice. "A girl. Nice girl. But I've stopped him from seeing her on weeknights anymore. It got way too serious, like he quit seeing his buddies just to hang out with her, and his room is a total wreck because he won't do anything but sit on the telephone and coo at Melanie. David had a talk with him about condoms and stuff. I hope the boy is careful, Mike. I wouldn't want him to make the same mistake you and I did and end up in a miserable marriage."

David prattled in the background; the little girl Hannah screamed a laugh. Trish said good-bye and hung up.

Shiller got another beer, swam through stark, familiar darkness to find it, then put on another videotape just as depressing as the kiddie fuck film. Only in this one it was Mike Shiller taking it up the ass from the district attorney. There were clips of press conferences and newscasts from the past year, about this time. November. Windy, gray, muddled by sleet and heightened crimes of theft and robbery.

A woman newscaster who looked like a Sesame Street muppet was a talking head.

"Today the district attorney announced that he will seek charges of homicide against an on-duty police officer who shot and killed last month a fourteen-year-old boy who was pointing a toy gun at the officer.

"Detective Michael James Shiller will be the first peace officer in the state to be charged with murder in a death that occurred while the officer was on duty. The DA said today that he will ask the grand jury to indict Officer Shiller for homicide rather than seeking lesser charges of negligence or involuntary manslaughter. If convicted of first-degree murder, Officer Shiller could receive a life sentence and spend no less than thirty-five years in prison. . . ."

He fast-forwarded to the district attorney on the screen, who by his appearance could've been a casino pit boss or a television evangelist. He was tall, with perfect gray hair that sat like a helmet, lean-faced, broad-shouldered. His eyes were the blue of a hot flame seen as it burns through a chunk of clear ice. The rage that went through Shiller at just the sight of his nemesis still made his mouth dry and his hands wet.

The Ivy League bastard pontificated. "I know perfectly well the implications of first-degree murder, and I fully intend to prove that Officer Mike Shiller killed Othel Middleton under the guidelines of those implications. He had many choices in that scene and was trained to distinguish between the right choice of defusing the situation or the wrong choice of shooting an innocent unarmed child. I do not believe the officer's first choice would have been to shoot a white child. I will see to it that the undercurrents of racism and disregard for human life that exist in Officer

Shiller's judgment are used as motives for his cold-blooded murder of a boy who could have done him no harm. . . ."

The phone rang. Shiller muted the screen, froze the DA's Mount Rushmore face into a frame of caustic resolve. The blue flame penetrated a spot on the TV screen.

"Shiller," he barked.

The quick reply, "Montgomery Raymond Jones."

Shiller rolled his eyes. "Hadeesh, what is this? Hit-men-drug-dealers for twenty?"

He first heard thunder behind Hadeesh through the phone and then felt it roll outside on the carpet of dark panning his living-room windows.

"No, sir, it is your first clue. Mr. Jones smokes Hoya de Monterrey cigars. Tire tracks have been washed away, but a witness can place him here at the time of the shootings."

Shiller looked at his watch. Almost 8 P.M. Rain falling like Niagara, promising by morning to turn to flimsy bits of sleet that didn't stick but made everything slick and gritty. He wasn't going to make it to his torts class tonight at the law school. He'd have to get his notes tomorrow from Nina the nymph who never stopped trying to feed and breed him.

He sighed. "Who's your witness?"

Hadeesh read his notes and raised his voice over the voice crackling on his car's police radio. "A Miss Phyllis Farmshore. She says she knows you."

Shiller chuckled wryly. "Miss Syphilis Forsure? We're old pals. I don't bust her for hooking anymore, and she don't try to shoot me in the head when I drive by on the street. Why would Syphilis drop Monty's dick in the dirt?"

Hadeesh was proud of himself again, having such forethought and all. "Well," he said, "she is angry at him, she says, because he is out with a white woman tonight."

* * *

Shiller's unmarked squad car coughed to a start. Through the blinking of his windshield wipers, he saw his dark house. He had left the district attorney's devious face time warped on the TV screen. The silver sheen that carried through Trish's forsaken lace curtains was like a beacon of hate and revenge emanating from the man who had tried to ruin Shiller's life.

David had told his son about condoms. Shiller snorted cigarette smoke cynically. Maybe Melanie would have more sense than Trisha. Maybe Melanie wouldn't get indignant and pouty when Corey pulled it out in the backseat and started to put it on.

Choices, he remembered the DA saying on TV. Officer Shiller had many choices. Fuck a beautiful high school senior without a rubber and then spend twenty years apologizing for getting her pregnant and stealing her youth. Face a fourteen-year-old boy with a gun drawn at Shiller's chest from four feet away, blow the kid apart and then spend his own life regretting an instant deadly decision.

Choices. Did Mike Shiller ever make the right one? He wondered. He pressed the accelerator and spun gravel up from his driveway. Shiller knew Monty Jones well. Nobody had more reason than Jones to want Mike Shiller dead.

7

The nightclub full of black people was too civilized to suit Allison's prejudices. Tables of well-dressed black couples talked low in the smoky blue-lighted haze. Between band sets, Aaron Neville crooned over the sound system. A leggy slick-haired woman in sequins blew white smoke and laughed lazily at something her handsome companion said.

A white maître d' appeared like a poodle. "Mr. Jones, nice to see you. You'll want a table up front?"

Monty looked askance at Allison and answered plainly, "Anywhere that everyone can see her."

The poodle yapped, thinking Monty was so proudly romantic. Allison smirked at Monty.

They noticed as Allison and Monty passed. Jaws didn't drop, but brown eyes drifted onto them a moment too long. The beautiful black women unconsciously raised one and sometimes both brows at the sight of the stunningly gorgeous white woman on Monty's arm.

"Vodka martini for her," Monty told the eager waiter, "with poison olives. Decaf for me." He studied Allison when they were alone again. "What? You thought the men in here would have bones in their noses and the women would be dancing with their tits hanging out?"

Allison demurred. "Well, maybe I did. Maybe I

didn't know that you people . . . socialized, you know."

His gaze was amused. "We do. Between shooting craps and having welfare babies."

A dashing black man approached. Monty stood, saying, "Senator, how you doin'? This is Allison Robbins. By the way, Senator, what time is it?"

The senator considered a gold Rolex in the dim lights. "It's eight-twenty, Monty. You staying out of trouble?"

"You better know I am."

The senator jerked nervously. "I took a swing for you with that last parole board, Monty. I want things to go right in all regards."

"Things are only going to get better, sir." They shook hands. Allison saw the small packet of white powder that left Monty's palm and slid into the senator's hand.

The senator went up some stairs toward the men's room. Allison gawked at Monty.

"You're not a good guy," she hissed. "You're selling the devil to innocent people."

Monty leaned forward. His cologne was musk. "The problem, lady, isn't availability of drugs; the problem is consumption. The senator himself said it on national TV last week, and he oughta know. I couldn't sell it if dumb motherfuckers didn't buy it."

She said with disgust, "You don't even use the shit, like that makes you some kind of hero. You're the reason kids and innocent people get killed every day. They kill and die for that horrible stuff you sell."

He glared. "I don't sell to kids, and I don't let none of my buyers sell to kids, neither."

"Yeah, like you know what they do with it."

He glared harder. "I got eyes everywhere. I make sure my shit only goes to worthless dicks like senators and bored, lazy, rich housewives. Now get the fuck outta my business."

Their drinks arrived. Allison's martini had onions in it.

Monty raised a hand. "Wait, son, this here's an onion, and the lady wants olives." He was gruff.

Allison touched his hand, "Montgomery, it's okay . . ."

"It ain't okay," he snapped. "Take this shit away right now, boy, and bring it back done right."

"You were rude to him!" she hissed.

Monty yawned. "The boy knows it ain't personal. You're going to drink a drink the way you don't want it? You are insane."

A phone in Monty's breast pocket rang. He flipped it out and open. "Yeah. Oh, you, I been looking for your ass all day. You done fucked up my bank account, you know that? It don't matter how I got your home phone number, asshole. You're lucky I didn't come down the chimney and talk to you personal-like. Now, listen here, the dumb shits who work for you said somebody accidentally put a freeze on my bank accounts by mistake, and I got all sorts of checks bouncing, chief among them the insurance checks for my car washes and my pawnshop. Looka here, you fix it. You write letters and you credit me with all them service charges you put on me. And if one thing goes wrong at my businesses before you clear it up with my insurance people, your sorry piece of shit bank is liable for every dime of whatever happens. Sorry? I need sorry like I need a bucket of dog dung in my lap. Monday morning I'm calling your ass early, first thing, and this better be all fixed up nice-like. Now, thank you very much, and pardon me if I was rude, but corporate incompetence really pisses off a decent businessman like myself, you understand? Uh-huh, okay, you take care and have a nice weekend."

Allison gulped martini—with two olives. "Your banker called you on a Friday night from home?"

"Yeah, because he knew that by Saturday morning if he didn't call me I'd be on his yard like a lawn jockey, waiting for an explanation."

"Wasn't he angry that you called him at home?"

Monty's brow wrinkled. "What do I care if some stupid banker is angry at me? He fucked up my day, I'm fucking up his night. Girl, don't be such a . . . victim, would you?"

The waiter stopped to ask how the martini was and to apologize again for the onion and olive mix-up. "It's fine," Allison beamed. "Don't you worry about a thing."

Monty stared after the boy and then at Allison. "How come you think it's okay to get bad service?"

She shrugged, her slender, bare shoulders catching Monty's eye. The martini was bombing her brain with calm. "I get embarrassed for other people, that's all. I don't want them to feel bad."

He laughed. "Girl, what does it matter who feels bad if you feel good? Are you too suicidal to dance?"

They swayed to nice music. His body was taut; her curves made him swallow too often.

"You're not going to kill me and rape me, are you?" She sounded and felt dejected.

He felt weak. "I guess probably the only thing better than fucking a crazy white woman is fucking a crazy white woman and then putting a bullet in her head."

"You don't mean that." She spoke with her head resting on his chest.

"No, I don't. Listen, about that rape stuff. If I wanted to have sex with a woman who was kicking and screaming to get me off of her, I'd just get married again. I ain't going to rape you. But if you smoke in my car anymore, I may go on ahead and kill you."

She looked up at him. He took an unexpected breath in the face of her angelic porcelain beauty.

"You've been married? Isn't it awful? Don't you just hate it?"

He felt her pelvic bone against his, pushed her back slightly to put space between her and his thoughts. "I've done prison and marriage, both. The sex and the food are better in prison."

She laughed. He felt a pang of pity. "Hey," he offered, "you want another glass of vodka?"

"You afraid that not enough witnesses have seen me yet?"

"Girl, I ain't afraid of nothing, and neither should you be. Not of bankers or waiters or husbands or nobody. Whatever they do, they can't eat you." He winked at her and outright laughed when she winked back.

8

Instinctively, as a newborn doe knows the sound of a gun cocking in the woods, Monty knew the feel of what was pressing the skin behind his ear as he sat. A pistol.

The familiar voice was cool over the band's music. "We're going out, nigger. Don't turn around, don't touch nothing, not the coat, not nothing. Let's walk."

Allison's new martini glistened in the fancy glass like mercury. She was in the bathroom up the stairs.

Monty said calmly, "Danny the Dictionary." He walked, face front, past the crowded dance floor toward the exit. "All your good work in the prison library must've got you sprung about seven years early."

"I'm out," the chain-saw voice said as a huge hand came around and held open the door for Monty. "And you're dead."

From the top of the stairs Allison saw Monty without his coat, eyes flitting every direction. His escort was shorter than Monty, had a shaved head, and wore an oversize peacoat. Up high she could see the jut of the gun in his hand.

Her first thought was, of course, oh shit. Now she was alone in a black bar with no ride. Now she would have to go home to her husband, to more physical beatings and verbal slams. Now her adventure was over, except for the dreary part of going back to reality. She had come to think that dying at Monty's hands would be not so scary. He would be gentle and quick, and she would die fast because he was an expert: no lingering wounds that left her merely paralyzed or hideously disfigured. After she told him her story, Monty would understand that he had to kill her, that it was the most merciful thing he could do for her. She stood there in the pulse of rainbow lights and dance music, feeling like a comatose person hooked up to machines, pleading on the inside to be let go, to stop the suffering and isolation, to be freed by death.

At the table she chugged down the martini. The adrenalin and alcohol made her fearless. She could go home and rot slowly in a tomb, pleasing her husband only by showing how much pain he caused her. Or she could follow Monty and probably die in a big way, maybe sound heroic in the headlines. There'd be no question then. The insurance money would go to her children. In death she would have quantitative meaning to them, a cash value. Dead, she would give them more than she ever had alive.

The keys were in the pocket of his cashmere overcoat. She yanked it up, put on her lynx, and—like the Lone Ranger—started out the door behind Monty and his captor. She was afraid, panting. Her heart thudded. There was danger at hand, maybe bloodshed, probably death, definitely big trouble.

She started the Coupe de Ville and couldn't help laughing maniacally. Her lily white hands were warm gripping the wheel; she was hotly alive. Her foot was heavy on the pedal as she floored it. How wonderful to pursue something instead of cowering or walking away or folding inward like a mummy.

She laughed. Mr. Hyde. Insane. Wild. Unbound.

Two streets over in a dilapidated industrial district, they led Monty up a stairway along the side of a building. Monty and one man went inside a yellow vacuum of light. Another man stood outside on the stairway platform. Allison crouched in an adjacent alley, pressed into the darkness.

She could hear and feel everything, as if the sharp sheen of fear had washed away a dried film of grief from her senses. Her mouth was dry. Her body shook uncontrollably. She struggled to breathe, like trying to take air through a tiny pipe. The wind blew sideways and leaves skated, rattled, jumped on the wet sidewalk and in the dark pit behind her. A siren flared in the distance. The man on the stairway platform tossed a cigarette and red sparks exploded, then rolled into a pocket of water in the parking lot. The darkness was profound. The happy man in the moon gave luminescence to the thick clouds that buried him in the sky. Allison shivered. The double-barreled shotgun felt foreign and volatile in her hands.

The alley stank of urine and vomit. At the other end, sunken in cryptic darkness, was Monty's car. She could go back to it now, drive away, park somewhere, call someone to come get her. Something behind her thudded. She gasped, turned to see a cat meandering, grimacing at her with equal ennui. A dead mouse dangled from its mouth. The cat prissed past her across the street, into another alley. She put the shotgun inside her lynx to protect it from the rain that was beginning to patter down more seriously. Her feet were cold. Her red satin Yves St. Laurent high heels were ruined.

What was her business here? she asked herself, jerking violently at every noise behind her. A crow pecking. A fat raindrop hitting a tin can. Her business here was simply not to be there anymore. Not in that house where she was told daily that nothing was hers. Not in that life where she was told daily that nobody cared. She started to cry silently. The tears warmed her lips. She couldn't sniffle, so she let the snot drip and wiped at it with her diamond-laden fingers.

She had married him for the money. She had never loved him, not one day, not one moment. They traveled in limos and Lear Jets. She was beautiful, prime property, the perfect trophy wife. The other wives hated her, of course, at all those garish business gatherings, because her body was incredibly beautiful. He liked for other women to hate her, she knew it; it made her superior to them, so he thought. And always he criticized her for being hated.

"My career would go much better, Allison, if you could get along better with these assholes' wives. Why can't you fit in?"

That was the beginning. She drank and got drunk to feel like one of them, to make a mockery of her superiority.

She got accepted into law school their first year of marriage. He begged her to postpone it so they could have their baby. Ellen was born. By then he'd had two lovers—a stripper and a bartender—and when she'd heard of it from gossipy friends he said he was sorry, but fucking a pregnant woman was just so repulsive and how could she expect him to go nine months without sex? So she got pregnant again right away to keep him from touching her. Jason was born.

By then he had a young woman lawyer living rent free in an apartment he owned. The only cost to the vulnerable young girl was to fuck the landlord every day.

Allison found out. She packed, babies and nanny and all, intending to head for an expensive condo across town while the divorce was settled. He never asked her to stay. But he fixed it so she couldn't leave.

Her family came the night just before she and the children were to make the move. He had gathered them unto him like sheep in his penthouse office. He told them how much he loved Allison, how worried he was, how living without her for a month or so was better than living without her forever after she drank and drugged herself to death. He wanted their help to have her committed to a mental institution where she could be treated for anorexia and alcoholism and cocaine addiction.

How Allison did scream that night. I've never done cocaine, she swore to them. I don't drink like he says I do, all day, every day, into oblivion. I fix breakfast and take the kids to school and do charity work. She begged. Please don't believe him! He wants me put away so he can have it all and owe me nothing! He's a monster!

She didn't go away. She locked the doors, huddled in bed with her babies, cried like an animal every night. He came to her one night.

"Come to our bed, Allison." Then he lay beside her, a poisonous asp slithering on her silky skin. "Stop trembling," he breathed at her. "Your family won't be back. They'll never be back. They told me that they don't care about you anymore. Drunks and addicts who won't get help are abandoned by all their loved ones. Don't contact them. They never want to see you again. All you have in the world now is me. And darling, if you leave me, if you go to a woman's shelter or try to disappear, I'll have you arrested. I'll tell the police that you're crazy and dangerous."

She was dry of all tears then, bereft of emotion as a dead body. "They won't believe you. I'm not crazy."

His eyes glinted in the dark. "The police will believe me. I own them. I own you. Now fuck me, Allison, and like it."

She lifted her head. The man on the stairway platform was gone. Then she saw him. He was coming toward her, clicking across the street.

She stiffened. Fuck it. Let him kill her. She wasn't going back. She was never going back.

But the man only wanted the cat, which had perched itself on the corner in the dusting of rain. He scooped up the cat like picking a flower and started back to his platform.

She stepped out. "Excuse me."

He turned. He was black, young, dressed like an FBI agent, but his complexion was hideously pocked.

"What the fuck?" He backed up, peered at her, dropped the cat which squirted away hissing.

"You have Montgomery Jones up there. I have a trunkful of cocaine and heroin you can have if you'll give him to me."

He moved for his breast pocket. Allison heaved up the double barrels. "I'm sorry to be rude," she said, "but all I want is Mr. Jones. Bring him down. I'll give you enough evil dust to make you a billionaire."

9

The man with the pocked face slowly dropped his hand from reaching for his gun. "Who the fuck are you?" He squinted at her through the veil of light rain.

Her acrylic talons didn't impede her trigger touch after all. "I'm a crazy woman. A crazy woman with a gun. Can you think of anything more scary?"

He swept his eyes up and down her, from shapely ankles and calves to breasts jutting from the opening in her lynx coat. "A goddamned good-looking crazy woman with a gun, honey, you got to know that. My, my, my. What the hell do you want with Mojo? You like dicks, my bulldozer of a cock makes his look like a damn little red wagon."

She wanted—actually salivated—to blow his head to pieces of brainless shrapnel. The double barrels pointed at his chest were raised to his head. She had a fierce look. He raised his hands.

She asked calmly, "You know who the real niggers are in this world? Women. We're the slaves. Slaves to roles we have to perform. Daughters are courteous and clean. Wives are thrifty and obedient. Grandmothers are trustworthy and reverent. Do you realize your race of black people was free before my gender could vote? What a bucket of shit it is, you standing there telling me about your cock before you even know for sure that I won't shoot you. A man about to die, and you're still trying to get laid. Well, I'm not playing a role tonight. Finally. For once. I'm a grown woman, not a Boy Scout. If you don't put your hands over your head and start up those stairs to where Monty Jones is, your bulldozer will be a Tonka toy when I'm through with you."

For a split second he considered going for his gun. The cat watched unblinking from its hiding place under a metal building overhang. Its eyes glowed gold.

He tried again, cool and playful. "Man, you ain't gonna shoot me. You look like all you need is some love. Me, you, going at it. You feeling good, not for free, neither. I got cash—"

A ball of fire lashed by his head, far enough to miss but close enough to drive his knees instinctively to the ground while he covered his head. He fell hard onto his chest and lay there on wet concrete.

Allison was strangely serene, the way she had been for a moment or so when an especially obstinate weed root had finally come free from the earth in her garden. There was relief, triumph, and yet in her view a thousand more stubborn weeds to attack.

"Mister, I don't know you. But I'm not feeling very friendly, helpful, or cheerful tonight. I'm just real fucking loyal."

He had caught some pellets in the face, sat up on his haunches rubbing the stings. "Loyal to Mojo? Jesus, why? He'd cut your head off and then piss down your throat while you died. Don't nobody give a shit about Mojo. Everybody just wants to kill him." The pellet had gotten his tongue; he bled a trickle from the mouth.

Allison commanded, "Who's up there with him?"

"Fuck you."

"Throw me your gun. Get up. Let's go."

"You go up there, white girl, they gonna kill your ass."

She shoved him ahead. "Good," she said. "Then this night was worth the price of admission."

First, Monty saw Ed "Black Bart" Riley stumble through the door with his hands raised, his overcoat stained and blood on his chin. Then Allison clomped in resting the shotgun on her bony hip. Her hair was stringy as if she'd just had a shower and put on a fancy fur coat to go out and get the morning paper in the yard. Because of the thick electrical tape on Monty's mouth, he had to gasp through his nose.

Black Bart Riley stood stoically in the amber shadows of the room. "Bitch says if we let Jones go we can have all the stash in his trunk parked down the road."

Monty thrashed. Riley and Allison and the two other hideous men ignored him. He was tied to a chair, making lots of noise but still tightly restrained.

The tall man, the composed one with the scar on his right cheek like a red ribbon, didn't acknowledge Allison at all. His eyes rose to bold-print exclamation points.

"All of it? What's that go for, about a million? Shit. Fuck. She'll give us that and all she wants is him?" He cocked a thumb at Monty, who was beginning to cry tears.

Allison's voice echoed in the empty office space. "I want him first. Then I'll come back and give you that . . . stuff."

The tall man with the scar looked from one thug to the other, and then he laughed. "No."

Allison swallowed dreadfully. "No? You don't want all that heroin and cocaine?"

There was a gold nugget ring on every one of the tall man's fingers. He fiddled with them. The room smelled like whiskey and Brut cologne. She was in some kind of nest, someplace she'd never dreamed of being, a land where restless, lawless addicts made their own laws. The three black men standing with her were criminals, killers, chain-smoking dope dealers. Soon, she knew, they would snap and shoot her.

He spoke. "Yes, of course I want what Monty's holding. He always has only the best. But first I want to fuck you, to lick soft white pussy, to taste nipples that are smooth and pink. You want him, this Mojo motherfucker piece of shit, take him, but not just for the drugs. Like I said, Monty has only the best, and that's what I want. All of it. Including you."

Monty stopped groaning. His silence was cryptic.

The room seemed to shrink. Suddenly Allison longed for the sweet breath of her baby girl Mary on her cheek. Mary was only five years old. Curls like roses on cake frosting. Allison went in every night to find Mary sleeping soundly under a mound of fresh blankets, flower patterns. She knelt there, listened to Mary inhale and exhale. The rhythm of peace. The drumbeat of human tenderness. She touched Mary sometimes, took little wisps of fingers in her hand and put them to her lips. Once, out of the depths of slumber, Mary had said in a sleepy voice, "They're still pink, aren't they, Mommy? You painted them pink yesterday. Did it come off yet?"

"No, sweetheart, your little fingernails are still pink. When you want me to, we'll make them red. Would you like that?"

A small face had come from under the flannel garden of quilts. "Mommy, I saw the stars tonight. You weren't home, but we sat outside with Nanny and we saw the stars. I want one. Can you get me a star?"

"Yes, oh yes, God, yes," she had cried. "Better still, sweetheart, I'll show you how to go up there and get a star for your very own self."

"I love you, Mommy. I love you so much."

The scar-faced black man lit a cigarette. In the blast of blue and yellow light he looked like a sneering jack-o'-lantern. He wanted to fuck her. She finally looked over at Monty. His stare bore through her, and she knew exactly what to do.

"Let him go," she said, "and I'll fuck you like there's no tomorrow."

Monty cried out when the tape was ripped from his face. The pocked man took out a huge hunting knife to cut away the ropes from Monty's hands and feet. Monty rose like an obsidian phoenix and seemed to snarl.

"Look at her, Danny. She ain't what you think."

Danny licked his wet black lips and blinked at Allison. "No, sir. She's better than I could imagine."

With clinical aplomb Allison announced, "I have AIDS. That's why I buy my shit from Monty. The medical stuff doesn't take care of the pain. If you fuck me, you'll get it. If you shoot me, pieces of my bone saturated with my blood may enter your skin, and you'll get it. If you try to wrestle me down and I scratch, cut, or bite you, you'll get it. If you touch me or let loose any of my body fluids in this room, you'll have AIDS. Let's go, Monty."

The pocked man let out a jungle scream, "Fuck you!" and dove for Monty's feet.

Allison threw the double-barreled shotgun. It slid slow-motion through the air, an explosive steel bomb heading for the black hands that caught it.

Once, twice, three times Monty fired. Shreds of lights and wooden walls rained between bloody screams. On her belly Allison scooted across the littered floor, over beer cans and discarded hypodermic needles, across wadded newspaper and containers of rotted fast food.

She hit the platform rolling, and then she ran. Down the stairs. Across the slick pavement. Through the pouring rain. Toward the light at the end of the alley where the car waited. She stopped once to yank the damned high heels off her small feet, took a breath as she leaned on a building, and heard two more sporadic shots. They were distant sonic booms.

In the car her chest hurt. She fell over in the darkness, and wept. The weeping, which she had held back for so long, eased the pressure and made her aching chest feel better. She sobbed, over and over, only one name.

"Mary! My darling! Mary . . . I love you, too."

10

Shiller wanted to be somewhere else. The hooker who'd flopped herself into his front seat smelled awful and was blowing booze breath onto him as she blabbed. His hair was uncomfortably damp under his cowboy hat. The windshield wipers sounded like knuckles slicing across a cheese grater. The n'er-do-wells who'd collected outside his car just beyond a filthy dive bar looked like spilled toxic waste to him.

Hadeesh was squeezed into the seat next to the hooker, fanning when she waved the cigarette in his face as she punctuated words with it. He was the picture of wholesome living. Shiller half-grinned at the boy's tortured expression, then watched as Hadeesh got out of the car.

Shiller said it with a tired sigh, "Shut up, Phyllis."

Her giant crisp wig swiveled toward him. One dagger of a purple fingernail pierced the air.

"You cannot talk to me that way. You cannot tell

me to shut up. It's a violation of my civil rights. You work for me."

He almost laughed. "If I worked for you I'd make a hell of a lot more money. And anyway, I work for taxpayers, not for whores who deal only in cash and never report a dime of it. Now tell me this story of yours."

She huffed. "Shit, why should I? You treat me like shit."

He leaned his face on the steering wheel. "What I don't do to you is what counts, Phyllis. I let you work. I don't haul you down once a week and cost you five hundred dollars in bail money, like I could do."

Her big lips pouted. Fake eyelashes clamped down on each other. "I was inside a car behind the five-twelve doing a little work, if you catch me."

Shiller muttered, "I do, all the time."

"I mean, if you understand. Mojo pulls up, sits awhile, smokes his cigar, checks his watch. A blonde—" A frown simmered in her bulging eyes. "—Not just any blonde, but some white rich bitch in a real leopard coat, flipping her hair, walking like she owns the damn world—she struts right up to Mojo's car and gets in."

Shiller yawned. "How'd you see all this while bobbing for balls?"

She hitched up her breasts under a low-cut sweater. "You gonna tell him I told?"

"Oh, sure. I'm a total dumb ass. Did I ever turn you around, Phyllis?"

She sucked smoke in like a fiery Buddha, then blew it back out. "You call me Syphilis behind my back. I should sue you for ruining my good name as a whore. I ain't got no diseases yet. Worst I ever had was warts down there, and once I had a kind of discharge for a month, but—"

Shiller grabbed air with the palm of his hand. "Whoa. Hey. Don't be cutting up that kind of info with me. I can't handle it. I'll never call you Syphilis again."

She eyed him, feeling sassy. "You gonna pay me?"

"Not to tell me about Jones. But I'll give you fifty bucks to never say the word 'discharge' to me again."

She settled back. Rain slashed sideways. Hadeesh hopped in place like a yellow buoy outside the window.

"We was through, me and my customer, the senator. You oughta watch him. While I suck him he likes to talk baby talk to me like I'm his mother."

Shiller groaned. "Lord. Is this planet a turd floating in midair? Go on."

"He pays by the hour, usually takes about two, the first hundred and nineteen minutes to get it up and one minute to come. I checked my watch. It was seven o'clock when the blond bitch sashayed up from nowhere. I watched while His Honor was counting out cash to me. That's all."

"Then what?" Shiller realized for the first time all day that he had been hungry until Phyllis fanned the fumes of rotten flesh through his car.

"Then we drove away. He took me back to my corner on Hemphill and Main. I didn't see no more."

She swacked down the visor and started applying lipstick. Shiller watched, nauseated at the thought of those gruesome lips anywhere on his person.

"How do you know it was a cigar and not a cigarette?"

"Monty don't smoke cigarettes. He smokes big fat cigars. What is that idiot camel jock doing?"

Shiller glanced. "He's trying to stay warm."

"Looks like he's having an attack of something. You sure about him?"

"You sure about Monty? Ever seen the blonde before? Did she get out of a car?"

"Not only have I not seen her before, I ain't seen nothing like her before except on the cover of white people's magazines in the Seven-Eleven. She wasn't buying no drugs, neither, because Mojo won't let you touch anything near him when you buy stuff. He don't want none of your fingerprints or hair around him."

"What'd she look like?"

"An actress. Playing a part, you know."

Shiller stared. "No. Tell me."

"Like one of them white girls that don't do nothing all day but fuck their boyfriends and spend their husband's millions. Like someone on a movie screen made up to look perfect. Perfect. That's it. Stupid bitch."

He fingered his bushy mustache. "Short hair?"

"To her shoulders. Kinda went around the collar of her coat like it was milk." She touched her own scouring pad of a wig. "Her skin was like that, too, like cream. Oh, and her shoes were red spike heels. Real nice." Her voice was thick with envy.

"Anything else?"

She snatched the fifty he held out. "Yeah. She wasn't scared. Walking down a dark alley in these streets full of killers, looking like she did, I mean just begging to be robbed and killed, and she wasn't scared at all."

"How could you tell?"

She patted his crotch and opened the door. "Because I'm scared every minute around here. I know how it looks to be afraid. She didn't have it."

Hadeesh sloshed when he sat down. The streams from his yellow slicker saturated the car seat. "Detective," he said breathlessly, "I am desperate for a woman, but for a woman like that I would remain forever celibate."

Shiller grinned as they pulled away. "We'll find you an all-American girl any day now, boy. It always happens when you ain't looking."

"American women hate me. They think I have socks or sausage in my underwear and that I aspire to own a convenience store. I'm a victim of stigma. No American girl will ever be in love with me, and I'm in love with all of them." He soured. "Except that one out there, Phyllis. She's horrible."

"You got to know one thing, Hadeesh, that'll make your life easier. With American women, we men are always victims of something. Me? I'm a victim of finances. The kind of women I crave are the ones who don't go around with broke old cops. I'm stuck with the kind of girls who bring casseroles and need gas money to get home."

"That will change, sir, when you are a famous attorney."

"Yep. Then I'll still be a victim of finances—stuck with the ones who only love you for what you can buy them. It's crazy, ain't it?"

11

As soon as Andy saw Detective Mike Shiller's unmarked car roll into the car-wash parking lot, he walked over and turned the Open sign to Closed. Old Beatty the shoe-shine man looked up. "I got another hour," he said in a hoarse rasp.

"I know," Andy said kindly, "but I got a lifetime of

trouble with this fucking cop. I'll make you up the difference in money before you go home tonight."

The brim of Shiller's hat hit the glass door as his hand reached, just as Andy turned the lock. They faced off through their own reflections in the bright lights.

"Open the door, Andy."

"We're closed."

"Says twenty-four-hour automated car wash on the sign." Shiller pointed upward through a glazed ring of rain.

"Take a rain check," Andy shouted.

Shiller stepped back. Andy relaxed. Maybe it was only a shakedown and not a real bust. Maybe Shiller was going on hunches and not an accurate hit list tonight. Then the stainless-steel Ruger loaded with Silvertips came methodically out of Shiller's belt into his capable hands and pointed at the door's lock. Andy lifted a hand, complacently turned the lock to the open position.

Shiller stepped inside the foyer, an encased glass cubicle of uncomfortable chairs flanked on each side by avenues into and out of the car-wash terminals. The lights were bright enough to be bruising to the ego and the complexion. Nobody in there could look pompous or pretty.

An office door along one wall was barely opened. Shiller pushed it so the door swung inward. Hadeesh ambled into the nook stained with cigarette smoke and oily smudges. "Where's the boss man?" Shiller asked.

Andy was a sixty-year-old stick of black muscle, tough as a dog's leather chew stick. His white hair sat on his head as if the wind had blown it upward. His chest was sunken, his hands and face beaten by both weather and the fists of cops and bad guys over the years. "Ain't seen him tonight."

Shiller replaced the gun into its holster. "Yeah? One

of my uniforms says Mojo pulled in here a couple hours ago, got out, and came inside. With a briefcase. Reckon if I called up for a search warrant I'd find that case in this here office, chockful of cocaine-stained hundreds? Shoot, Andy, then I'd have to bust you for possession of all that dope, and then you'd be implicated in the shooting where that money came from tonight."

Andy didn't flinch. "Yeah, then you'd have to hang around here about six hours to work the bust and then whoever you're looking for who really did that shooting would coast on down to the river and get rid of the guns, so you wouldn't have no weapon to go on when you finally caught him. You are one dumb motherfucker, Shiller."

Shiller scratched his head, set back the Stetson onto his hairline. "Yeah, but you're on parole, so I don't have to prove the dope is yours. I just have to catch you in the same remote vicinity where it is. And you go back to playing honeymoon every day in the shower with twenty horny sons of bitches who outweigh you by about six cock inches. Hadeesh, radio for a warrant. Or maybe we'll just go in there on probable."

Old Beatty said without looking up from where he was stuffing bottles of shoe polish into a box, "Seems to me, boy, you'd be wanting to stay way the hell far off from Mojo. Only reason you ain't dead is 'cause he'd be the first suspect. 'Sides which, he don't think your honky ass is worth killing. Way you carried on, crying on the TV news, he figures your life is already a pile of dog shit. I wouldn't be backing Mojo into no corners if I was you, boy. A man who's been done like you did to him is likely to snap and wouldn't nobody blame him in this town."

The detective's face burned red with rage and regret. Suddenly the wafting shoe polishes smelled like the putrid fluids that had assailed him when he had watched Othel Middleton's autopsy that stifling airless night the year before.

He walked to the hunched-over old man, took hold of a shoulder soft in muscle and brittle in bone, and pushed Beatty against the wall. With the nozzle of Shiller's gun jammed into the flesh of his jowls, Beatty made a bleating sound, dropped the box. Shoe polish splattered and flowed like art deco. Hadeesh froze; he knew Shiller was crazy. Andy bristled; he knew even better than Hadeesh that Shiller was crazy and dangerous.

The click of the hammer resonated against the crackling sound of rain on the tin roof. In his grip, Shiller could feel Beatty's heart rate thicken and quicken.

"Old man, I won't be needing your permission to do my goddamned job no matter how many people I kill to get it done. I realize that all them political, liberal-type fake intellectuals think every fourteen-year-old gang member is a national treasure, our way of apologizing to you for us being white, but in my way of seeing it, the little sawed-off fucker had a gun pointed at me."

He moved into Beatty's face so his breath was warm on the beads of sweat on the old man's forehead. "You know what it's like to have a gun pointed at you?" He was down to a whisper that sounded like blood coursing silently. "And to wonder if the crazy bastard is really going to shoot you? You know what that's like? Scary, ain't it? Real fucking scary."

The long moment simmered. Beatty wanted to cry. Shiller wanted to vomit, hated himself, felt no choice except to let his insanity work for him and save him as it always had. Hadeesh put a hand on Shiller's shoulder.

"Detective, I will go outside and ask if anyone in the crowd saw Mojo. Meanwhile, you decide if you are not smarter and stronger than these enemies. I think you are."

A brassy blond whore in tight red leggings and a feather boa waddled over to Hadeesh outside under the prism of fluorescent raindrops. Shiller slumped behind his steering wheel. His hands shook, though he was too numb to feel the cold. He recalled crouching over Othel on the sidewalk, feeling and smelling the mush of blood that flowed like steam from the boy's throat. The gun coiled in the kid's hand was plastic. Even now, Shiller had to clinch shut his eyes at the horror of the lightweight toy smattered with blood. He had picked it up, held it in mesmerized disbelief while the boy made gurgling sounds, sprawled like a war-zone victim. Sirens wailed. Shiller had screamed so loud in his agony of the moment that the sirens seemed to go mute in the night.

He didn't duck or bend or even resist when Monty Jones approached him at Othel's evangelical funeral. In the bright sun, amid the gospel singing and the horrible shrieks of grief from the congregation, Monty Jones hit Shiller square and broke his jaw.

They had not crossed paths since then. Shiller pressed no charges and Jones never came to finish the beating he had begun that day. Tonight, Shiller knew, would be a command performance for both men. He shivered. Hadeesh slammed a car door. "He was here about an hour ago, dressed nice, so we should check the nightclubs in this neighborhood. The woman with him is, they said, very beautiful, fragile, and yes, she is white, but not the type, they told me, to be working by the hour."

"Then what the hell is she doing with a known murderer and cocaine dealer?"

"She was in the backseat. Perhaps a hostage? I suggest we try the Iguana Club first. Would you like me to drive? You look pale."

Shiller lit a cigarette, exhaled heavily, pulled into the morose row of cars stopping to buy gruesome girls and good drugs.

"Jones said if he ever got me in his sights again he'd kill me."

"He will not have a chance, sir. I am here with you. I am at your back. Besides, we are friends, yes?"

Shiller laughed. Hadeesh saluted.

12

She stopped crying when she heard the eerie thud on the hood of the car. The luminescent eyes looking at her through the windshield were angry and had red, unhuman centers. She sat up, wiped her nose with her furry sleeve. The cat regarded her from where it sat near the Cadillac's front grill.

Suddenly a man was in the door and on top of her, mauling, grunting. She was knocked backward toward the passenger seat and smelled an unfamiliar pungent odor. Gunpowder.

Monty was panting painfully. They wrestled awkwardly as he shoved her away and she grabbed to see if he was all right. Instead of words they were reduced to a series of silly, meaningless grunts. He threw the car into drive and the rear end sat suspended a moment before it met the wet pavement and they were moving.

"You're okay?"

Like a mommy she was reaching to monitor the feel of his forehead. He slapped away her hand.

She took hold of what was in his lap. Silver tape. Rope. A doorknob. Shreds of evidence that he might have left in the room, things that had touched his skin or his fingers.

"I am in big, big trouble. I got to get rid of her. I got to do something with this shotgun. I got to think, think, Monty." He talked to himself hysterically, not to Allison.

"I got to figure something out. Too many people saw me leave the Iguana Club with Ed; nobody knew he was carrying on me. It looked like I went along on my own. Shit. Fuck. They'll rap the ammo out to this gun as the same ones from the 512 Club. I'm fucked."

He was perspiring, twitching.

Allison said smoothly, "Slow down. This is not the time to get pulled over for speeding."

He glanced, then in a heated warp he swerved, slammed against a curb, and took her by the throat. She couldn't breathe.

"Look here, fuck your stupid little games, girl. This is some bad shit I did. This is death penalty shit I did, multiple homicides. You understand?"

She made gagging noises. Through her nose she could taste only the slightest slivers of air. He was choking her to death, waiting for her larynx to collapse. She jerked reflexively, feeling herself want to control her muscles but reacting to dying the natural way that any suffocation victim would do.

She felt something like the first wonderful headiness after a martini. She did not struggle to stop him. Finally there was no air at all. She felt her face bulging, suffered the anguish as her body fought to make her gasp for air that wouldn't come.

She saw a movie, a hologram of deep dimension that intrigued her as she began to die. She forgot wanting a breath. She remembered distinctly why she never did want another moment of this life.

The beautiful blond apparition was crying. He was brutalizing her again, having her hair wadded around his hand like an elegant bandage, and he dragged her. She scrambled for her feet because her knees were growing bloody, but she couldn't get a stance because he pulled so fast, as if she were a heavy human trash bag he was hauling to the curb.

The force of his hatred was like flames lapping the air. She made crying sounds that he could hear and that he enjoyed. "You want to leave me, you fucking drunk slut? You don't love me? No-fucking-body walks out on me, you stupid bitch." They hit the brick stairs of the patio. With his strong free arm he flung open the door to the house. Her arms were bloody from scraping the edges of the narrow stairs.

She was screaming. "Don't, please don't hurt me. I just want to go! I'll go away! You can have it all. Just let the children and me go, please. Don't hit me."

But he did. Smack in the belly with his fist. She tried to fall in pain, but he held her by the hair like a damaged marionette. "Children? You goddamned whore. You leave me, you'll never see these kids again. I own these fucking kids. I'll fix it in court so you're not allowed within a hundred goddamned yards of any of them."

There was the rusty taste of blood on her teeth from where he had slapped her when he pulled her out of her car when she tried to drive away. She begged. Pitiful, pathetic, in such mammoth physical pain and emotional terror. "Just let me leave. If I stay you're going to kill me by accident. One slam too many. You won't mean to do it, but I'll be dead. Why, why do you hate me so much?"

He raised his fist. He was a dragon. "Because I love you, and you don't deserve to be loved. You can go."

She took a remotely hopeful breath that night. "I can?"

He smiled, a torturer's sick reward. "You can go if you come and tell the children you're stupid and worthless."

She sat on the floor calmly. He brought the babies in, sleepy and rumpled in their pajamas from the television room. Ellen rushed and bent to her.

"Mommy, you're bleeding. Daddy, what happened to Mommy?"

She was barely seven years old. Jason was two years younger and Mary was a month from turning three.

The dragon commanded, "Get away from her. Sit on the hearth."

They huddled, fire at their backs and a cold, lifeless mother in front of them.

Allison's voice quivered. "You need to know something, my little sweethearts. I'm . . ." God, how she had wept! "Mommy is really, really stupid and worthless."

Jason, pink cheeks and burr haircut and footballs on his pj's, had chirped, "I don't think so. I think you're really smart. Remember you taught me to ride my bike without training wheels, all by yourself?"

Mary's tiny, flimsy porcelain arms had reached. "Mommy? Can I hold you? Are you going? Can we go?"

"Your mommy," he said with the power of a man transfused with new bad blood, "doesn't love you. Isn't that right, Allison?"

The chest pain doubled her over. "Yes. That's right."

Jason clamped shut. Ellen wiped a tear. Mary bellowed loudly in sudden overt sadness. Allison, for all purposes, died.

But he didn't let her leave after all. He led the children away, came back, and somberly knocked Allison unconscious on the parquet game-room floor. She stayed in bed for days with the heavy drapes drawn until he needed her to appear with him at a dinner party where the news media would be watching them. She bought a six-thousand-dollar beaded dress. At the party when the lights came up and the applause began, he ceremoniously kissed his wife and whispered to her, "You . . . are . . . nothing." She got very, very drunk very, very fast.

Monty had suddenly released his choke hold. He was cursing, not at her but at himself. She was limp, able only to cough as mucus and saliva dripped from her mouth and nose. The hologram had faded in a swarm of stars as oxygen flushed her again.

Monty cradled his head. "I should fucking kill you. Why don't I fucking kill you?" He struck a thinker's pose. "Do I like you? No. Not one goddamned bit. Do I feel sorry for you? Shit, no. Crazy bitch. Got all the chances in the world to make something and fucking up all of them because your big white daddy don't pay you enough attention. Do I want to fuck you? Is that why I'm keeping your stupid ass alive and carting you around like I'm some damned social worker to drunk, rich, neglected, worthless broads? Honestly, I believe I'd rather fuck a beehive than you. Least if I survived I'd have me some honey. You, I fuck you, I got nothing when it's over except a witness. Shit. Goddamn it."

Allison's breathing was troubled, and she had only begun to regain muscle control. She coughed out some words.

Monty ignored her, groused more, slammed a fist into the steering wheel. "I could blow your head off. Wouldn't bother me none at all. Bitch. Dump your body right here in this gutter and let all the white cops go in and watch the autopsy just to see your pretty tits. Why don't I?"

She was crying. Because her throat hurt and because he wouldn't stop insulting her.

He spoke some words, angelic in their honesty. "You want to drive your son-of-a-bitch husband crazy, woman? Yeah? Then live. Go home and get well and turn out to be okay. That's how you get even with somebody who tries to take you down. Somebody hates you bad, you dance while they can't do nothing but watch."

He stared at her, a mixture of poignance and disgust. "You know why I won't kill you? You know why I'm a good criminal, Allison Robbins, and not a great one? Because I have a conscience. Weren't for that, me, I'd be famous."

She had been light-headed when he choked her, maybe lost awareness for a time. Sparks had cascaded in her vision. But she was breathing now, able to talk.

"I'm sorry, Montgomery. I didn't mean to be so much trouble."

"Fuck sorry. I don't need sorry. I need the impossible. I need an alibi."

"You were with me."

He chuckled unkindly. "Yeah? And why would any fucking cop believe you? Look at you, all messed up with that shit running down your face, that black eye-makeup stuff. Your dress is all wrecked. Your hair's kinda—" He studied her. "Kinda nasty and wet. How the hell you going to tell anybody anything that keeps my ass off death row after what I did tonight? Who the hell do you think you are?"

She dreaded it but said it. "Allison Robbins."

"Right. That'll do it. Mr. Officer, you best believe I'm innocent because this shabby-looking skinny blonde whose old man won't pork her says I am. Forget all them dead bodies and the fact that I happened to be in each choice location at the time of the killings. The blond bitch says I was with her. Cop says to me, who the fuck is she?"

She lay her head back, considered a star dangling between parted clouds as if it was winking at her. She told him quietly, "She's Allison Robbins. She's the wife of our esteemed and upstanding district attorney."

He had some sort of comical seizure, leaping from the car and spinning around on his heels, screaming. It was an African scene almost, as if he beckoned some jungle god.

He blithered and yelled. "What? What? What? No. Yes? For fucking real? I've killed five people and you're the chief prosecutor's old lady?" He laughed, something hysterical, a chant, an animal sacrifice. "God. Oh, God. Shit! Death row? No, too good for you, nigger. I'm the fucking district attorney and I sentence you to life in prison sharing a cell with the fucking Osmond Brothers who'll never stop singing. The DA?" He bellowed laughter again. "No? Yes! I can't kill you. Do you see that? How 'bout we make a deal and you kill me? Least I won't be butt-fucked by Aryans for fifty years first. Yeah, bitch, you got us into this trouble, now you owe me. You get that gun and you kill me. Oh, shit. There won't be no flute playing in prison this time. Death row. Jesus. That's what I'll do. I'll find Jesus as my personal savior and then I'll beat your ass until you don't remember this whole evening . . ."

He carried on maniacally. Allison smoked, stood by the car, worked on her smudged face with a tissue from Monty's glove box. She spoke without fanfare.

"He beats me. I hate him. I'll help you any way I can if you'll just kill me so I don't have to go home."

The cat had gotten spooked when Monty went manic, risen to its feet in an explosion, and darted into darkness.

Monty seemed to have just run four miles, sweating, panting, jumping in place to cool down. "Get in the car. The cops are looking for us. We gotta get rid of this evidence and this gun. You know, you didn't need to make up that AIDS shit. Just tell 'em who your old man is and they'd have shot themselves in the fucking heads. The DA? No shit?"

She answered him truthfully with a dull, unblinking

stare across the top of the car where they faced each other.

"I didn't tell you because I knew you wouldn't help me die. I can't go home. I won't."

He shook his head like a dog. "Get in the god-damned car. Maybe I can figure a way to save both our asses."

The dainty star poking through puffy clouds led the way as the car lumbered into the tunnel of thunder and lightning creeping up on the distant horizon.

13

The old house listed sideways in the darkness like a sinking ship. Its clapboard sides were peeling badly and were muddy from splashes of rain off the bare dirt of the lawn. The house was a cracker box, the porch barely wide enough for two people to crowd onto under the one grisly yellow bulb.

Allison huddled behind Monty's massive shape as he rapped on the crumbling door. They stood in stony silence.

A few of the other houses in the dilapidated neigh-borhood bore condemned signs on what was left of their kicked-in or rotted-away doors. The occupied ones on the dirt road were merely overhead shelters with lawns laden with junk—mountains of plywood, rusted cars without tires, ratty furniture tossed aside. The yards were mud. The people she could see through the bare windows were mummies bathed in the blue sheen of televisions. No children played outside.

A train whistle made a bleak, angry tone in the background. A stretch of sleek freeway curled up into the sky nearby and made an abrupt turn away from this relic of a government housing project. Cars whooshed on the wet pavement. Allison smelled exhaust fumes and other exotic scents such as boiled vegetables and marijuana.

She shivered. "Where are we?"

Monty's knuckle cracked once on the wood. "The slums."

She was one step below him, pulled her lynx in closer at the throat, felt his rear end against her chest. "My God, people live in these horrible little houses? They haven't even enough room to give dinner parties."

Monty didn't turn. "Very funny."

The wind carried his cologne like veils touching her face. "I was joking. I mean, whose house is this?"

The wooden door backed in on itself, letting light and incense and Ravi Shankar music gush out. There were clicking noises and a shadowy form in the doorway. When the globe of weak yellow porch light hit the form, Allison saw that the clicking came from beads that drenched the woman's flowing African robes.

Monty's voice was soft as a distant church bell. "Mama," he said to her, "I need some cleaning up."

She was the most beautiful woman Allison had ever seen. Big as an opera singer, vibrant as a kindergarten teacher. She enveloped Monty in a wave of kisses and hugs and called him baby and darling. Her skin had a golden sheen, something of a young island girl, and her teeth were white as pearls when she smiled while caressing Monty. He stepped back obediently as she swept her eyes to Allison standing pitifully just inside the door.

"Just look at you . . ." she swooned, coming toward Allison, opening arms like a giant jaw and consuming her. ". . . All wet and shivering." Huge breasts under the vividly colored robe parted on Allison's body like two more droopy arms. She was inside a loving cocoon.

The voice was a minister, soothing, promising, forgiving, hopeful.

"Allison," the woman repeated after Monty, then stepped back and looked as though she were seeing a fabulous museum painting. "My, that is a lovely name." The gaze swamped Allison with affection. Great hands with snow white palms swept the air, and bracelets jangled like wind chimes.

"You are good, Allison. I'm seeing your aura, darling. Orange because you are friendly, likely the life of the party. Yellow because you are optimistic even in troubled times. Pink!" Her eyes swelled. She took a deep breath, moving her hands around Allison like a metal detector. "Pink because you love someone—or several someones—unconditionally." Her tone rose in alarm. She searched Allison's eyes.

"But baby . . . oooh, honey . . . why do you not have this unconditional love for yourself, darlin'? Now just look at this black *X* that goes right across your heart. God is calling you to love yourself unconditionally, and oh my, how you do resist loving yourself. You must, baby. You will. God is in you, moving around, loving you, waiting for you to learn that you are part of Him and you are good."

Wind chaffed the house. Things rattled. Allison was afraid that any moment Jesus was going to appear before her, all bloody.

The woman spoke again, full of conviction. "Monty, this child needs a robe and a bowl of stew, both of which Mother Marie is going to get for her while you pour her and me a big ol' Jack Daniels."

She paraded from the room into a tiny hole of darkness. A light came on. She hummed. The East-Indian music moaned.

"She's . . . fantastic," Allison gushed quietly.

Monty clanked booze into glasses on a small end table; no ice, she noticed. He extended her one.

"Did you grow up here, Monty?"

He slumped into a soft, badly worn couch and reached to switch off the lamp. He was hoarse. "No. We lived in the projects downtown until Mama had no more kids living at home. Then she had to get out." He glanced around with sudden disdain. "I could get her a better place but she won't take my money. She lives here off what she makes telling fortunes."

Allison sat in an upright dining table chair in a slant of light that seemed to carry the humming on it like a bridge. "You have brothers and sisters?"

Monty yawned. "Had. My brother Clark died in Nam. They always sent all the brothers out to do the most dangerous stuff first, draw out the enemies. His platoon got lost, nobody came to look for them. He was gutted with a knife. I was seventeen then. And last year my little brother Othel was shot and killed by a cop."

Allison flinched. "That was your brother? My husband tried to personally get that cop the electric chair. Shiller, that's his name. Your mother had a fourteen-year-old son?"

"Adopted. He died, she moved here. And I'll kill Shiller yet."

Marie appeared like a glamorous movie queen and set a tray in front of Allison. "Chitterlins', baby. Nice and hot. Here's a gown for you, angel. It's your size." She smiled and Allison did, too. "See, Marie got your size because I knew you was coming, honey. These are some slippers for you. You go get nice and dry, baby, and eat before your stew's cold."

Monty watched Allison step lightly into the house's only tiny bathroom with a door into the only bedroom. He watched his mother sip whiskey and sigh with great satisfaction. "Mama, you have any readings tonight?"

"No, I blocked the evening off when I had the vision of you coming here. What is it, baby? What do you need?" She leaned forward heavily and lighted the many candles set on a round table between them.

"I killed some people tonight. A white son of a bitch who was selling dope to kids, two baby fuckers and three assholes who were about to cut my throat if I didn't stop them." He hung his head. The candles flowed warmth into his eyes and flowery scents into his nostrils. "She saw some of it. She's the district attorney's wife."

He raised his head. "She plops from nowhere into my car tonight behind the five-twelve, asks me to please kill her. I was hiding her in my car when the thing went down with the baby fuckers trying to pass off films instead of money. The other three ambushed me and she followed, saw the whole thing when I had to take them out." He looked toward the bathroom. "She saved my butt, I'll tell you." A vague, tired smile came to his face. "Busted in there promising to fuck everybody if they'd cut me loose. They went blind thinking about some pussy and did what she said to do. Otherwise I'd be dead by now. She wants me to kill her, Mama, and I think I might have to do it. For my own reasons, not hers."

The candlelight illuminated her gold eyeliner and red lipstick. When she spoke she sounded like the wind scurrying leaves and raindrops outside on the porch. "He beats her. He has paid someone to kill her. Ah, five thousand dollars cash. He cannot divorce her because the financial investigation would reveal great amounts of money he has stolen from his brother in a business they own together."

She looked squarely at him. The train whistle in the distance sobbed. An ambulance siren wobbled. Thunder. A strange breeze ruffled the candles though no door had opened. Monty's skin went cold.

"Who's here, Mama? Who is it?"

She closed her eyes. "The devil."

"Why?"

"He . . ." she strained, then relaxed. ". . . He wants events to happen. A husband murders. A woman suffers treacherous physical pain before she dies. Children . . . ah . . . sweet children lose their mama. Satan wants it, wants to vanquish the Lord, to delight in such human suffering."

"So why is he here in this room?"

One candle flared as a moth dived into it. The sparks of the moth's ashes were colorful. Marie opened her eyes.

"He's here, baby, because you're in his way."

Allison appeared, wrapped in silk of gold and red swirls, her hair thrown elegantly up on her head. Her face was scrubbed bare of cosmetics and was even more beautiful unadorned. Monty ran a hand through his coarse black hair.

Allison said to him, "Did you just call out my name while I was in there? Someone did."

Monty's heart thudded. Marie gasped. The rain bled heavily.

14

Before entering the Iguana Club, Shiller and Hadeesh had unhooked the straps on their pistol holsters; it was police policy within the perimeter of the Stop Six beat.

The glaze of colored lights swallowed them just inside the door. They could feel the floor vibrate from the music and the patrons stiffen from the presence of cops. As was also policy in Stop Six, Shiller and Hadeesh had called for backup. Two uniformed officers heeled at their sides.

They parted at the step down toward the room of crowded tables. A lanky black man in slick black leather played a saxophone up on a stage veiled in smoke while a black woman and a white woman dressed in matching sequins swayed together and sang loudly about loving a man.

Stormy weather . . . Shiller had the remnants of it on his drenched long duster. Across the room through the haze, he saw Hadeesh's mouth move as he bent to question the deadpan bartender. The lantern-jaw uniform stayed at Hadeesh's vulnerable back, facing the crowd.

Shiller headed for the men's room and motioned over the loudness for the redheaded woman uniform cop to wait outside. She touched a palm to the butt of her .45 and nodded.

His voice bounced on the tile floor and mirrored

walls. He caught a glimpse of himself—big black Stetson dripping at the edges, sand-colored duster stained with rainwater, mustache drooping long at the edges of his mouth, a hairy perpetual frown, bags under his eyes, a five o'clock shadow now decayed into a ten o'clock stubble.

The assorted black men at the urinals turned in unison when he yelled, "Lord, look at those dicks! If inches were dollars, this here would be the Bank of America."

He leaned on the door. No out. No in. The silence was robbed only by a flush from one of the stalls, then the clanking of a belt buckle. Four faces turned to him, various heights and haircuts, but all grim.

The old one, whom Shiller recognized as an ex-con named Hatchet because that had been his trademark tool when he went stalking through a park looking for his wife and the man she was having an affair with, thirty years earlier, raised a stern hand.

"Catch you some yonder right now, Shiller, while your motherfucking white ass can still walk. That door behind you don't swing outward, boy."

Shiller pushed up the brim of his hat. Water made a dripping echo in a sink. Nobody stepped toward him. A tall skinny man in an orange zoot suit and a hat sat smugly on the sink, his legs angled out like tentacles. With his hand he made a gun-shooting motion at Shiller.

"I'm looking for Monty Ray Jones."

The zoot suit risked it. "That your woman he's with? Nah, fucking nah, man. Fine bitch like that wouldn't have no use for your ugly ass, unless she needs traffic jams directed while she walks down the street."

They laughed except for one, the one Shiller recognized as a newspaper reporter. His shirt was crisp and tucked in, but he was drunk, defiant by status but respectful by profession. Shiller eyed him.

"Evenin', Ronald. You seen Jones here tonight?"

Ronald cleared his throat to try and sound sober. "No, man. I just got here." He put his hands up. "Last time I saw Mojo, he was busting your jaw at his brother's funeral. I got my first front page byline for catching that story."

One who was clearly a youngster about twenty years old—big shoulders, high-tops, baggy jeans, surfer on his tee-shirt—wiped repeatedly at his nose, sniffled constantly.

"You got a cold, boy?"

The boy slurred. His eyelids drooped. "I ain't got shit, man, 'cept my daddy the senator out there waiting for me—" He put a long finger into his own chest. "—to come carry his water bucket, you know." He sniffled again, wiped his nose, blood smeared on his pale palm.

"Your daddy taught you to use, boy? He fucking buys you that poison, and you don't whip his ass?"

The zoot suit chimed in. "The fruit don't fall far from the fucking apple tree of sin, man."

They laughed again. Thunder shook the ground like an alien crawling through the floor beneath them.

Hatchet, the old man, growled, "We your prisoners?"

Zoot stood. "No. Maybe the motherfucker thinks we his slaves."

The reporter stepped in front of Zoot. "Shiller, you can't do this. You know it. You can get a warrant for Jones and then detain us in public in the presence of other officers or subpoena us downtown, but you can't do this bad honky Kojak shit and shake us down like—"

Shiller hit him. Half-force. Fist in the gut. Ronald crumbled first, then stumbled backward into a paper-towel rack jutting from the wall, then to his knees, where he leaned onto the floor and made gagging sounds.

Zoot sat back down. The kid started to cry, sob as if his dog had just died in his arms. The old man went to the reporter.

Shiller spat on the floor. "Let's see, Ronald, as witnesses you got yourself a panel of fucking up-standing experts. An ex-con who ain't supposed to be where people consume alcohol, a minor whose father would sooner tell him to piss from the steps of the White House than testify against me, and, of course, you got Zoot Suit here, out on a weekend pass from the psyche unit at the county hospital where he's been since they found his girlfriend wrapped neatly in butcher paper in his freezer last month. Fuck you, Ronald, shut up. You can't make news; you just write it. I can't break the law; I am the law. Just consider yourself in the wrong place at the wrong time and chalk it up to waking up with fleas. Now, any of you dog motherfuckers seen Monty Jones tonight?"

The door behind Shiller budged. Hadeesh called out. "It is me, Detective." He stepped in, saw the reporter belly-down on the tile floor. "Does he need an ambulance? What happened to him?"

Shiller lit a cigarette. "He resisted arrest. And no, he don't need an ambulance; he needs a reliable source, but this don't seem to be his lucky night."

Hadeesh helped Ronald up. "You were arresting him, Detective?"

"No, but he didn't know that. C'mon, Zoot Suit, you and me's going back to the nut ward. They don't let you out of there so you can go get all drunked-up and then start seeing demons have sex in the trees so the only way you can stop them is to hack up a hooker. Let's go."

The tall Zoot began backing up, sat fully in the yellow stain of the urinal. "He left with Danny the Dictionary. The blond bitch ran out after them."

The old man muttered, "Got'dam . . ." The senator's smart-ass son laughed. The reporter bent to wash his face, then vomited.

He groused, "If I have broken ribs, Shiller, I'm suing your ass."

Shiller grinned, stomped out the cigarette. "If this son of a bitch Jones has murdered anybody else while your lying ass protected him, boy, your next headline will be when the guards at Huntsville take the electric razor to your scalp on your first day. Remember that thing you wrote about me in that big story of yours?"

The anger was like a tongue between their almost-touching faces. "What? When I wrote that you had as many police commendations for bravery as you did citations for stupidity?"

"No. That part was true. I'm talking about when you wrote that I showed no emotion at Othel's funeral."

"You didn't. You killed a little boy and you didn't even cry when you stood by his dead body."

Standing at attention, Hadeesh said, "Mr. Reporter, we are law officers. If once we begin to cry, we will never stop. I would appreciate it if all of you would put your hands on your heads until the detective and I are out of the room. Thank you."

Shiller ambled in front, feeling as if the world was the deep end of the pool and he didn't know how to swim. Hadeesh yanked at him from behind. Shiller leaned through the screaming music. The uniforms skidded to a stop behind them.

Hadeesh hurt his ear yelling into it. "Detective Shiller, over there at the bar is a woman I would like to meet. If I don't, as you say, seize the moment, then the moment will be gone forever."

Hadeesh wiggled his brows. Shiller laughed. He saw the young black woman lounging over the bar with a malt liquor. Short hair. Long legs. Stiletto heels. Silver leggings. Cigarette holder.

He yelled and knew he was hurting Hadeesh's eardrum. "She already knows you're in love with her. Everybody's in love with her. What she don't know is what you can do for her. What can you do for her, Hadeesh?"

The wiggling eyebrows caught an arch and stayed there. "Well, sir, I can lick my eyebrows."

"Go tell her that."

The large brown eyes and silver leggings turned momentarily toward the spiffy black cop uniform and beholden face.

When the pretty girl's drink sloshed with force into Hadeesh's innocent face, Shiller burst into laughter. So did the uniforms behind him.

Jumping through spattering rain toward the car, Hadeesh sighed at Shiller, "It did not work, sir."

Shiller slapped him on the back. "I know. It never worked for me, either, but I was always hoping to see it work for some brave warrior. Where to, Sherlock?"

"An all-points for Jones, sir."

The radio crackled in the dash. Shiller shivered and turned the heater full blast. They stared at each other, troubled and yet not surprised.

Three men shot dead in the warehouse district nearby. Shiller hit the siren.

Hadeesh said without malice, "She threw her drink on me. I smell like liquor."

Shiller grinned again. "Good for you, boy. Now the other cops on the scene will finally trust you."

15

The two ambulances in the warehouse parking lot somberly went dark; the paramedics knew there would be no need to rush to a hospital. Only cop car lights made blue strobes across the shiny wet parking lot. Up the stairs in a dingy room littered with needles and trash, the crime-scene officers stood over dead bodies and took photographs.

Shiller and Hadeesh moved back when they were through with a terse examination of the bodies. Uniformed officers around them collected bits of strewn garbage and even tagged as evidence a straight-backed wooden chair that had been shot up into three separate pieces.

"If Jones was here," Shiller began.

Hadeesh clipped him off. "Then he was forced here by Solomon because of the information Jones gave to the FBI about Solomon's drug and racketeering organization."

Shiller gnawed an unlit cigarette, glanced dryly at a flash of lightning outside the door. He pointed at the rotund and lifeless body of the black man who had wanted sex with Allison and said, "Buddy Solomon and Danny were under heavy federal indictment for drugs, prostitution, you name it, all sorts of dirty shit. They must've suspected that—"

Hadeesh barked, "—that Monty Ray is the informant who will be the FBI's main witness next month at the hearing, which is not true, because the main witness is Alexander Johnson, Solomon's top most trusted sidekick in the drug cartel. It was Johnson, I believe, who made bail for Solomon and Danny, almost six million dollars, quite a lot of friendship, if you ask me—"

"Which I didn't."

Hadeesh waved at the smoke Shiller blew in his face. "No, sir, you didn't, but I am learning to anticipate your thoughts so that I may be an excellent partner."

Shiller yawned. He wanted a beer and a burrito supreme from the fast-food joint on the main road to his farm. "So Solomon has Danny take Jones here, thinking Jones is the snitch, but where's the evidence putting Jones here? I guess somewhere there'll be—"

"Yes, fibers from Jones's hair and clothing, but in this mad array of debris the chances of finding even a fingerprint are remote. How am I doing?"

Shiller glared. "You get any more clairvoyant, Radar, and we can go on a talk show and amaze the world. So now—"

"—If Jones was here and they restrained him, he took the stuff with him after he shot them all and is now hiding them while we stand here watching cops kill roaches."

Shiller tried again. "Maybe it—"

"—Wasn't Monty, maybe the woman got the drop on Solomon and the others while Monty was restrained. Although if it was the woman she was a very good marksman, I must say." He stared at Shiller.

"Shit, no," Shiller snapped. "I ain't even gonna start—"

"Well, you are wondering where we should look first. At his home out there on the lake, at the airport, his car washes. You are thinking that by now the shotgun is melted to a very sturdy metal doorstop and the suit with the matching fibers is ashes. And you are wanting a burrito."

Shiller choked. Hadeesh clamped him on the back and said, "But that is not clairvoyance, sir. I heard you say it to the other sergeant over there earlier. About the burrito."

A burly Hispanic cop stepped as lightly as he could amid the shattered glass and filthy rags and bags. "We're done here, Detective. Amid all this bullshit you can't really tell evidence from assholes, but we got what we can. There might be prints on the chair, but the powder burns fucked that up pretty good. If there's fibers in here the fucking roaches already ate 'em. I got the shotgun casings, but you know that whole drill."

A plump white larvae was rolled past them on a stretcher, Solomon's dead hand dangling and dripping blood. The uniformed cop sighed with ardent fatigue and rubbed his weary face.

"I know you'll do it up right, Shiller, but ask yourself who gives a flying fuck about these dead grunts."

Shiller grinned dryly. "These men were only indicted, Paco, not convicted, and that means a great deal to me, to see that each citizen's rights are upheld equally as I strive to protect and serve without prejudice."

Paco grinned, too. "Oh, yeah, I forgot that part. You know how Solomon made most of his money? Running young girls up here from Mexico, telling 'em they were going to work for nice families, then putting 'em in snuff films, tied up, tortured, murdered. Yeah, I'm gonna miss him."

Hadeesh looked pale even for his cinnamon-stained skin. Shiller asked him, "You all right, boy?"

"I am sorry Solomon will not receive a trial and execution."

"Well," Shiller said, popping his hat against the duster and plugging it back into his hairline, "seems to me that tonight he got both."

A blond woman cop stepped inside from the landing, out of the misty rain, and called out to Shiller.

"Call for you. They're putting it through to your unit."

They shivered in the police car. Shiller yanked up the phone when it buzzed in the seat beside him. It was a voice he had hoped never to need again, a voice that had cost him a huge piece of lakefront property he had worked all his life to finally own. Nicholas Wolf needed to chat, he said, which meant the clock was ticking for three hundred dollars an hour again. The lawyer's voice was the sound of a boiling cauldron, choppy but regular, always the sign of trouble brewing.

Shiller pictured Wolf plucking at his suspenders, leaning back so his belly pointed upward at the fancy scrolled ceiling.

"Mikey, boy, how you doin?"

Shiller cringed. "Take me off the fucking speakerphone, turd. I paid you enough to hold the fucking phone in your hand while you jack me off."

Wolf laughed, not nervous, not exactly amused. "Got this letter here at my home on the fax machine. Got it about an hour ago, been making some calls on it. Thought you ought to hear it from me instead of the news media."

Hadeesh leaned back, looking very asleep. Shiller shouted, "Wolf, do you think that for three hundred dollars an hour you could use goddamned pronouns when you talk to me? How's the fishing on my lakefront cabin?"

"I sold it to a developer, turned a pretty profit, too, but not as much as I'd have made if you'd paid my bill outright in cash."

He droned on about the tax penalty he paid for

making revenue on the property, but Schiller could only sink into a hole of agonizing sadness. The beautiful property he had taken a million moonlighting jobs to pay for, the little cabin and dock he had built with his own hands, thinking someday he and his son would fish off it together—gone, again, with as much grief as when he signed the deed over to Wolf to pay legal expenses a year earlier. Now it was on the chopping block for some developer, and instead of fishing there with his boy, Shiller would no doubt go there someday to work a robbery at the 7-11 that stood where his dream lake house crumbled.

Hadeesh raised his head, poked Shiller, pointed at the speaker where Wolf was pontificating, waxing paternal, like a pilot telling the passengers the turbulence was just no-big-thing-at-all.

"—Why he's got this hard-on for you I can't say. Did you fuck his wife when she didn't want you to or maybe you didn't fuck her when she wanted you to? Anyway, it won't go anywhere, I'm sure. I'll go down there in the morning and handle it so you shouldn't be publicly arrested again like fucking Oswald, like you were last year."

Then what Wolf had said sank in and Shiller's chest began to burn with fear. "What new evidence?" he asked with a mouthful of dry cotton.

"Doesn't say here in the motion that he faxed me, but I hear from sources that now he's got a witness that says you put the toy gun on the kid, that there wasn't even a toy gun. Seems Mr. DA is going back to the grand jury right away for another homicide indictment. Now, listen, don't get excited, don't do anything stupid like last time, cussing on TV so that all the news bites of you were just a bunch of bleeps, taking a swing at a couple of cameramen like you did. Just let me handle it and call you tomorrow."

There was no room for Shiller to take a breath. The

grief and fear and pain were all panting fast and using up all his oxygen. He hung his head, felt Hadeesh's hand on his shoulder.

Wolf muttered more bromides that were supposed to be reassuring but only made Shiller's throat tighten more, until he couldn't swallow at all.

"I gotta take a walk." He stepped out of the car and ignored the lightning and thunder and harsh winds. His breaths were furious and labored. His steps should've shook the earth as he reached the street, crossed under a streetlight, and lowered himself into the darkness of an alley.

"Lord, it's all gone. My wife, my kids, my chances for promotions, my faith, my friends. I ain't asking you to bring any of it back—most of it I pissed away on my own, so since you didn't take it you can't revive it. Just don't make it any harder. I'm only asking you to please not make my life any harder because—"

His voice cracked. He was alone but embarrassed. His face tightened. "—Because whatever you bring on me I'm gonna have to face it alone. Give Marshall Robbins a heart attack, Lord, or smash his car up, anything, just take the rotten bastard off my back so I can live my life and try to make something good enough so maybe I can feel love for somebody again. You see?"

He took his Stetson off, covered his face with it, and cried right out loud.

Hadeesh straightened when Shiller approached. He said, "Detective, the shotgun shells are all collected, but you know that they can only show like-and-kind to the shells at the Five-twelve Club tonight."

"I know. The casings are never identical. But it'll be at least some kind of remote link between the shootings," Shiller said flatly. "Let's buzz Jones's house, get some black-and-whites to cruise his car washes and hangouts. You know what I'm thinking?"

Hadeesh said with kindness, "Yes. You are thinking

that Jones may be at the airport, so we will go there with a dragnet. And you are thinking, sir, that before you will go to prison, you will put a bullet in your head."

"Fucking-A, brother. Let's go no-blow to Jones's joint. Get dispatch to notify airport security."

The car would move with lights only, no sirens, toward Monty Jones's expansive redbrick bachelor pad and crime headquarters, which sat passively on a manicured neighborhood street near the lake and a stone's throw from a serene Catholic school.

Hadeesh spoke respectfully into the radio dispatch. Shiller lost the feeling in his face and hands. The only sensation not deprived by the moment's acute anxiety was the salty taste of dried private tears on his lips.

A sliver of moon winked from between blurry clouds. It was a nice moon, Hadeesh said retiringly, but Shiller didn't respond as they drove. Beneath the same shimmery moon, he knew, lurked the demon district attorney whose vendetta made Shiller's life pure hell.

"I wish—" Shiller began weakly.

"Yes, sir. For a beautiful, kind woman to love. Me? Well, I wish for an average-looking woman to simply sometimes let me see her breasts."

The impossible happened; Shiller chuckled. So did Hadeesh.

16

The crunching of the rain stopped against Marie's tin roof. The sudden silence was eery. He sat in the darkened living room. The fake animal-skin rugs that overlapped on the floor were the perfect exotic bodies to the monster heads that grew and shrank on the walls from the candles' lights. The skins almost seemed to move, a slithering, soundless stampede, as if at any moment one would turn and lash a fiery claw.

Monty was among them, caged by tension. He sat erectly on a kitchen chair pulled up to the ratty curtain that looked over the muddy yard. Lightning sparked off his shiny car like knife blades.

In his reflection on the window his face had a round hole of fire that bored through his jaw like a red-orange bullet hole. He toked the cigar, played with the smoke as it hit the glass and careened back into his face almost dutifully, returning to caress the master's hair and cheeks. He was not scared, though he knew they would come soon. Shiller would come soon. The scene in his mind quickened his breathing. He would kill Shiller, no matter how many cops surrounded the sad shack or how many bullets riddled his own body within seconds of his blast through Shiller's chest—no matter all that. He thought of killing Mike Shiller the same way he thought of loving Othel Middleton. The emotions were opposite, but the rushing they welled up inside him were identical. He drifted, seeing the sheer willowy image of a small boy's soft black face behind him in the glass, then the smile on the boy's face, a white star that rose on an opaquely beautiful young mouth.

The voice was an angelic echo. "Aw, man, Mojo, this is no good. The preacher yells and alls I do is sit there in these funny clothes and itch . . ."

"You got to go to church now, boy. I promised Mama Marie that you always would. You got to do in life what you promise God you'll do."

The star twinkled, mischief winked. "Yeah, then maybe I'll promise God that I won't go to church no more. . . ."

The boy faded. Monty's momentary grin wrinkled in pain. He would be fifteen years old now. He would be a freshman baseball star on the high school team. He would be honest, do good in math, stay away from gangs, respect the Lord. He would have by now one hell of a change-up pitch. Othel. Monty sighed. Cigar smoke rushed out and then back at him like comforting foggy fingers to embrace his face.

Shiller. The killer. Shiller the killer. Monty's fists twitched. It was time, he thought to himself, not for some movie-screen horseshit showdown, but for two real men to finally face the hate. It was time for Mike Shiller to get shot and gurgle and choke to death in his own blood and urinate on himself and cry for his mama and lie dead on a rainy sidewalk and look up last at the sky as it spun down on him to suck him into nothingness, emptiness, death.

The cigar had toothmarks now. The window had wet streaks of evaporating rain on it. He thought of Othel, baby Othel, with the fresh skin and the mischievous grin and the toy gun. Bang-bang, Cop, you're dead. When Monty slid sideways that night on the scene in his Cadillac and leaped from the car and knelt over the boy's body there had been . . . oh,

Lord . . . there had been streaks on Othel's dead cheeks. Tears. His boy had lived long enough to weep for his mama as he drowned in blood that filled his lungs and throat.

The killer. Shiller.

She was behind him, a white apparition that vaguely glowed in the window's reflection. She held out something that was clumpy and heavy.

"Your shotgun. Marie melted it with a torch of oxygen and acetylene in the shack out back. Look. It's nothing now but a doorstop. Here's a sweater and some slacks your mother had for you. If you'll give me the suit and shoes, she'll burn them while she still has that gas-mask thing on."

She knelt beside him. All he saw were ribbons of dark bare eyelashes making wispy lines on her porcelain white face in the moonlight. He looked away quickly.

"Monty. They can't catch you now. You don't need me as an alibi. The rope and the tape that man used are nothing but smoke in the air. Monty, please, if I go back I'll die slowly, a little every day. That's no way to live. Please, do it quickly. Do it now."

He looked down at her. She was coiled, all skinny legs and sinewy white arms and falling hair. And she was faceup at him, as if she'd stopped amid some modern dance and was just waiting for the cue to twirl and flail her pretty limbs in supplication.

"Divorce him."

"I can't. He says he'd have me put in a mental institution, that he would get people to testify that I'm a danger to myself. He says he'll take the children and fix it so that I never see them again. He says that the money is all his, the kids are his. He says if I leave he'll frame me for a murder—think how easy that would be for him to do, Monty. He slaps me. He holds me down and rapes me. He forbids my mother and sisters to see me, told them that I wouldn't quit doing cocaine until I reached some bottom of isolation. I don't do cocaine, and they won't take my calls. My sisters, Monty. He took away my sisters. He'll take my babies, too. Don't you see?"

She started to cry. He turned his back to her, listened to the sniffles and broken words.

"After my last baby, after I had Mary, I started bleeding badly at home. Marshall had to take me to the emergency room or let me gush blood all over his handwoven carpet. On the way there to the hospital . . ."

She was there again, gushing blood from her vagina, handing a prunish new baby over to a drill-sergeant nanny, screaming.

"My God! Marshall! Help me! Please, take me, call an ambulance." It pooled foul at her feet. He yanked her, slung her into the backseat of her own car.

"The baby, Marshall, I want to bring the baby with us, don't leave her, she's only three days old . . ."

"I know how fucking old she is, Allison, and I'd just like to ask you if they put you back in the hospital what the fuck am I supposed to do with a three-day-old baby. I have a job." He was screaming now, his neck veins rippled, reaching back to grab her hair and toss her forward onto the floorboard. "You fucking bitch. I'll go slow, maybe you'll die. That'd be good, wouldn't it? Why don't you just go on and fucking die?"

"I hate you, Marshall. Please don't hit bumps in the road, oh God, it hurts my belly when you hit bumps like that. . . ."

He had laughed. Laughed right out loud as if somebody had said a punchline. And then he had driven as far as he could on the bumping, agonizing shoulder of a jagged road. Each time she cried out in pain, he had laughed louder.

"Monty," she whispered hoarsely. Lightning licked at the far-off skyline. "Don't make me go back there."

He turned to her. "Get on your knees."

She lifted herself, bowed her head. He moved behind her, pressed the nozzle of the gun behind her ear.

"It ain't you, Allison. When you're gone, after they find you murdered in a ditch and have you a right nice funeral and the whore girlfriend moves into the mansion with him, after Allison has chickenshitted out and they all sit around sipping champagne and talk about what a fucking sorry drunk you were, picture this. He's gonna beat your boy and fuck your little girls. They're going to cry for you. But just like you now, stinking weak and stupid down there on your knees, just like you, those babies will cry out for someone to help them. And they'll die a little every day, too."

He leaned in. She smelled orange Tic Tac on his breath. He whispered in her ear. "Mama . . . Mama, help me."

He cocked the gun. With one slender finger she reached, ran its coldness along his warm hand. And she pushed the nozzle of the gun away from her head.

He towered over her, wiped sweat from his aching brow, opened the window so fresh air could rustle her gold hair and dry her tears. He was almost out the cranky front door when she spoke softly.

"I have no options."

"Sure you do, Allison Robbins. You just now chose the most important one. Tell my mama I'll be back. I hope."

His car skidded tracks in the mud, out to the illuminated freeway. She did not think he would ever be back.

17

Marie looked like Winnie Mandela wearing welding goggles and a gold turban. The screened back door slammed behind her in a gust of wind as she stepped into the small bedroom where Allison sat quietly.

"He's gone?"

"Yes," Allison answered dryly. She was embedded in deep, colorful quilts on an antique bed in a room crammed with photos and knickknacks in every square inch.

Marie's gold makeup flickered in the serene yellow wash of light from one bedside lamp. With a Velcro ripping sound, she removed the goggles.

Allison watched, asking, "If they ever search your house, won't they find that tank of stuff out there that you use to melt his guns?"

From one of a hundred atomizers on an ancient bureau, Marie squirted herself with perfume, globbed a mound of lotion into her oversize hands, rubbed it in lavishly.

"I'm a sculptor in metals, baby," she said brightly, moving her huge body and flowing robes easily among all the debris, the delicate chairs and plant stands and endless picture frames. "And my specialty is doorstops. There is nothing they can do, darlin', with all those hunks of scrap steel I got out there. No ballistics, no fingerprints. Only way my boy's guns can help the cops after I get through with my magic torch is if a policeman has a stubborn door that won't prop open."

She had put the goggles in a drawer, applied lipstick on her lips in the shadows of the mirror, swigged whiskey from a decanter on a bookshelf, slipped flat house shoes onto feet as big and round as dinner plates. Then she stood before Allison like a coiffed Egyptian goddess, raised her arms so the flab fell out of her billowy sleeves.

Did she summon that peal of thunder, Allison wondered, or was it coincidence that a belch shook the floor?

Marie raised her face all outlined in gold to look up at her hands. The electricity flickered but stayed on. A distant ambulance whined. The wind made mournful sounds as it swept through the house's many crevices and cracks.

"Allison, angel," Marie boomed, "it's time to do magic, but first," her face came down, eyes aflame and leveled at the blackness of the window, "before we feed the spirit world, we'll feed our bodies. Come in here, baby doll. Marie's got powdered doughnuts!"

At the table they sat, talking loud over the crashing thunderstorm, a box of sugary white doughnuts open between them, two glasses of milk.

"Honey girl," Marie sang out, "eat another one. There's nothing under your skin but bones, child! You look like you live in a concentration camp."

Allison pushed away the mug of cold milk, held herself in a hug. "That's an interesting way to put it."

Marie gulped, sighed. "It's not true what you are thinking, that there is no way out of this except to die. Starve yourself to death? Drink and smoke yourself to death, honey baby?" She clamped a meaty palm onto Allison's forearm. "Allison, you listen here to me: you are not responsible for what your husband does to you. You are not weak or stupid or dirty or any of the things he calls you, sweet angel. He has gone and made you sick in the mind, made you believe that you're his property. Well, sweet baby, it ain't so. You need some help." She squeezed gently. "And I'm right here."

Allison sighed dully. "I'm such a failure."

"Why?"

The words were dry as crackling leaves. She pushed back a blond strand that fell into her brows. "I married him for the money, because I was twenty-eight years old and tired of working as a paralegal, and because I figured that at that age my chances for offers were diminishing. He was a fantastic young prosecutor. We socialized, you know, with the right people, docents and wheeler-dealers who could help his political career. One night I put on this beautiful red sequin thing, and he said to me, 'You're not going to wear that, it makes you look like a whore, change your clothes.' So I said, 'Screw you. I dress how I like.' And he threw his drink at me in our living room. The glass hit me and cut my chin. It starts like that. To avoid trouble I changed clothes, made up a story about my chin, and . . . that's how it starts."

Marie sat reverently. Allison continued, the memories so vivid she could taste the smoke from his pipe in the room.

"If he came home and my friends were there by the pool with me or sitting in the kitchen talking, he would slam doors until I asked everyone to leave, then he would jerk me around the room by my arm, and he would scream at me that when husbands came home they weren't supposed to find a patio full of fucking drunk bitches. They stopped coming over, of course, and stopped inviting me out because I was getting so drunk before I left them to go home."

Marie ran a finger along the rim of her milk glass, did not meet Allison's eyes. "Yes, Allison, sugar, he was beginning to isolate you. It helped him control you if you had no support."

A day came into Allison's mind. "I had surgery on both of my hands, carpal tunnel syndrome, so painful, I recall . . ."

It had been excruciating to get dressed that evening. Her hands were swabbed in bandages and immobilized by wrist braces. With one finger she had applied tons of eye makeup and eased into a fancy dress, taken two pain pills. The thought of not going crossed her mind, but the anger it would spark from him wouldn't be worth it, she had thought.

He puffed his pipe, drove, talked crisply on the car phone. She became woozy from the pills, weak from not eating, tired from the pain. And she said to him, "Marshall, let's not stay long. My hands really hurt."

He had glanced. She could see it now, flame blue daggers that sliced her throat when he turned his face to her.

"You always do this to me, Allison. You always fuck me up any way you possibly can. These people are important, these people will matter someday when I'm ready to be governor, but the whole world's supposed to stop because your fucking hands hurt . . ."

It went on, the yelling, the cursing. She ducked a couple of slaps. ". . . Everyone already thinks you're a stupid whore, Allison, everyone in town hates you, everyone knows you're a whore, you look like shit all the time, nobody can stand to be near you . . ."

"Marshall," the whimper came. "I—"

He swerved off the country road. The nearest civilization on this road into the city was a desolate mobile home park about two hundred yards away. "Get out."

She cried. He ignited, reached, opened the door, shoved her out onto the shoulder of the road, reached, slammed the door shut, drove away into the night. She lay in a heap, bandaged hands burning with pain. And she cried more, until her hair was wet and her back ached. A police car shone a light on her. She climbed in for a ride home.

"What the hell happened?"

"My husband shoved me out of the car about an hour ago."

"You? With your hands like that? What a son of a bitch. Who is this asshole? Let's go press some charges."

"We can't. He's the DA."

The cop bristled. His big droopy mustache eased to a grin. "Good. It goes double, then, that he oughta know it's a crime to pop your old lady out of the car. I'll go in with you and talk to him."

"He's at a party. At Senator Vilblosk's house. Don't. Just leave it alone. Turn here. That's my house."

He came around, opened the door. His eyes were black, the kind of eyes you would see in a cowboy movie from over the rim of a robber's bandanna. Glassy hard, suspicious.

"I'll walk you in."

"No. Thanks." She hobbled, mired in self-hate and pity. He watched, leaning on his squad car, smoking effusively. She turned once, looked back. He straightened. She shook her head, hobbled on up the drive to where her two young kids—the third one yet to be—splashed in the wavy lights of a glimmering pool.

He called out, "Hey . . ."

She turned, a refugee leaving the safe coast.

He had put a giant Stetson on his head, flicked away a cigarette, jogged to her. "He's gonna kill you."

"No, he won't. It would ruin his career." She smiled sadly.

"By accident, I mean. It happens a lot. A man throws you. A man slaps you and you hit your head.

They don't ever mean to do it, to kill you, but you're just as dead as if he put a gun to your head and pulled the trigger. You oughta go to the shelter, take your kids, get away from this motherfucker. You know?"

His face was pleasing, kind of chiseled and lean, older than his years, dark skin, cleft chin.

"Thank you, I will," was all she said. While she watched her kids play in the pool, she sat on a porch swing, vodka-rocks cradled between taped and bandaged fingers, variously praising one kid or the other for fancy dives. After enough vodka she felt, in the only way she could, that she had left Marshall Robbins. Drunk, she felt no pain.

He beat her violently that night, because the cop had buzzed the party and asked to speak to Marshall outside. She didn't know what was said. To smooth things over and give his career the sheen of a happy marriage, she got pregnant again.

Marie poured coffee into their mugs. The box of thirty-six little powdered doughnuts was gone.

"This cop, what was his name?"

"I don't remember; it was years ago."

"When your husband beat you that night, did you go to a hospital? Is it documented?"

Allison almost laughed. "Oh, no. I don't want anyone to know what I let him do, Marie. I'm so ashamed."

She wiggled her brows, clanked her mug to Allison's. "Shame, angel face, is the abuser's tool. I am old, pretty baby, and I know two things now that I didn't know when I was young. Never buy cans of food that are dented or bulging. And if someone in this world wants to come and put his mean, lying, ugly ass in my place on my deathbed, then and only then can he tell me how to live my life."

Allison chuckled. Marie took Allison's hands and pressed them to her face. "Child, one day you will be strong enough to stand up for yourself. Until then, you must let others stand up for you. Okay, baby?"

Without guile, Allison's backbone instinctively straightened. "I need to get my little kids away from him, safely, the right way, where he can't hurt us."

"Ahhh . . ." Marie's face glistened. She closed her eyes. "The children. My Monty. My Clark. My Othel." She let out a long breath.

Allison lit a cigarette, dropped the match into the milk cup so it sizzled. "You know what Monty does."

"I know what Monty is, baby. I watched him. He got so tired back then, in the sixties, knowing that everything he wanted he had to ask the white man's permission, everything he bought he had to get the white man to sign for. 'Bout fifteen years old, in Nineteen sixty-five, he beat a grown black man to death 'cause he came upon the man using a board with nails in it to beat the man's poor wife in the backyard. He did some time down at juvenile in Gatesville, and he wasn't ever the same. He was lost to himself, you know, darlin'. But he wasn't lost to me, and he isn't lost to the Lord, neither. Pray with me, Allison, would you?"

They leaned their heads together. It all came from Marie, a spiritual done with operatic finesse.

"Oh, Lord Jesus, hallelujah, praise Your name, yes." She hissed, pressed her warm palms onto Allison's chalky cold cheeks. "Jesus, sweetness, we want gifts from You. Teach us instead that You are the gift, You are the gift, with You standing up for us, all will be well in the end. We despair, Lord, we cry, we fail. Be with us, yes, because we love You."

The storm finally licked out the lights. Allison tensed. Marie raised their hands together in the dim candlelight.

"Thank You, Jesus, darlin' boy, for the darkness, for in it we come to know the joy of the light!"

"I want to go home to my children," Allison said after a long silence.

Marie poured more coffee for them. "Bring that candle into my room, child. I want to show you some photos of my family."

She asked Marie as they walked, "The woman being beaten with the board of nails, you know, the one whose husband Monty killed, did that woman die?"

Marie turned. The candle she held made prisms of light and dark on her aged face. "No, honey, I did not die."

Allison jarred. The coffee mug and saucer jostled. "Monty killed his own daddy?"

"Monty saved his mother. I've never been nothing but proud of him."

They sat together on the floor, photo albums spread open so they could peer through the candlelight. Marie kept an arm draped all the while over Allison's shoulders, hugging her close, pointing to long-lost but beloved faces, a smiling Monty among them.

"Marie," she asked during the conversation. "Are you a witch?"

"Huh," a quick laugh. "I reckon the men who serve with me on the board of directors at my church would say I am. I take no shit off nobody, even big holy preachers and deacons. They can all pass the plate and kiss my ass if they don't like the way I play the organ at church Sundays. A little rock and roll never did hurt nobody every now and again, did it, sweet Allison?"

18

Monty figured driving his mother's car would give him about an hour's head start on the cops. Nobody would be looking for him in a Chrysler New Yorker or whatever the hell it was, he thought as he looked for some brand name somewhere in the interior.

He had bought it for her, took her to the lot one day with a wad of money in his hands and stood around while she shopped for what she wanted. He paid cash, didn't ask what kind it was, followed her home in it. Since then he wasn't sure it had been out of her driveway, where it sat in front of her house as if some gangster had stopped off in the ghetto.

He talked to himself in the rearview mirror. His face had a green cast from the lights on all the dashboard gadgets.

"Fool. Fucked big-time now. Take a drive with the district attorney's wife and stop off to murder a few brothers while she keeps the heater in the car warm. Yeah. Fool.

"Oh, but you ain't through, are you, Mojo? Naw, uh-uh. One more to do, one more nigger to off just to help out a piece of white pussy you ain't never even gonna get. Shit.

"Do you want her white pussy, Mojo? Well, let's see, I'm driving my mama's car and talking to myself while the cops are hunting me down all over the city."

He looked down at himself, a pained expression. "My fucking suit's wrinkled, man," he whined. "White women. Got'dammit. A black woman, she'll rear back and sock your stupid ass right to the moon if you look at her wrong. White women, naw, man, all they got to do is cry, then all the white men go bumping around like Mexican jumping beans, buying them white girls Jaguars and fur coats if they'll just stop crying.

"White men, spending all their lives thinking that to earn the pussy you got to marry it, buy it a house, and never fuck nobody else. Fools. Me? I'm cool. I'm the brains. I'm stone. Yeah." He mocked himself.

"I buy women Jaguars and shit when I'm through fucking them, a safeguard, you know, so they won't come kill me in my sleep. I tell 'em, honey, if I'm gonna fuck somebody else 'sides you I'll either tell you straight out or you'll never ever know. Ignorant white guys, they don't have the courage to tell a woman they're gonna fuck somebody else and don't have the sense to do it without getting caught."

He sighed, drove slower. The rain was blinding. "Do you want to fuck Allison Robbins, Mojo? Huh, do you?"

He bit the tip off a cigar, flamed it with the lighter. "Ha. I want to fuck all good-looking women, man. I mean all of them. Short mean ones and tall icy ones and married easy ones and single ones who like to pretend that they're hard to get into bed. Yeah. All of you pretty girls, come to Monty.

"All of you except the goddamned crazy white goddess who's married to the district attorney and has witnessed me shoot five people tonight. You, I'm not fucking. You understand? Why won't I kill you? I'd like to, oh baby, look how you fucked up my night. I mean bad, too. No, I won't kill you. I could strew this city with dead black men's carcasses and nobody would care. I drop the white babe, I'm frying, I'm telling the prison chaplain as we walk that the bitch wanted me to do it, to kill her, so he says to me, well, Mojo, I hope at least you got some white pussy first, and then I'm crying like a baby, no white pussy plus the death penalty. The math don't work, I'm saying to you.

"It's this way. A man can feel like a fool for a woman. But there's no excuse for him to act like a fool. That's it now. You get back, you take the girl home. That's how it's gonna be."

He turned the car next to the alley, killed the headlights. The sides of the two abandoned buildings were piled with trash that he had to step around to find the unmarked door. The rain had made the trash wet and slushy so some of it stuck to his shoes. He cursed, ducked the wind that whipped through the narrow space not much wider than his shoulders. The door pushed inward with a vacuum-packed sound, and he was in the dark hallway of a slum apartment building where only a few elderly black people lived.

There was a greasy, grimy pay phone on the wall. He could've gone in firing cannons and none of the old people, most of them in wheelchairs or on walkers, would have cracked a door to see what the noise was. The place had a smell that made Mojo retch—urine, cat shit, boiling cabbage—so he put a white silk handkerchief from his jacket over his mouth. He touched the phone receiver with a rag from his car, as much for sanitation as to avoid leaving fingerprints. It was an archaic rotary dial that made grating chinks and chunks as it turned both ways. On the second ring a man answered. Mojo did not need to announce himself.

"Yo, Stomp, who's doing the hit on the DA's old lady?"

"You want part of it, boy?" The voice was old and broken.

"Hey, if I wanted to be asked questions, I'd call me

up a schoolteacher, you know? Cut it up with me. I'll leave the packet outside your door."

"Alex Johnson."

Mojo frowned. "Johnson. Solomon's ass licker?"

The old man laughed into a crusty wet cough. Mojo grimaced and instinctively cleared his throat. The old man said patronizingly to the gangster czar Mojo, as if Mojo were simply a punk thug, "Shit, boy, you oughta get somebody sometime to read your ass a newspaper. Johnson turned state on Solomon, sang about all the drugs and gambling and running whores and snuff films like a canary with a firecracker stuck up his yellow feathered ass. Alex was in the federal witness protection program until tonight. Nobody to prosecute, no witness to protect. Now shit, let me go. Jackie Gleason is coming on Nick at Nite."

Mojo worried. "Wait, Stomp, Johnson's on the streets?"

"Fuck you, homeboy, you killed his goddamned golden goose. You oughta know. Good news is ain't nobody got no way to prove you did it, so's I hear. Bad news is all of Solomon's boys thought it was you doing all the talking to the feds. Run on out, boy, and change your name to Patsy."

With the silk handkerchief, Mojo rubbed through his damp hair. "Fucking cops. They told that honky horseshit to some of Solomon's boys so he'd kill me tonight. I coulda popped him in self-defense if I did it. When's the hit on Allison?"

Mojo cringed, squinted. The old Stop Six barber caught it but let it slide. "Whenever she's alone without some goddamned kids or something. It's supposed to look like a kidnaping for ransom. She dies. Johnson goes with his new identity to some island where they bought him a bar to run."

"Except that won't work now that Solomon's dead."

"The DA will say that Solomon's boys are after

Johnson. He'll get the brother out of the country somehow, long before they find the decomposed remains of the much-loved Mrs. Robbins. Uh . . . Allison, to you, dick-brain. Say, homeboy, that white pussy as good as they say?"

"Listen up, Stomp, that white boy who took your daughter from that convenience store and beat her to death with a tire tool after he raped her with it, he still dead? Never even lived long enough to have a trial, did he?"

The crusty laughter died. "I'm clear on what I owe you, brother. Bring a white woman to get next to me sometime. Must be the best pussy you ever had, this one. You can tell the good stuff; it's the one a man won't make jokes about."

Monty took the rickety stairs, gagging from the stench of frying fish heads and old men's farts that hung in the hallway. He set down the bag in front of a door, knocked once, waited at the bottom until he saw a hand reach out like a starving leper.

Shiller was looking to arrest him. Solomon's boys were looking to kill him. The rain was blowing sideways like sandpaper. He had a half-million dollars in a bank in Mexico. He could shave his head, put on glasses, get one of his fake identifications, get on a plane, and forget it all.

"Big hero," he lambasted himself again in the car's rearview mirror. He gave his own eyes serious consideration. "You doin' this 'cause you like her?" Then he smiled wryly at himself. "Naw, man, I'm doin' it because this gangster shit is fun."

And he laughed riotously, just like a villain in a Disney movie.

19

He stood outside the paper-thin door, smelling chocolate cake baking, hearing a television blare, tasting the delicious sex already. He knocked, tried to be funny. "Honey, I'm home!" Straightened his tie.

The hatchet blade that shot through and stuck in the door from the other side barely missed his nose.

"Go away, Mojo! Rodney, turn down that television!"

Mojo stood to the side. "Jasmine, baby, throw down your weapons and open the door. I brought—" He fished in his pocket, found one Tootsie Pop and a caramel. "—Candy."

She was just on the other side. The meat-cleaver blade stuck out at him like a tongue. "You better back your butt away from my door right now, Montgomery Jones. You're not getting in and you're not getting out of what you did to me tonight."

Her boy's plaintive voice behind her. "Mama, he's got candy."

"Jasmine, baby, it ain't like you think."

"I think you stood me up for dinner because you were out with a white woman. And don't lie because about a thousand people saw you at the Iguana."

"Jasmine, a thousand people called you tonight?"

"Jackie Crittendon called me, that's who. She saw you, you sorry piece of no-good vanilla sponge cake."

"Vanilla sponge cake? Whew, you are angry. Baby,

Jackie Crittendon has an earring in her nose. You would take her word over mine? Yo, Rodney, help me out on the candy thing."

"Mama, just reach out and get the candy. Then you can shut the door on his arm and break it."

Mojo yelled, "Yo, Rodney, don't help me no more on the candy thing? Okay?"

Her fingers wiggled through the crack in the door. He put the two sweet tidbits in her palm, then the door slammed.

He leaned, mindful of the hatchet blade. "Yo, baby, you smell good. You going out?"

"Mama gets off at the hospital at midnight. She's sitting with Rodney. I'm going dancing."

"Can I go?"

"To hell, yeah. Your white date had to dump her black stud and go home to the good side of town?"

"I hate that white woman Jackie saw with me. She's crazy as shit. I mean it, Jazz. She's got like this spooky demon brain and her life's all messed up, and I did whatever I had to do to get shed of her tonight. Think of it more as me being an escort tonight for the mentally handicapped, like if I took a deaf person out to the park or something. It wasn't a date, baby, I swear. Would I take a date to the Iguana where a thousand people would see me?"

"Jackie said she's major beautiful."

"Hey, I don't know. Lassie and the Statue of Liberty and the musical *Porgy and Bess* are all beautiful, too, but I love you, baby. Open the door."

The chain slid. The door opened. He was ready for her fabulous face, but instead found Rodney's contemptuous, beady black eyes smirking up at him.

Mojo petted him. "Hey, Rod, a haircut today, huh? Not too much, though. You don't want those three sixes to show there on your scalp."

"My grandma hates you. She says you're a pervert. What's a pervert?" The Tootsie Pop stick bobbed.

"Where's your mother?" He pried the hatchet out of the door.

"She told me to watch you here while she loads her gun." The kid was annoyingly deadpan. "I'm watching *Godzilla.* I want to be Godzilla when I grow up because he doesn't have to go to school ever."

Monty threw his coat on the couch. "You're in luck. It's in your genes. Your grandmother was the bride of Godzilla, did you know that? Jasmine! Where are you?"

He found her in the kitchen frosting a cake calmly. "You threw a hatchet at me again, Jazz. It's a bad habit."

"I didn't have a flamethrower handy."

She was alarmingly pretty. Five foot ten, legs all the way up. Flat belly, broad shoulders, athletic. Her complexion was flawless, her hair short, close to her head, not as kinky as some black women's, but the rest of her was exotically African-American. Strong physically. Sexy and soft in the best places.

He went behind her, slipped his hand into her robe, and found her nude beneath. A fire slithered up the middle of him while he played with the furry part of her that was just at his reach from behind.

"Who you going dancing with?" He kissed the back of her neck.

"Maurice Templeton. You can diddle me all you want. I'm not doing you."

"It's wet." He whispered it.

"Yeah, it should be. I get pretty excited about chocolate cake." She turned in his embrace. "I don't ask anything of you, Mojo. Not money, not to daddy my kid. I just want you to respect me, is all. I got dressed tonight for dinner with you. You didn't show. You didn't call. It's a game and I won't play it. Now go away."

"Maurice Templeton? The preacher? He has a limp."

"He got hurt in Desert Storm. He was an Army chaplain. A real hero. Who's the white woman?"

He kissed her a long time. She didn't resist. "Jazz, do you want me to give you money and daddy your boy? I will."

She put the chocolate spoon in his mouth. He lapped it. "I work real hard, Mojo. I'm almost graduated, and then I'll be a nurse, and then I'll buy Rodney and me a big house. I don't want realities from you. What you give me that I like the best, honey, is the unrealities. The slow dancing. The long walks. The trips to Las Vegas and San Francisco."

"The sex?"

She wiped chocolate off his chin. "Especially the sex. I got plenty of real-life stuff. You're my fantasy. You shouldn't disrespect or mistreat a woman who only wants you to be her fantasy."

She went into the bedroom. Mojo stopped in the living room, watched Godzilla crush a bridge and then fall into a big net.

"They trapped him," Rodney said plainly. "But he'll get out."

"How do you know he'll get out?"

The kid strung popcorn into his mouth. "Because he's Godzilla. Besides, I've seen it a hundred times."

"Oh, this is a Godzilla movie. I thought it was your grandmother's wedding video. Say, Rod, here's five bucks to not come banging on the bedroom door."

The kid snatched it, looked flatly at Mojo. "I don't see how you can be a black stud like Mama called you. You got chocolate on your face."

He opened her robe, found her breasts, nibbled a nipple. She arched, moaned when he put a finger in her moist center, found the bulb, massaged it lightly with his palm. She took in air when he trailed his tongue along her narrow ribs to her triangle of coarse hair. Afterward, after she had come and cried and laughed, she used strong, manicured fingers to take open the buttons on his shirt, to lower his slacks, to pull off his socks. He rocked on top of her until her chest and neck shined and his back dripped sweat. When he came, hard and long, he said twice, "I love you," and she whispered, "I know."

They talked awhile like that, locked by fingers and lips and pelvic bones. She made him laugh. He made her reality gloriously unreal for an hour.

Godzilla was eating a train. Rodney was eating his third piece of cake. Jasmine was showering.

Rodney chugged milk.

Mojo put on his overcoat, patted the kid's head, saying, "Sorry it took so long. Here's another five."

The kid's stare was fixed on Godzilla. "It's okay. She didn't stay in there with you as long as she did with my dad, and he didn't pay me nothing."

Godzilla ruthlessly stomped a bespectacled Japanese scientist. Monty knew pretty much how the guy felt.

It took twenty minutes of driving around to find the sporting goods store, closed up tight for the night, where Alex Johnson and his black buddies were holding a poker game inside. It took two minutes to call from a pay phone and get word to Alex that Marshall Robbins needed to meet him immediately at a Denny's four blocks away. It took one minute of aim through Alex's interior car light to get him in Monty's rifle scope, and two seconds to pull off the shot that went right through Alex's ears, in one and out the other. It took two minutes total to uncork the vial of sulfuric acid and pour it down the barrel of the rifle, less than a minute to put the rifle beside Johnson's car. Monty ate a Tic Tac, put the surgical gloves in his pocket, and drove slowly through the stormy night.

20

Shiller finished the last bite of a hot dog he had bought before the call about a shooting behind a South Side sporting goods store. They were surrounded by cop cars in the parking lot, the same exhausted crime-scene specialists. They stood several yards away from the car where Johnson was slumped dead, gook oozing from his head, his window shattered and car door dinging.

Shiller talked with his mouth jammed full and mustard on his breath. "Robbery?" He gulped coffee that tasted funny. "What is this shit?"

Hadeesh looked up from the flashlight beam on his notepad. "Vanilla cinnamon cream flavor. No, he wasn't robbed. Rolex and wallet still on him. The crime-scene guys are going over it all now."

A gruff uniformed cop called out from over near the body, "Shiller, can you come look at this guy's ID? It's a doozy."

He shouted back, spitting pieces of hot dog. "Yeah, in a minute. Right now Hadeesh and I are having a General Foods International Coffee moment." To Hadeesh, "Weapon?"

"Remington Seven hundred, in thirty-oh-six, he must've been close, he only had a four-power scope on it," Hadeesh answered. "It's over here."

They walked toward the yellow tape boundary and were signaled in by the gruff cop, meaning the evidence was all in. Johnson's body had slid sideways, as if he were reaching to open the passenger door, except for the pool of goo sliding out his mouth and eyes onto the console. Hadeesh pointed to the Remington lying flat just beneath the dinging car door.

He asked while putting on gloves from his pocket, "You are through with this, yes?"

The gruff one. "Yeah, boy, but I wouldn't—"

It was too late. Hadeesh upended the gun and instantly spots on his black overcoat began to smoke like speckled small fires. While he watched in disbelief and everyone else yelled laughter and backed away, the sulfuric acid globbed from the gun barrel like watery ketchup, and within seconds Hadeesh's wingtips exploded into smoke.

"Get your shoes off, boy!" the gruff one hollered between belly laughs, over loud, irreverent applause and whistles. Hadeesh slung his smoking shoes. Some cops including Shiller ducked, and just as Hadeesh's socks started to sizzle and smoke, Shiller yelled out.

"Socks off, boy, and run right there to that water nozzle at the Seven-Eleven gas pump! Water, son, hurry!"

They watched, laughing so hard that one of the old uniformed veterans threatened to pee his pants. Hadeesh narrowly made it across the busy street, dodging cars and slinging his socks backward in the air. He hit the convenience store's gas pump water nozzle in the nick of time, before the acid started to eat his skin.

The gruff one wiped tears from his eyes as they watched Hadeesh hopping at the pumps and spraying his feet with water. "Oh, god, Shiller, I needed that laugh. Man, what's the deal with Monty?"

Shiller yawned. "I don't know, but if he keeps killing bad guys like this, he'll be our solution to prison overcrowding. He left the bolt closed in the Remington?"

He blew his nose, took some deep breaths, recovering his composure. "We ain't got shit on ballistics. The acid took care of that."

"Fingerprints?"

"Yeah. Right. Hadeesh's," the gruff cop said. "My guess is Jones used two pairs of surgical gloves. He's damn good. Why don't he work for us?"

"Dope dealing gets you more pussy and better cars than police work. Well, there goes Johnson to the morgue. I guess I'll stop at Payless so my brain surgeon of a partner can get some shoes, then I'll head to Monty's mother's house. God, I hate shaking down old ladies at one o'clock in the morning."

A gruff but brotherly slap hit Shiller's shoulder. "You want some backup, Mikey?"

"Shit, no. I killed this woman's young son. Least I can do now is spare her the embarrassment of having a fucking police raid on her privacy. Monty ain't there, you know that."

The slap became a gentle squeeze. "I'll give you thirty minutes then do a squad car drive-by, see how you're doing." He peered curiously. "You need a vacation."

Shiller shrugged, smoked. "Word is that by noon tomorrow I'll be on nonpaid suspension if the DA has his way."

Rain began to spatter. The gruff guy lifted his parka hood. "Yeah, word is the DA beats the shit out of his sweet little wife and kids. Real hush-hush deal, she's too scared to do anything about it. What's his hard-on for you?"

Smoothing his droopy moustache, Shiller said, "Aw, I took him out of a party a few years ago and sort of told him that if he wanted to hit somebody, how about me? He declined."

A gruff smile from a kind face. "You ain't ever sort-of said anything."

Shiller smiled, too. "I think it was my fist clamped on his balls that he didn't like."

"Now he's got yours, huh?"

"Seems that way."

His alligator cowboy boots clomped across the wet pavement toward his car, and he got there just in time to hear the phone ringing. From the computer screen on the dash he could see the number being called from, and he groaned and hit the speaker button. "Hi, Nina."

She talked like a first-grade teacher, which she was by day, not at all like the whiz-kid law school student that she was by night. "Hi, Mike! You missed torts tonight."

He rolled his eyes. "I know."

"I got all the notes transcribed for you. I'm at your house now dropping off some chicken and dumplings. There's some girl's panties and socks draped over your couch."

He grinned grimly. The cowgirl ladled butt-up naked over his recliner seemed years instead of only hours ago. "An obvious break-in, Nina. Call the cops. How'd you get in my house?"

"I figured you left a key somewhere. Since you're a cop I figured it was someplace obscure, so I looked under the last hay bale on the left in your barn, and there it was. You coming home tonight?"

He had been leaning back, Stetson over his eyes, but now leaned forward to glare at the screen as if she could see his disapproval. "I'm tracking a heinous killer." He yawned again.

"Well, I'll leave the notes and the dumplings. If you'd come home I'd give you a back rub and, you know, other fun stuff."

"Nina, honey, my idea of fun stuff is a blow job and a nap. Your idea of fun is to bleach my tennis shoes so they'll be white and to put lemons in my garbage disposal so it'll smell good."

He sensed her puffy bottom lip. "You don't want your disposal to smell good?"

He honked for Hadeesh, who was playing grab-ass with a pimply clerk, nodding too strongly at her and faking a roaring laugh, obviously explaining why he was barefoot and two of his toenails were burned away.

"You know what I did the last Christmas Day of my marriage, Nina? I worked. I went to this house where they thought the baby had died of sudden infant death syndrome, to make a police report, then I go in and see that this precious little newborn has frozen to death in its bed because there's no heat. I get home at two that morning, and my cute little wife didn't want to make love to me because her turkey had split apart from the breast bone and she was worried it would be dry."

He knew that she had flipped her long blond hair back from her shoulders. "What's that got to do with anything?"

"It means that we're all ninety-seven percent sane, but there's a three-percent part of us that's totally fucking nuts. The thing is to find someone whose three percent you can live with."

She screeched into the phone. "What's nuts about me?"

"Nothing. You're wonderful. You're just not my type."

A huff. "Oh? And what's your type?"

"Raquel Welch definitely, and probably this leggy blonde I picked up off the side of the road about five years ago after her son-of-a-bitch husband had shoved her out with two broken hands all bandaged up." He was talking to himself by then, remembering. "I went back there in the bushes and watched her with her kids. She didn't scream when they splashed her by the pool, she just smiled and brushed water off her cheeks, even in her fancy dress. With broken hands, she stood up there and applauded those goofy little dives the kids were doing. One of them fell, and she didn't leap right up, she kind of waited to see if the kid would call to her, she kind of ambled, letting the boy find out for himself if he was okay.

"She took off her shoes and put her feet in the water, and she didn't go nuts when the little girl put on those expensive high heels and clomped around the grass. She pushed them in a hammock real high and didn't yell about how they were going to get hurt going so high. That must have hurt her hands, I guess."

He came back to earth. Nina was silent on the line. "I think women are no damn good, Nina, honey, until they've had kids, like mares are so much more reliable than fillies."

She was gritting her teeth. "You hid in the bushes five years ago and watched a woman and you're in love with her? You're sick. I'm right here. I'm nice to you. I cook and clean. You should marry me."

Hadeesh slid into the seat wearing a pair of Dallas Cowboy thermal socks he'd bought in the 7-11.

"Well," Shiller barked at Nina, "that there's your three percent, honey, that I can't take. Thanks for calling."

The dial tone slapped at him. Hadeesh stared.

"She likes me, Detective, that clerk does. She did not spit at me or throw anything."

"It's a start, son." They began to pull away. "Nice socks. Maybe before we confront an armed and dangerous multiple-slaying suspect, we should get you some shoes."

The clerk was waving in the rearview mirror. Shiller stopped, and she tapped on his window. He rolled it down, face-to-face with her pimples and braces.

"Hey," she said to Shiller, "aren't you somebody?"

"My mama thinks so."

"No, I mean didn't you used to be that cop that caught that serial killer two years ago who had butchered all those teenage girls all over Texas? Weren't you on *Inside Edition* last Christmas?"

She had a chit of paper. Shiller signed it.

"Nice of you," Hadeesh said with real admiration.

"No shit," Shiller snapped. "I wrote your name and phone number. Say, Hadeesh, my boy, you like back rubs from women?"

Hadeesh crinkled his brow. "Yes. Especially when they are free or I have a coupon."

"You have a garbage disposal?"

"Of course. I am an American now. Why?"

Shiller hit the pedal dangerously hard for wet streets. "Nothing. I'm just thinking, is all. Let's get shoes and then hit Monty's mom's house."

21

Monty came through the door silently, shut it lightly. Flicked a light switch. Nothing.

"Mama?"

"In here, baby. Pick up a candle and come in."

Allison faced a mirror, a candle blooming light up into her face that made her look ghoulish. She was back in her own clothes, the seductive strapless red leather dress, and she had used Marie's cosmetics on her face. She looked as she had the moment she had stepped into Monty's car.

But something was different. She was smiling.

"Hi," she said, like ice cream melting on a hot tongue.

Marie was on her hands and knees in the corner, fishing under the bed, her butt up like a hot-air balloon.

"Mama, what are you doing?" Monty asked.

"Looking for my crystal ball. I can't find it anywhere. Maybe the tarot cards will tell me where it is. I'll go get them." She waddled past, stopped to kiss his cheek. She smelled like Jack Daniels and scented candle wax. Intuitively, she shut the bedroom door behind her.

Allison watched Monty in the mirror. It was the first time all night that she had been afraid of him. He was angry. Behind her he looked like a mountain. The candlelight made deep holes where his eyes were, and she could hear his fast breathing. He spoke in a low voice.

"You've seen me murder people tonight." He put a black gloved hand on her shoulder, a slab of onyx on porcelain.

She laced her fingers together. They were ice cold and numb. "I want to go home, Monty. Your mother has given me the courage to do what I need to do to stop the abuse and save my children. I want you to take me home."

His other hand slipped gently to her other shoulder, two black claws set heavily on her tender white neck. Thunder rolled. She was afraid, wanted to scream for Marie, but sat still while his fingers played on her throat, feeling the first tears grow warm at the rims of her eyes. She couldn't see Monty's expression, only deep gouges in a black skull hidden in flickering candle shadows.

"I've been in prison, Allison. I ain't going back. Laying up all night listening to brothers scream and cry, hearing bones crack in the next cell while white guards beat a man with clubs, knifing people who are begging me to butt fuck them. I ain't going back. I got rid of every single thing tonight that can put me at any of those killings, except for one thing. Except for you. Now what am I going to do?"

She stood, faced him. "You're going to tell me how to murder my husband, some way that I won't get caught. Then I'm going to go home and kill him. I'm not going back to prison, either, Monty. No more beatings or rapes in my world, either. That's what you're going to do."

She lifted a cigarette to her mouth, shaking violently, feeling nauseated, yet excited, relieved. "Now," she said, mouth as dry as desert sand, "before you tell me how to murder my husband, can I have a light?"

He raised the candle. Their eyes were lighted. Hers had flecks of gold. His had shards of amber.

He whispered so that the candle went out. "You know about guns?"

They were in the dark. "No."

"Poison?"

"No. I could hire someone. You?"

"Not me. I'm too hot now. No third parties. They get greedy and drop you in the grease. All right. There's a way. It's simple. It's clean. You can do it."

Lightning spangled the room long enough for him to see her bloodred lips parted in a smile. Monty smiled, too.

And finally she reached for him. A hug. Slithered her lily white muscular arms up around his neck like a schoolgirl. He embraced her.

"I'm scared, Monty."

"Don't be, baby, or you'll fuck up. Be quick. Heroes don't hesitate. Do exactly what I'm going to tell you."

They stayed like that a moment or so, cigarette smoke and perfume and white skin encircling him, she enveloped in a strange, virile, ebony affection that she had never known existed.

They heard the knock at the front-room door.

They did not touch mouths, but were close enough to feel each other's lips move.

"They're here, Allison."

"I know. You've been with me all evening. We met at six at your car wash, talked awhile, left my car there, went to the Iguana around eight."

He took over. They were not frantic. "Danny came in to tell us that your car had been stolen, and I got him to drive me to where he thought he last saw it. Then we dropped him, alive, at the warehouse. We came here, had dinner, then I went out about ten-thirty to see my girl Jasmine. I was back by eleven-thirty. She'll tell them the times I was with her."

"You were back by eleven-thirty, right. And how did we meet, how are we friends? I know, when you used to play the trumpet at the Women's Club luncheons, I was a member. I really was, but I never went to those chamber music things. No one can prove that. You called me to have dinner tonight; we're old friends."

He lightly kissed her forehead. "Don't you ever contact me again. Okay?"

"Yes. Now give me your hand. Let's walk out there together."

He stopped her by the arm. "Allison, I played the flute, remember, not the trumpet. Good luck out there."

22

Monty wanted to charge the room and do a full-body slam. His arm, back, and jaw muscles were tensed into hard balls. But behind Shiller in the doorway was a tall plainclothes guy and about ten uniformed cops stringing down the porch into the yard and peering in the windows of the living room from both sides of the house. They'd seen Monty's car and called for backup.

He stood erect and motionless as Marie said, "Come in, Officer. There's no need for trouble. Monty's right here."

Shiller swaggered forward, eyes hidden by the shadow of the familiar Stetson, hand Napoleon-style inside his damp duster, fingers no doubt on his gun.

"Monty Ray, I'll be needing you to turn around and put your hands on the wall. Mizz Jones, you sit down here at the table. You, over there in the dark, come sit by Marie, move slowly, keep your hands where I can see 'em. Hadeesh, find a light switch."

Marie's voice was strangely cheerful. "Lights are out."

The blonde stepped into a pool of white candlelight. She had dancer's legs under a dress short enough to not even have to lift when you laid her down for lovemaking. She moved gracefully, confidently to a chair. He squinted but couldn't see her face clearly. She crossed her legs and they made a swishing sound, which made Shiller's eyes water and his crotch burn for a moment. He shook his head like a dog sneezing.

Hadeesh had Monty cuffed and turned and parked low on the couch.

"Get Al to take Marie," Shiller barked at Hadeesh, who nodded. "You take Monty to the car and get some answers. I'll see what Blondie here has to say. Monty, I've got a search warrant. We'll call and get the lights on immediately. Don't fuck with us."

Monty looked straight ahead as Hadeesh led him by the elbow. The handcuffs, arms twisted behind him, gave him a choking feeling. He looked backward at Allison's obscured face until his head wouldn't twist any farther. Marie and the gruff cop followed. She wasn't handcuffed. She walked proudly, like a queen leading a commemorative parade down a fancy avenue. She thanked Al when he held the door for her. He closed the door, leaving Allison and Shiller in a gulf of chilly silence.

He shoved a candle under her nose, glared at her face, moved the candle back, shoved it to her again, staring and blinking. Then he sat back and slapped his knee and laughed, not ha-ha laughter but like that from one who was about to say, I'll be damned.

Then he said, "I'll be damned. Fuck me every way but up. Shit." He blew a big breath, stood, sat, slapped his palms onto his face, and rubbed as if he was waking up from a bad dream. "Lady, please don't tell me your name is Allison Robbins."

She said nothing. He hung his head and made growling sounds, slapped his knees again, drew in a whole bunch of air, and said with an immensely amused, bright smile, "I cannot fucking wait to hear this." He shook his head, the night black Stetson brim cutting the air while he chuckled. "Lord, this is gonna be good."

He folded his hands on the table and bent forward

into the flickering candle beam. She drew back, not having been ready for him to be that handsome up close. She flipped through a mental file of the last time she had seen a man whom she had thought was good-looking. Couldn't come up with one. They came at her and went by her like pasteboard movie heroes all day long, everywhere she went, with their stupid lines. While she shopped for groceries. While she browsed a bookstore. While she waited for the valet to bring her car at a snazzy restaurant. While she watched her boy play tee ball or her girls leap at gymnastics. They had these lines: "That your kid? She's good. Your husband must be proud . . . A pretty girl like you shouldn't be sitting here drinking that martini and reading a book alone . . . I was just watching you; you're so beautiful, can I join you?" She looked up at them, each and all, and with a whip of her eyelashes turned their ignorant asses to stone, not because she was virtuous, but because she was so incredibly fucking bored by them.

This one, the edges of her puffy lips twitched, this cop, he struck a long-numbed chord. He lit a cigarette and offered her one. When she said yes, he lit it in his mouth and handed it to her, a gesture of sexual intimacy that made the hairs on her arms flutter. He laughed again and rubbed his eyes, and she liked his hands, not white and manicured but brown and rough. She interrupted his laugh.

"Are you going to arrest him?"

He pulled at his cheeks. "Yes, ma'am, I believe so, seeing as how I have a witness who can put him at a double-shooting scene tonight behind the Five-twelve Club—" He leaned forward. His eyes focused ominously, like a leopard watching a lion cub. "—With a blonde in a red leather dress."

He puckered his lips, narrowed his eyes. She liked his jaw, a male model's facial bone structure, and she'd bet he didn't know that, which made it more alluring.

"Tell me about that," he commanded.

"Do I need a lawyer?"

"You committed any crimes lately?"

"No." She pushed back a string of blond hair that had fallen over her shoulder and between her breasts.

He wanted to throw this gorgeous babe right over his shoulder, walk outside, and tell the boys, "Hey, it don't matter who Monty killed, I'm taking her to the Bahamas for two weeks and do nothing but crawl all over her and buy her stuff. Y'all call me when this is solved."

What he said, matter-of-factly, readjusting his Stetson nervously on his dark mane of hair, was, "What happened behind the Five-twelve?"

"We weren't there."

He giggled like a girl, in a strange burst. "Imagine my surprise."

She did not plead or whine, just stretched out her luscious arms toward him on the table and sighed. "I went to the car wash at six to take Monty to dinner. We talked awhile, then went to the Iguana about eight or so. Monty's friend named Danny came and said my car had been stolen from a side street and that he thought he knew who did it, so he drove us around, but we didn't find the car, so we dropped him at some warehouse. We came here for dinner with Marie. Monty went to see his girl Jasmine about ten-thirty or so. He was gone about an hour. Marie and I talked here. That's the only time he was away from me tonight."

He chewed his lip. "Why would you alibi this asshole? It's a fucking crime to impede justice, don't you know that?"

She lifted one delicate eyebrow. "It's the truth."

"I can polygraph both of you."

"It's inadmissible."

"I can arrest you for suspicion."

"It won't stick. You've got no evidence."

"Where is it all?"

"In your silly suspicious dreams."

He got pissed off and grabbed her wrist. "This is some bad shit you're in, lady. Is he your dealer or your pimp?"

She slapped him. Hard. It stung his cheek and cut his bottom lip. He let go of her wrist. The lights came on in the house.

He looked away from her, licked a small pearl of blood off his bottom lip. "What'd you have here for dinner?"

"Chitterling stew."

"How is it that the district attorney's wife is out hobnobbing with a convicted felon?"

"I'm a member of the Women's Club. The prison chamber orchestra plays there for us some Sundays. You know, bridge the societal-racial-economic-political gaps. I met him and liked him. He plays the flute."

She was better in the light. Skin like a big bowl of cream he could lick and suck, eyes he could do stupid things to amuse and impress, a voice that could make mundane phrases into soothing ballads.

"Oh, Lord," he mumbled, alarmed at himself. "You want to take a walk?"

They ambled through police cars, past the lighted one where Monty sat stiffly, leaning forward off his hands behind him, talking to an intense Hadeesh who was scribbling on a pad. Shiller told a few loitering uniformed guys that the lights were on and they could search the house now, and they all scrambled inside with their bags of special equipment. The street was paved but uneven because the city didn't really devote much neighborhood improvement to this rotting area of town. Her high heels clicked. His boots shuffled.

There was a run-down abandoned house. He led her to the steps and they sat side by side.

"I know what to do," he said, trying not to see the wind rustle her hair back so her sculpted face was open to his mouth. "Run you both in, interrogate the crap out of you, beat you with water hoses and all that. We'd get it, one way or another. Monty fucked up somehow tonight. We'd find it."

He looked up at her where she sat a step above him. His expression was regretful. He said aimlessly, "A cool cop in the movies or in a novel would tell you all about how this is a career case for him, how it would redeem him in the department, get him a promotion, how Monty is a slimeball killer, how you're obstructing justice. A cool cop would definitely not do what I'm about to do."

"What are you about to do?" She scooted closer to him. The breeze was bitingly cold. He didn't dare touch her.

"I'm about to tell you that I don't give a shit about much. I'm fucked up about a lot of things. My job. My kids. My divorce. Money." He stood, took off the cowboy hat, and fooled with the brim. Hat in hand. It made her smile.

"Without you, I can't pin anything on Monty tonight." He glanced at her, then back to the hat brim. "And if I involve you, your husband will hit you. I know that. I am not fucked up over whether that's something I want to be part of."

"I didn't use my charms on you," she said, feeling guilty if she had been coy. "At least, I didn't mean to. I knew from the first moment that you're not a fool."

"Oh, yes, ma'am, I am a fool. I got dead bodies piled up at the morgue like you wouldn't believe, and I know who did it. Those cool cops in novels, they'd say to you, 'Baby, I wish I could save you, but I'm a cop first, and he's a dirty rotten killer, and that's the way it is.' Clint Eastwood would grit his teeth and haul you in and go drink some whiskey. Mannix would give you a big wet kiss and then take you downtown by the hair."

She was laughing gently. It sounded like ballroom music to him.

She asked, "What about Mike Hammer? Or Kojak?"

He plunked the hat back on, plunged his hands into his duster pockets. "Hammer would fuck you on his desk and then make you leave the country. Kojak would just shoot you. He was really cool."

Their laughter trickled away. They were left with silence.

"Really, Mizz Robbins, I'll do what I can. But you need to go on home now. Report your car stolen. With your credibility, Monty's ass is pretty covered. If they polygraph you, take a Valium before you go—nothing will show when you lie. I'll try to make it so nobody, especially your husband, ever hears anything about you being in this."

She stood. "He's trying to have you reindicted for the shooting of Monty's son."

"I know." He cocked his head. "You mean Monty's little adopted brother."

She came down the steps with the grace of a beauty pageant winner. "Othel was his son; Marie told me. The boy's mother died when he was a baby. Monty wanted Othel to believe that Marie was his mother."

Shiller's chest hurt. "I killed his son?"

She huddled deeply into the lynx coat, dug a high-heeled toe at the sidewalk. "I overhear a lot, Officer, when my husband talks on the phone at home. There's a man who's going to testify that he saw you put a toy gun on the boy that night. He's in the witness protection program. His name is Alex Johnson. I heard my husband tell him exactly what to say."

"He talks about that stuff in front of his wife?"

A tongue skirted her lips. He wanted it to skirt his moustache and his teeth and his belly.

"No. He talked about it in our game room where my daughter was taking a nap. She's four. She has asthma. I keep an intercom on her all the time when I'm in another room. Guess I didn't turn it off a few nights ago. You're being framed."

A huge wind whipped them. She was a few feet from him, wearing a coat that cost more than his own pickup truck. Her diamond drop earrings danced like glittering angels in his eyes.

He told her, "Alex Johnson is dead. Shot tonight."

"By whom?"

He looked toward the car where Hadeesh and Monty sat talking. "I guess we'll never know."

They walked. She cautioned severely, "Officer Shiller, don't ever get caught alone with Monty. He'll kill you."

The bitter wind ate the words, but he heard them first. He briefed the other officers. Not enough to go on. Monty's story matched Allison's, Hadeesh said. No holes. They'd check the girlfriend for times. The house and cars had no drugs or weapons in them. Shiller wondered how long ago Marie had burned it all, wished he had somebody in his life who loved him that much. Monty was uncuffed, stood on the front porch like a panther, pacing. Shiller started to approach him, but turned away.

Hadeesh said in the car, "Very good alibi, the DA's wife, yes?"

Shiller didn't answer. He was thinking hard about how he would feel if someone shot and killed one of his precious sons, down on a sidewalk like a yard dog. There was a string of blood dried on his lip. He licked it away.

23

She sat two feet from her sleeping husband. Her pink silk robe looked almost festive. She could have been sipping coffee in the floral Chippendale chair, watching her beloved lover there in the predawn murky darkness. The storm was moving out, pushed by bleak and gusty winds.

She was not sipping coffee and admiring her betrothed. She was fidgeting with the small plastic sandwich bag that Monty had given her, and she was waiting for the strength, the nerve, the courage to walk over and kill Marshall Robbins. He looked almost angelic there in the vast swirl of expensive sheets, his hair tangled boyishly, his face in repose. He was breathing steadily.

Monty's eyes had penetrated the sheath of dark between them in the car when he brought her home. He had told her exactly what to do. And she was going to do it. Now.

She stood, found weak legs, held the chair's arm a moment, tightened the sash around her tiny waist, took a step. Something scratched at the bay doors. A tree limb in the gusts. She stopped, watching for a figure to move in the dapple of limb shadows and moonlight outside the sheer drapes. The house inside was quiet as a morgue at midnight. A grandfather clock chimed five times, echoing reverently. Her children were tucked away, smiling in their dreams. When she had looked in on Ellen, at the canopy bed, at the prepubescent body that soon would blossom into the track star that the girl wanted to be, she had caught a gasp in her throat that entangled her heart. She had lifted covers over Ellen.

In Jason's room he was sprawled on the floor, a cereal box stringing Cheerios he'd eaten as a snack, the TV blaring snow. She had actually smiled at the disheveled sight of him. His scalp was buzzed to a burr; he had begged Allison to tell the barber to do it, and so she had. Now when she touched his head lovingly, it felt like rubbing a horse's coat the wrong way. She turned off his television and stepped over him to close his door.

Mary was captive in her bottom bunk bed among a jungle of stuffed animals. They looked at Allison. Simba. Pongo the Dalmatian. A lithe and heavy-lidded princess from Aladdin. Others, garden-variety bears and rabbits and cats, puppies, and a huge smiling green boa, and something like a Tasmanian devil character. Mary was a lump of curls cuddled beneath them. She had a bruise on her left thigh. Allison straightened in alarm. Bastard had spanked Mary the previous Sunday for forgetting to close the back door. Allison had stepped up, fists raised to stop him, and later that evening as she bent in the sink washing her hair before her bath, he had held her head under the water with his strong hands. He turned off all the cold, had her pinned there, screaming. The hot water burned blisters on her neck the next day. They were gone now. Mary's bruise was almost gone. "Never," he had said with his teeth gritted, "correct me in front of the children. When you start paying a few bills around here, you can have some say, but right now the power is all mine. You got that?"

Tonight she had tiptoed down the long winding

stairs, found the packet from Monty in her purse. She wound her way through the dark house, aware of every sensation and sound.

The scuffling wind. The bright green of the numbers on a microwave in the kitchen. The luxurious cushion of the carpet on her feet. Heightened sensations of fear as her heart raced and her breaths grew shorter.

The bruise on Mary.

Allison stopped then at the bottom stair and sat on it, letting her hand grip the brass rail, and she had wept so noiselessly it seemed she was in a silent movie scene, shoulders wobbling, snot drooling, hands contorted in the air, twisted as if they were arthritic. But no sounds.

If she left him, it wouldn't stop. He would always have access to the children, even if by some miracle he didn't fight her for custody and win. Ellen came into her mind. The glasses on bright blue eyes, all in forest green tights and leotard up on the split beams. She turned in slow motion that day to look at Allison and Marshall, teetering but firmly upright and so proud. He had shouted to her, "Stop shaking!" And Ellen's face fell just a touch, just enough to dim the smile. Not good enough.

Jason made a goal at soccer, ran toward them in the bleachers with his arms raised, his eyes glowing, and Marshall said, "It wasn't a clean goal. You could've kicked it in a lot straighter." And Jason's face hardened just a little. Not good enough.

Mary had cried after her spanking that Sunday. "Mommie, I can't remember everything like closing doors and stuff. I'm just a little girl!" She buried her face. Ashamed.

No more. The packet in Allison's hand made no sounds as she put its contents into her palm. Marshall Robbins did not move as she stood over him where he slept on his side. Like Monty said, she had taken ice water from the refrigerator door, put it in a cup, put the needle into the cup, and drawn the cold water into the syringe. That was it, that was all. Liquid instant death.

If Marshall woke he would be surprised to find her in his bedroom. He would not know that she hadn't been in her own room all night. But Marshall was not going to wake.

Her hands trembled. She had to wait a moment, take some breaths. He flickered, made a horse sound, twitched his strong, sinister hands.

She put the flashlight beam onto his ear. He didn't squint. His eyes were moving back and forth in dream stage. The needle went deep and fast into his eardrum. The cold water slipped instantly from the syringe under pressure from her thumb. It was done. Good enough.

He opened his eyes, had time to furrow a brow. Opened his mouth, didn't have time to form a word of pain. He had a wrenching body seizure that lasted less than one minute. Allison leaned against the wall, seeing millions of herself in the mirrors all around her. She was foam white, emaciated, gasping. His body contorted one last time, arched upward in the middle. His hands clutched. He relaxed. And then she knew he was dead. A sound came from her, the sound of someone who had just tugged something very heavy from under a bed. "Uhh." She slid down the wall. "Oh. God."

She drove out the driveway without car headlights. On the street she went slowly, as Monty had said. Attract no attention. She felt nothing. Nothing. Just drove to the bridge on the country road a mile from their house. With the window rolled down she tossed the syringe and the needle over the bridge into the rushing waters. The rain had created many flash-flood warnings the night before, and the creek tumbled with rapids. She did not get out of the car.

At home, she had a sudden nosebleed. She stood in her bathroom with a cold cloth on her face, head back, until it stopped. She got into bed with Ellen.

"Mommy?"

"Yes, honey."

"Is it time to get up?"

"No."

"You should turn up the heat, Mom. You're shaking all over."

"Ellen, does Dad ever hit you?"

Hesitation. "He doesn't mean to. I make him so mad."

A few stars lingered outside the window in the fading night sky. Allison fell asleep.

Mike Shiller pulled onto the bridge as soon as Allison's taillights were out of sight. He skidded down the muddy banks of the creek and looked furiously in his giant beam of light for what she had thrown. It was stuck there in a mound of dirt like an arrow she had shot into the horizon.

A syringe with a needle in it. In his nightscope, watching from behind her, he had known, just somehow known in the blurry, obscure images he saw that it was a large hypo.

He sighed. "What the hell, darlin', are you doing?"

With a white cloth he dropped the hypo into an evidence bag, sealed it, stuffed it into his duster pocket, and climbed back up onto the road.

The sun was a pink line at the edge of a misty black drop-off in the distance. He was tired. He was scared.

He was in love.

He headed home for some sleep, saying only to himself, "Oh, my God."

24

Everyone who passed Shiller in the glossy hallway of the medical examiner's building congratulated him. The new acting district attorney, sworn in on the courthouse steps that morning just hours after news of Marshall Robbins's death, had postponed Shiller's suspension and the investigation of Othel's shooting.

Shiller had slept until noon, then gone for a haircut and a boot shine while he read the paper. The newspaper didn't have the story of Marshall's death yet, but the barber shop television blared the story. With one boot shined and his hair still stringing below the collar of his starched white button-down shirt, Shiller had bolted from the shop.

Now he was striding smoothly toward the autopsy room where the cowgirl receptionist had directed him to find Benjamin Elias, chief medical examiner and king of the condescending personality. Only his strides were smooth; his insides were swirling like fence posts in a tornado.

He passed through the complex of offices where loitering county employees who knew him perked up when he passed. Some ME investigators—burly, florid guys with military haircuts and wearing khakis and flannel shirts—motioned with waves and said collectively, "Congrats, Mike, now you'll get some fair treatment."

When he entered the tunnel that led to the windowless ominous row of autopsy rooms, he was so focused on finding Dr. Elias that he almost missed the five-foot-ten brunette whom he'd flirted with now nearly every day for the year that she had worked in the building.

She shook her fluffy long curls at him, clutching a stack of black X rays to her chest like a favorite pillow, and he was past her before he stopped and turned.

"Oh, hey, Valerie. What'd you say?"

She was eye level with him, blinking as if she had something painful in her eyes, but smiling as if she had something aching in her underwear. "I said, don't you ever smile?" With an alarmingly pink long fingernail she thumped the brim of his Stetson.

Yesterday he would've played coy with her, like he did on the weekly or daily occasions when he came here on homicide investigations. But today she looked different, kind of like a hick in after-five dressy shoes and a polyester print dress that screamed Kmart. Yesterday, before he had sat on the steps and basked in the reticent elegance of Allison, he would've thanked Valerie for the blow job she gave him the week before in his truck outside a bar where they had shared two pitchers of beer and six dances.

Today he felt sheepish and sleazy, as if he'd used her, which he had, and he had a twinge of conscience that he didn't know and didn't want to know her last name. It wasn't that he was a better man for taking a walk with a gentle woman like Allison, but at least now, Shiller thought to himself, he wanted to be a better man. The memory of himself in that pickup truck a week ago, reaching under Valerie's dress as he had done, ripping her panty hose at the crotch, using his thumb like a vibrator until she screamed like a steam engine, actually made him ashamed suddenly.

"Sorry," he said with a mindless shrug. "You doing okay?"

Her pink lips tightened. "You said you'd call me."

He wanted to push a remote control button and put her on mute. Instead he offered, "Well, I shouldn't have said that. We had a shitload of shootings this week, and I spend almost all my time studying for law school and—"

She took a step toward him. The X rays were now her shield of armor. "You spend a year traipsing through here, flirting with me like a dog in heat, then I give you what you want and then you don't like me anymore? Fuck you, you son of a bitch. You tell anybody what we did and I'll tell everybody you're a fag. Asshole."

She wheeled. Shiller indignantly straightened the tie he was wearing, the only one he owned, and turned to let her go.

Ben Elias was hunched over a shiny metal countertop near a huge metal sink. He was draped in more protective gear than if he were about to enter a nuclear accident scene. All Shiller could see besides gloves, mask, paper shoe covers, wrist wraps, and white coat were Elias's round eyes and a swatch of gleaming bald head. The body splayed open with a Y cut on the autopsy table had the top of its head removed as if it had been scalped by Indians. Shiller recognized Alex Johnson. He also recognized that Elias had gruesomely sliced Johnson's head in half to analyze the bullet wound that passed through the dead man's ears.

"Ben? What the hell happened to Marshall Robbins?"

The fat doctor's fat little hands kept scribbling on the paper. "Massive cerebral hemorrhage. Did you see Max in the hall just now? He went for Cokes and fell in a hole."

Shiller stepped around the gore of Johnson, whose giant feet and hands were all that remained intact. He leaned on the counter next to Elias, who wrote quickly and didn't look up. "I saw Max going into the men's room with a magazine, Ben."

"Great," the befuddled doctor mumbled. "I can't do more till he returns, so what is it, Mike? I'll have preliminaries on all your shootings by noon tomorrow." He finally righted himself, eye to eye with Shiller's sport-coat breast pocket.

"I'm more interested in Robbins."

The doctor dropped his mask and his bushy beard fell out. "Why? It's natural causes. This is a non-smoking building. Either put that cigarette out or give me one."

Shiller grinned. Elias inhaled deeply.

"You do a drug tox?"

Knobby short fingers rubbed tired eyes. "Everything but a Pap smear. I found the aneurysm. It was waiting to happen. Something increased the pressure and it was like a pin popping a balloon."

Shiller strained to sound casual. "An air bubble?"

Elias frowned. "No. Air bubbles go to the heart. He had no cardiac involvement." His tone became conspiratorial. "You're investigating this as a homicide, Mike?"

Shiller's belly churned. "Naw, Doc. I'm just checking. This is a big deal to the public and all. We just want to cover our asses." He faked a yawn. "Poisons, maybe? Acids, alkalies, corrosives, cyanide?"

Elias laughed a plume of smoke. His paunch jostled. "Jesus, no. No chemical agents. No legal or illegal drugs. You are paranoid." He peered. "Maybe you're afraid they'll think you did it. Robbins died between two and six A.M. today. Where were you?" His petulant grin died when Shiller didn't smile. "Look, Mike, I have no forensics to indicate anything but an aneurysm. Do you?"

It was momentarily hard for Shiller to swallow. He wanted to sound cool. He tossed the cigarette into the metal sink. "If I did it, I'd have tortured him first.

You'd have found ligature marks all over him. You can't narrow down the time he died?"

Elias peeled off the gloves with a smacking sound, fished in a cabinet for a fresh pair. "That is narrowed down based on body temp, stomach contents, and bleeding. It's all written for you in the report. And you, Dirty Harry, are safely in the clear, too. Pathology indicates to me that Marshall Robbins wasn't tortured by a long-haired, filthy-mouthed cop with a reputation for catching killers and lying to girls."

Shiller smirked. "You got no respect for me."

"Of course I do. You've done to every woman who works for me what I'd like to do if I were just six inches taller, thirty pounds lighter, and had no morals or conscience." He replaced the mask so only his bulging eyes showed. "Except some of them I might do twice, which I hear is not your style."

"You find anything weird on Robbins?"

"A microscopic trace of blood in his inner ear. He must've had an ear infection recently."

"Was he taking antibiotics? Is there a record of any recent doctor appointments for an ear infection?"

Elias stood over Johnson's mutilated corpse like Dr. Frankenstein. "No antibiotics. The other is your department. Whether he had an ear infection or not, the man did have a ticking aneurysm. There's nothing in his brain except what's supposed to be in everybody's brain."

Shiller said hoarsely, feeling his heart pump a weird series of beats, "Water."

"Water," Elias grunted. "Do you want me to hold him? Unless you do, my report is complete and he'll be released for cremation—his last will and testament."

Max the criminalist, who only needed a stovepipe hat to be Abraham Lincoln in a lab coat, returned with two cans of Coke. "Hey, Shiller," he chirped in a reedy voice, "you staying? I'll get another soda. By the way, Valerie just told everyone in the break room that you're a homosexual. Want to go to dinner sometime?"

Shiller smiled drearily. "I ain't staying, thanks. Ben, you hold on to Robbins's body till I call you, okay?"

He heard the grating sound of the buzz saw start up and hit pay dirt in Johnson's body as the door sucked itself shut behind him. The bright sunlight outdoors hurt Shiller's eyes. He put on his Ray-Bans, hoping to dull the images of what was now so clear in his mind.

She shot water into his brain. Monty told her how. If there was any trace of her husband's blood on the syringe—and he knew there no doubt would be tracings—then Shiller had the evidence to convict Allison of premeditated murder. He could ask Ben Elias to do a special test, to splice Robbins's eardrum, magnify the cross sections a zillion times. The needle hole would be there. The sudden aneurysm would be explained.

"Crap," he growled, dusting lint off his navy blue sport coat and hoping to wipe away some of the ether and formaldehyde smells. "I arrest her for murder, I never will get her in love with me. Cops let worse people walk for reasons not nearly as good."

His car phone jangled. Hadeesh barked in his ear, "Detective, I know it is your day off, but you should come here to the station. A woman is here to confess that she murdered Marshall Robbins."

25

Monty sat at Jasmine's crummy Formica kitchen table, his head buried in his folded arms, looking like a sobbing man. But he was laughing aloud.

"Bitch did it. Yeah, so she's got nothing on me anymore. Hallelujah." He laughed again in spasms. "Oh, Lord, she did it. Motherfucker won't be beating up on her tonight. Hoo-hah, no way. Tonight old motherfucker Marshall Robbins will be running like a scalded dog from all those brothers he put down there in prison who got the lethal injection. Man, I hope that son of a bitch shows up in Hell with his track shoes on . . . ha-ha-ha."

Rodney stared blankly. "Who you talking to?"

Monty raised his head. "I'm praying. Don't you know it's rude to interrupt people who are praying?"

Three soggy letters of the alphabet floated in the soup in his big spoon. "People don't curse when they pray. You wasn't praying. I don't like you baby-sitting me. Baby-sitters are girls who know how to play Nintendo."

Monty glared. "You think I enlisted for this shit? You're supposed to be in school while your mama's at her school. I'm supposed to be making deliveries all day. We all got shit we're supposed to do, but you get sick and mess up the whole deal, so now I got to sit here and watch your ass practice tying shoelaces and pretend to be a Power Ranger. You think I begged your mama to let me stay with you?"

He said dryly, "I got diarrhea."

Monty winced. "Please, boy. Eat that soup."

He slurped, kept his eyes on Monty like a mannequin. "Anyway, what do you deliver?"

Monty examined his solid gold cufflinks. "Flowers."

"You ain't got no flowers in your car down there."

He felt a surge of impatience. "I got flowers at my flower shop down the road."

Utter insouciance from the boy. "You do not. You deliver drugs, that's what everybody in the building says. Don't you know how to just say no?"

Monty sighed. "I know how to just say shut your ass."

The boy shrugged, slurped more soup. Monty cleared his throat and asked cautiously, "These big bad liars, do they tell your mama that I deliver drugs?"

"She don't believe 'em. She tells the ladies at the church that you're a li-ti-gi-mate businessman. You got car washes, she says, and a couple pawnshops. She says that someday she's gonna bring you to the church on Sunday and let all of them see how good you are." He had the gaze of a puppy dog. "I had this blanket. It was a good blanket. Before my daddy died he used to put me in it at night between him and Mama, then when I went to sleep he'd carry me into my bed alone in that room, but since I still had on that blanket I still felt safe."

Monty was examining his manicure, hardly listening, but now he looked up at the child's compelling face.

"Then one day Mama told me that I needed to know that the blanket wasn't really magic or nothing. It mighta made me feel safe, but the blanket wasn't what kept me safe. She said I was safe because of the people who love me—her and Grandmother and my dad—so I let her put the blanket in a box in the attic."

"Child, what is your point?"

He drank soup from the bowl, wiped his mouth with his forearm, and dutifully placed his bowl in the sink, then turned to face Monty like a miniature philosopher.

"My mama's gonna put you in the attic someday when she figures out that you ain't what she thinks you are."

Monty bit the end off a cigar. "You want some ice cream, kid?"

"I ain't supposed to have ice cream today, my mama said, nor no milk. It irritates my bowels. You want to play checkers?"

Dejectedly, Monty admitted, "I don't know how."

The boy giggled. "Come on. I'll show you."

Rodney brought the checkerboard to the table. Monty didn't resist when Rodney crawled into his lap. It felt good, real good, as if just for a moment it was Othel's warmth pressing into his chest.

The last television news bulletin he heard before he and Rodney fell asleep together on the living-room couch was that the medical examiner had given a preliminary ruling in the death of Marshall Robbins as natural causes. Stroke.

Funeral plans were pending. Monty lifted his head. The DA's body would be held until Dr. Ben Elias released a final cause of death ruling to the police.

He listened to Rodney's peaceful breathing on his shoulder. No cause for alarm. Allison will call. I gave her my beeper number, everything's cool. He fell into Rodney's comforting cadence of breaths, and then fell into a deep afternoon slumber while stroking the little boy's soft hands.

Sweet Jasmine, he thought as he drifted deeper. She

needs a new couch, a new car, a new everything. If only she would let him, he would buy her the world. He would buy her a beautiful house someday, preferably one without an attic.

26

Allison was surrounded by a sea of police officers in stiff black uniforms. Beyond that layer, which made a half halo behind her where she sat in the first pew of the church, were fifty or more sheriff's deputies in pale brown uniform shirts. Spilling out like paper dolls behind the deputies were hundreds of civilian dignitaries. Congressmen, senators, the Catholic bishop, the mayor, endless judges and public prosecutors and defense attorneys. They filled the city's cathedral in a collective sullen hush.

Allison was flanked on one side by her older sister Angela and on the other by Marshall's sobbing mother. She lay her hand on Caroline Robbins's scrawny pale arm. The heavy diamond bracelet that encircled the old woman's frail wrist felt exceedingly cold, like a surgical instrument.

The memorial service was brief. Allison planned it that way. There would be no funeral. A medical examiner's investigator had told her that the body was being held for some routine additional tests and that they expected to release it for cremation within a few days. She had caught a twitch in her body when the woman investigator said it so sublimely, as if it were true. That was on Saturday. This is Monday, she recited silently to herself. If they've caught me, I'll know within just a few days.

When a magnificent choir sang "The Battle Hymn of the Republic," she had stifled a smile. Such grandiose pomp for such an extraordinarily cruel and hypocritical man, like a requiem to Satan. A girl two rows back from Allison cried aloud once, buried her face in a sullen police officer's offered handkerchief. Allison glimpsed and suppressed another angry grin.

So you're the latest one. And you're weeping because he's dead and now you have to pay your own rent.

Her sister Angela set a solemnly oblique stare into Allison's eyes. The stare said: "Can't you at least dredge up a tear?" Allison bristled. Angela gazed complacently again at the governor, who was eulogizing Marshall as "a man whose life was a monument to justice." He pointed to ten or so rows of people who were there representing the Victims of Violence, people whose loved ones had been murdered, and he said it was Marshall Robbins who had given those poor people the relief of knowing that the deaths of their loved ones was avenged. He didn't mention Marshall's virtues as a wonderful husband and father. Allison had called him on the phone and told him he'd better damn well not deify the son of a bitch as a human being. She knew the governor by first name, had kept him overnight drunk in her guest house after a dinner party many times. She'd told him, "You say what you want, Jerry, about what kind of lawyer Marshall was, but you spout off that he was a good friend to me or a good dad to my kids, and I'll stand up in that memorial service and call you a fucking liar. You got that? Now, thanks for your time."

Monty would've been so proud. Her lips flickered. She pressed a finger to them. They were angry that she wouldn't let the children attend the service, her sisters were. So she said to them, "Yo Angela, yo Dana, it's my fucking kids and my fucking dead husband, so unless you want to put your ass in my place on my fucking deathbed, then don't be telling me how to live my life."

They had left her house and gone to stay in a fancy hotel downtown, to talk about how out of control she had become. How dare she set some limits in her life and make them respect them!

Marie would've been so proud.

The choir sang "Ave Maria"—Allison picked it because Marshall hated it—and she let her eyes wander around the room. When she met his eyes, her mood sank.

It wasn't his eyes that she met; they were hidden behind staunch Ray-Bans so that no one could see where Detective Mike Shiller was looking. He stood by a wall, under a stained-glass window of Christ stumbling with the cross. If her eyes met his, he did not acknowledge it. He was in a black suit, crisp white shirt, and black Stetson, a black moustache covering any semblance of his mouth. He looked stern, as if, if you approached him he would snarl.

He did not move, did not uncross his arms or lick his lips or check his watch or wiggle an eyebrow. Like cold metallic beacons, his lenses bored into her. She looked away and then back at him. No change.

She felt a rising panic, a choking kind of desperation to get the body cremated. The panic caused the tears that came. They welled up fast under her eyelids and fell in hot sudden streaks. Caroline Robbins patted her grieving daughter-in-law's knee. "There, there, darling. I know you'll miss him. We all will. Be strong for his admirers."

Shiller was gone when she looked back to the wall. The space beneath the crumbling Christ was vacant.

She wanted a limo alone after the service. They had balked about that, too, her flapping, yakking sisters. Marshall deserved a show of family togetherness, they argued. They were standing then in the lobby of the hotel, amid tinkling piano music and noontime business lunchers, and Allison had told them that after the service she would ride alone, that there was a separate limo for them to share with Marshall's mother.

Angela, a duplicate of Allison, only ten years older and with black hair, had snapped, "Just for once why don't you act like something matters to you."

Dana had echoed, "Allie, really, we should all ride in the same car. There's national news coverage here. It'll look funny, like we don't get along."

In her swingy little black dress, looking more colorful and rested than ever, Allison had retorted, "Girls, if we weren't sisters, would we be friends?" Angela rolled her eyes. Dana sighed. Allison said, "See, when you believed all that bullshit about me being a cocaine addict, when you saw me wasting away to an anorexic death mask, when you sat in conspiracy with him and planned to put me in a mental institution, when you did all that—without once coming to me in private—you helped him batter and abuse me. He used you to control and isolate and hurt me."

Angela put a tissue to her lips. The limo driver dutifully opened the door. "We regret that, Allison. He was very convincing. He told us he loved you."

Allison had said before the door closed, "I'm going to see a family therapist. You do whatever it takes to feel better about what a mess we are as sisters and friends. If in order to get along I have to earn your love, then I don't want it."

She found Shiller again. He was seated at the end of the first row where she sat. The memorial service ended. An usher came to lead Allison away before the large crowd dispersed. Mike Shiller followed stoically.

He slid, uninvited, into the limo beside her. The sunglasses came off. The sexy eyes floated up and down her. She liked it.

"Does the funeral home mind if I smoke in here?"

She punched the lighter. "It doesn't belong to the funeral home. It's ours . . . mine."

He smoked. "How'd he get so rich on a county salary?"

"His family is very rich. He invested well."

"Those your sisters?"

A twinge of sorrow squirted through her numb veins. "They used to be, I guess."

"Trouble in paradise?"

"They don't think I live my life right."

"Fuck 'em. Can the driver up there . . . can he hear us?"

"No. Oh God, not another winter storm. Every time there's a storm my children barrel into my bed and I get no sleep."

He put his arm behind her but not around her. "When you come into a room, say a restaurant, do all the men quit talking and all the women start fidgeting and frowning? I bet they do. I got a picture of it. You step in. The room gets quiet. Men go 'Whoa, jeez, she's beautiful,' and women go 'Whoa, jeez, I'm an ugly piece of shit.' Is that pretty much what happens?"

"Why can't you release Marshall's body for cremation, Detective?"

"I can. Soon as you tell me how you did it."

She wanted to curl into a fetal position. Instead she sat straighter. "He had an aneurysm."

"Yep. I got a big color picture of that in my mind. You throwing a syringe over the Silverbrook Road bridge. Me fishing it out of the dirt. It didn't hit the water like you and Monty cooked up. I've got it in an evidence bag." He looked squarely at her. "In my pickup truck."

"And you can lose the syringe if I fuck you." She said it so wearily.

"Now, you see, Mrs. Robbins, I ought to slap you. That's quite an insult."

She would take the children and leave the country. Her mouth went completely dry. Her hands shook; it was hard to breathe. She would tell Caroline Robbins that she and the kids needed some time abroad, and they would take the Lear Jet to New York tonight, fly straight to Switzerland.

Shiller talked as if they were sitting on fence posts sharing beers and barbecue. "Doesn't your conscience bother you?"

She had begun to cry. "What do you want?"

"I want to know how—not if or why. See, murder's real easy. If it wasn't, they wouldn't need platoons of guys like me to go and catch people doing it. It's damn hard to catch people, because killing somebody's so damn easy. I just want to know if my theory on how you did it is correct."

"He had an aneurysm."

"With a little help from his friends."

"What do you want?"

"I want you to pick up that phone and tell the driver to let me out at the next bar. I want you to know that nobody, least of all me, really cared about Marshall Robbins. He was a tyrant and a liar. I want you to get some psychiatric counseling and then be a good mom to your kids. I want you to know that if you tell anybody you did it, then I'll go to prison, too, because suppressing evidence in a premeditated murder is, uh, not the smartest thing for a cop to do. But we do it, baby, all of us, every day. We turn our heads."

She asked dully, "Why?"

He studied her unwavering and put a hand on hers.

His hand was warm, steady. Hers was an icy skeleton's claw. She realized that she had been looking into him intently, and it seemed for a time as if they were all alone on a calm, balmy island.

He said quietly, "Because sometimes it's the right thing to do."

On his white collar a lock of his soft hair was curled, set there like a half-moon jeweled pin he had worn. She touched it. He kissed her wrist as it passed his mouth, more a light dusting of quick passion than foreplay.

"I am a good mother, Detective."

"I know. It's important. Good mothers are the only thing that might save this gun-toting, gang-infested world, honey."

Her smile was sad. She touched his cheek. "Did I have options?" she asked innocently.

"Yeah. But you didn't know it. Battered wives never do know it."

The car rolled into the gravel parking lot of a square brick beer joint with the door propped open and country music pouring out like hot syrup into a cold gray day. Allison peered at the run-down facade.

"I don't think we should leave you here. It looks dangerous."

Mike Shiller winked gallantly, making fun of himself. "Danger, baby, is my middle name."

They smiled kindly at each other. Then he was gone from her.

27

It had begun to snow before dawn the next day, if Texas snow can qualify for the term. There were no gale-force winds or blinding blizzards. These snowflakes simply floated to the dry frozen grass like soft white confetti, all different sizes and shapes.

Monty and Jasmine were in bed. She had sent Rodney to his grandmother's and had come to Monty's house the night before. They had made meatloaf and death-defying love. Now they were talking, holding hands, hearing only the chimes that lined his screened-in porch (Marie had put them there) and the squeal of gulls diving for breakfast in the nearby lake.

Monty was sorely troubled. He linked his fingers through Jasmine's, kissed her hand. She wanted to know why he was troubled, why she had found him alone in the living room by the fireplace at 4 A.M. in his boxer shorts and robe, sweating like a prizefighter. When she came to him from behind and touched his shoulder, he had almost slugged her.

"It's not something I can talk about, Jazz."

She stroked his arm, made the hairs stand up with pleasure. "Monty, please don't get in trouble with the law. You promised me, no more."

"I feel like I'm lying on a bed of nails. My chest hurts. I know what I've got to do—what I'm going to do."

She lifted her face from his shoulder, looking like Nefertiti with oddly green eyes. "Monty," she hissed, "you'll lose me. You may get away with whatever it is, but that doesn't mean I'll forgive you."

He cupped her bronze breasts in his hand, played lovingly with them. She listened to him, fixated and terrified by each word.

"That white woman, Jazz, her husband was mean, real bad mean to her. He beat her up and raped her. The worst part is, he tortured her mentally, you know. Nobody ever did that to me in my life, nobody ever put me in a place in my head where I couldn't take care of myself. But this guy, this husband of hers, he kind of . . . brainwashed her into thinking that she's nothing to nobody. He got everybody away from her and then started making her think that the way he treated her—the slapping and the insulting—were what she deserved."

Jasmine was unblinking. She traced a finger along his lips until he spoke again. As a film of dawn lightened in the window, they could see the snow speckling the pewter lake water.

"She came to me and told me all this, and suddenly in my head I started knowing this husband of hers as every white motherfucker who ever wouldn't hire me when I was a boy. He became every white prison guard who ever kicked me in the ribs while I lay on that floor refusing to scream, pissing on myself. Her husband, in my mind, became all those white sons of bitches who beat up people because they can, because they're white, because there's nobody with the power to stop them."

She could feel his heart racing under her palm on his chest.

"I told her how to kill him, Jazz, and she did it. Last night she beeped me. She had this warm-and-fuzzy story about how this heroic white cop found the evidence on her, but he's not going to use it because he's such a wonderful human fucking being. He's going to turn his head, she says with hearts and flowers on her breath, because he hated her husband so much. It's all wrong, Jazz, it won't go down like that. The cop's got what he needs on her, but he doesn't have anything on me."

He rolled her toward him.

"Monty, you're frightened." Her voice wavered, quivered.

"I know what this white cop's going to do, girl. He's going to tell her soon, very soon, that he'll lose the evidence on her if she gives him what he needs on me. He's going to cut her a deal. Her life or mine. Because he can. Because he's white. Because he's got the power and nobody can stop him."

He was panting, gripping her arms too tightly.

"Let go of me, Monty. I'm going home."

"Jazz, please, if God wants a man to do things a different way, why doesn't He show Himself?"

She sat up. Her slender back muscles were flexed in alarm. "God doesn't choose for us. There's no devil, Monty, who makes men do wrong. Men choose evil. Men like you. It has nothing to do with God."

She got up and started to dress. Monty felt his mind going, felt his thinking start to slip like a train off a track. One thought crashed into the back of another one so fast that all thoughts ended up broken and twisted.

He whispered. "I don't want to do this. There just isn't any other way."

She was a silhouette against the stark white outside the window. "I'm leaving you, you know that." She covered her face a moment to fight the tears, then gained composure.

"Don't come around Rodney or me. Whether you kill a cop or not, don't ever come near me or my boy again."

"Mike Shiller killed my son. I have the right to take his life, don't I?"

She was so pretty. He reached for her. She backed away.

"I love you, Monty. I'll pray for you. I'll pray that the love of our Lord God somehow saves you. Good-bye."

He lay awhile feeling her side of the bed grow cold, hearing the wind lash the froth on the lake, remembering a sultry summer day when Othel had splashed there, diving off the dock. He was about Rodney's age that day, just a little eight-year-old black boy waist deep in golden water, shimmering, smiling. Gone forever now.

28

Hadeesh leaned very close to the stony face of Senator Frank Vilblosk, like an ophthalmologist checking for cataracts. The senator was upright in a wingback chair at his desk in his den with classical music swooning in the background.

Hadeesh said, "Dead."

Shiller replied, "Good." With a pencil he picked up the syringe spilled next to the rubber hose on the desk. "The only thing better than a dead politician is two dead politicians. Let's go shoot a congressman."

Hadeesh cautioned, "It is against the law to say that."

Behind him a uniformed cop barked, "Not in Texas," and all the cops in the room laughed loudly.

"Heroin," Hadeesh pronounced crisply.

A uniformed woman cop said wryly, "Well, that's one way to teach your son the dangers of illegal drugs. I've popped his boy Daniel twice already for possession. Maybe he'll get the message."

The reporter whom Shiller had socked in the ribs sauntered into the room, notepad smoking as he wrote.

"Hey, puke," Shiller sang out, "this is a crime scene. Step back behind that tape or Officer Connie there will get you in a leg lock and suck you till your head caves in."

Ronald smirked. "I thought you were through. This is a sad, sad story. He was a fine senator."

A lanky young cop guarding the hallway quipped, "Yeah, what a shame. Now who'll sell the world its snake oil?"

Shiller chuckled. Ronald shook his head. "You guys are so irreverent. Can I go in now and get a description of the scene? I've got all the statements I need from here."

Shiller stepped back. Ronald went through, followed by an entourage of other reporters and television cameras.

"This'll be a first," the lanky young cop muttered. "All those cameras and that son-of-a-bitch heroin addict senator without a word to say." His hip radio crackled. Dispatch was asking for Hadeesh, who was a member of the police sharpshooter team. The young cop told Shiller, "They want him at a possible hostage scene. Some kid ran to a neighbor and says a guy has his mom in her apartment."

Shiller scribbled the address and yanked Hadeesh to the car. While Shiller drove, Hadeesh put on his bulletproof vest and assembled a cache of weapons from a case he kept in the trunk of the police unit.

When they arrived at the apartment building in a lower-middle-class government project, the streets were cordoned off and the SWAT team truck was in place. Hadeesh sprinted, ducking and darting, to the position the captain had outlined to him. Shiller watched Hadeesh go bravely, almost gladly, into what was sure to be a shootout if things went the way they usually did in this neighborhood. For his partner, Shiller felt an odd pang of pride.

"That's a good boy there," he remarked to a uniform standing next to him.

"Hell of a shot," the cop said. "I wouldn't want to be in his sights if he was gunning for me. You want to question the kid? He's in my unit over here."

The little black boy was petting an enormous and regal German shepherd police dog with the K-9 force, who was panting with pleasure. Shiller knelt. The kid peered out from behind the beautifully gold and black dog. He had been crying, but now seemed to have stopped. He stopped petting and the dog whimpered, so he petted heavier, lavishly.

"Hey, son, what's your name?"

The boy's voice was a nervous, tenuous chirp. "Rodney."

"You want to take a walk over there to that store with me, Rodney, and get a Coca-Cola? My name's Mike. I'd like to talk to you so that I can help these police officers get your mama away from that man."

Rodney slid out, slipped a trusting little hand into Shiller's. The dog barked, lay down, made begging whimpers. Rodney looked back at the dog as Shiller took him across the wide street that was usually busy but was now deserted because of the barricades.

"You need you a big ol' dog like that, don't you, Rodney?"

With two hands the small boy held an orange soda

can and drank from it. "My mama's too scared of dogs. You a cop?"

"Yeah. Detective."

"I might want to be a cop, but first I think I'd like to be a professional wrestler. I ran when that man came into our house. My mama said run, so I ran, but if I were a wrestler I'd have stayed and saved her."

Shiller opened a Butterfinger in the store that had been evacuated when the SWAT guys took position on the block. He broke it in half, gave some to Rodney, and took a bite out of his half.

"Tell me about that."

The boy talked as if he was describing a TV cop show plot. "I'd have head-butted him and then done a choke and then—"

Shiller smiled. "No, I mean tell me about the man. In your own words. Okay?"

Rodney chewed and talked at the same time. They leaned on the rusted beer cooler.

"I was in my room doing my spelling lessons. My mama was in her room folding laundry. A man came past my room and went to Mama's room and then I heard her screaming for me to run, so I went out the door and down the stairs and told Mr. Mensy who runs the Laundromat that I thought somebody was hurting my mama."

"How'd the man get in? Was the door locked? Did he use a key?"

"There was a sound like Godzilla makes when he smashes a building, like maybe the door got kicked open."

"Was it open when you ran out or did you have to open it?"

The kid tilted his head. "I don't know."

"Do you know the man? Have you seen him before?"

Rodney shook his head. "He's white. I don't know any white men, except our doctor and it wasn't our doctor."

"Was he . . . hitting your mama?"

His face sank. He stopped chewing but wouldn't look at Shiller. "It sounded like a body slam, like in *Wrestle Mania.* How come you aren't dressed like a cop? Don't you have a gun?"

Shiller lifted the edge of his overcoat. "I got lots of guns. This one, one in my boot, and a big one in the back window of my car, a great big rifle. I'm what's called plainclothes. I don't wear a uniform."

The boy nodded. "Like Dirty Harry."

A policewoman came through the jangling door. "Shiller," she called out, "they're getting no answer on the phone in there. No communication at all. From the descriptions we're getting from people on the street, it's a white male around thirty who parked in the supermarket lot and walked the half block to her building. They noticed, you know, 'cause there's not many white guys strolling around here. We've got his car, checking it now. So far, nothing. He closed all the drapes." She looked askance at Rodney, licked her lips tentatively. "SWAT's thinking he may have . . . finished up and run off when the kid bolted. Hadeesh is in the next apartment hearing nothing at all. He's gearing up to go into the apartment pretty soon if they don't get any noise."

Shiller had straightened and bent again to be even with Rodney's face. The boy shook his head no to each question. "Son, does your mama have lots of jewelry? Does she have different men come up to your apartment at night and stay just a few minutes and then leave? Does she keep lots of cash around?"

Rodney's face cracked as if he was going to cry. "Naw, sir. My mama ain't a fence or a whore or a drug dealer. But she's got a boyfriend, and he's not a Christian. They all say in our building that he's a gangster and sells drugs." The tears and snot began to stream down his shiny face. "She don't see him anymore, though. She told me this morning that Monty Jones wasn't coming around anymore. Ever."

Shiller rested his elbows on his knees, cradled his face in his hands a half second, and then pulled Rodney into an embrace. Shiller spoke to the policewoman.

"Tell somebody to get Montgomery Jones down here. One of his enemies is trying to get a message to him through his girlfriend. Rodney, you come back and sit with Striker, the big German shepherd. He's missing you by now, I'm sure."

Rodney went quietly, trying hard not to cry. But all he could think about was how he shouldn't have run away. He even said so to Striker, who barked his agreement. In the store where Rodney and Shiller had talked, Old Man Turner kept a handgun, Rodney knew it, right on the counter under the cash register. It was for shooting thugs and punks, and it was loaded. Old Man Turner had sent Rodney back there plenty to get his cleaning rag and spray wash so Rodney could do the shelves and make five dollars. He had told Rodney never to touch the gun, that guns were only for when there was trouble.

"There's trouble," Rodney said to Striker, who began to bark wildly and run in circles when Rodney slid past him and out the police car. But Striker couldn't leave the car. He had to stay put in case his master needed him. Rodney knew that. He'd seen it on TV. "I'm gonna get that gun," he told the frantic dog. "I'm gonna help the cops save my mama."

29

Allison had awakened early that morning and tried to stretch but couldn't. She was boxed between slumbering children. Ellen was placid alongside her in the bed, almost as tall and with the same coils of gleaming blond hair as her mother. Mary was a snoozing, snoring clump with tentacles splayed everywhere—legs across Allison's waist and chest, tiny arms looped around her mother's neck. Jason was an elongated anonymous lump under the covers at the foot of the bed.

When the wind had swirled during the night and made things creak, the children had floated sleepily to be next to her, one by one, slithering or flopping into the king-size bed to snuggle up against the only real security they had ever known. Allison.

She wiggled free of them quietly and shut the door of the master suite behind her, leaving them in peace. With the great drapes drawn back from the endless den windows, the muted winter morning light was enough, somehow comforting in its organic sensuality, a sensuality that no fluorescent or synthetic lamplight could manifest. She made coffee, torched logs in the den fireplace, and then sat serenely down at the glassy baby grand piano.

Gently, so as not to disturb the children or the gracious light of the morning snowfall, she played

Chopin's Nocturne in E Flat. Opus nine, number two. And then Beethoven's *Sonata Pathetique,* the adagio. It came to her to play *Pavane for a Dead Princess* by Ravel, but she hesitated.

He had hated for her to play the piano. She remembered a day, saw it in her mind like a marionette show on the mantel shadowed by fireplace flames. She had been then, as always, the culinary master, setting for them, even just the two of them, elegant and lavish tables. Napkins folded to form roses. Ribbons tied on the crystal stemware. Tapered silver and gold candles. Menus that took her hours of shopping and special devoted preparation. Quail and Cornish hen. Yorkshire pudding. Praline mousse. Even on Mondays!

That day, the one swirling into her glimpses as she fondled the ivory keys, she, the young doting pregnant wife, stunning in a red satin kimono, blond hair piled, skin aglow from the hormones of their first girl inside her, that evening, she had poured his after-dinner brandy and said with hushed pride, "I learned the Ravel piece today that I've been working on. You should have seen me, possessed by the notion that I finally could get it just right. It was funny. Me, between tressing hens and grinding quail and seducing mousse and pampering the damn Yorkshire, me, running back and forth to the piano. I set the table and then sat at the piano and didn't let up for more than two hours. Marshall, honey, would you like me to play it?"

He had glared. One lip curling. "Thanks. But I know how it goes."

She and Jason one day (it brought a smile to her lips now with the proper crescendo under her light fingertips) had invented a goofy language. She would pretend to say something in a garbled gibberish, and baby Jason, up for the game, would blather back at her nonsensically. A little game for a boy and his mommy, that they could understand each other even when what was being said was ridiculous. They showed Marshall as he sat at his desk upstairs. They went in and stood before him, she and the eager three-year-old, and when a nonsense sentence was finished between them, they cackled laughter. "Bee-sabuttle bootagosh?" Allison would ask. And Jason would answer with a serious face, "No, dozzel dweeze oof hummeltwerp." His face would break in joy.

And he said to them as they giggled, Marshall did that day, with his Rushmore frown and his villain's growl. "Jesus, Allison, you really must have nothing to do all day."

She switched to a waltz now. Brahms.

He threw her against a wall one Christmas Eve. Lifted her by her throat and the belt of her robe and tossed her like a shot put, where she collided with the mural on the bricks and then slid to the floor. He shut himself in his bedroom. She dragged presents from the attic alone and set them under the tree and then drank herself into a gagging, weeping oblivion in her own bedroom.

It began when Allison went to his office upstairs and hit the redial button on his private line. All she said to the raspy young woman who answered was, "This is Marshall's wife. I'd like him to come home tonight. It is, after all, Christmas Eve."

"Drunken fucking whore!" he had screamed two feet inside the game-room door as he lunged for her. "I'll fucking kill you. I'll destroy you, do you understand? You don't own a goddamned thing. You're nothing, you'll live on the fucking streets and never see these children. I can do anything to you I fucking make up my mind to do and there's not a goddamned thing you can do to me! I own this fucking town and that fucking divorce court and I fucking own you! You ugly, stupid cunt—"

He had panted in her face as he held her on the bed. Then came the hoist and the toss and the wall knocked her dumb for a few minutes. She remembered calmly setting out the presents, bikes and a dollhouse and baby-doll furniture. An angel spun happily on the top of the massive glittering tree. She poured vodka from her nightstand drawer and gulped it straight. It stung the cut on her lip. So she drank more.

And now she could see Marie. "You are good, Allison." The voice was a salve. "Friendly . . . optimistic . . . Pink! Because you love someone, several someones, unconditionally . . . God is in you, waiting for you to learn that you are part of Him and you are good . . . shame is the abuser's tool . . . Jesus, we want gifts from You, teach us that You are the gift . . . Be with us . . . God is calling you to love yourself unconditionally . . ."

She played *Clair de Lune.* She loved Debussy, so fluidly innocent and yet taunting, almost coy.

"Mommy, look," a small voice lilted from the bay doors across from Allison's back. She turned. Mary was there, spinning to the piano tinkles, an undulation of cotton gown folds and bunny slippers and snow white curls, spinning with her flimsy arms upward like a real ballerina. She was a blur, a wisp of, yes, pink air. Pink.

The snow fluttered. Allison played. Mary danced. They laughed.

"You're very good," Allison called out.

Mary, bending in a waist bow before another tippy-toe kick and spin, sang out, "I know, Mommy, you tell me that all the time."

The logs burned, licked by blue and yellow killing heat, as would Marshall's body later that day at the crematorium. No one would be there to say good-bye. An urn of his ashes would be ceremoniously delivered to his mourning mother. In the glowing ashes Allison saw the rubble of her fears, the debris of her self-loathing. If she was not proud of killing him, she was at least relieved. If murdering him closed forever her gate into Heaven, it also opened for a while in this life, the only one she knew, a pathway out of earthly hell.

Mary flew more than floated back and forth on the plush carpet. Allison played Ravel. *Pavane for a Dead Princess.* Playing it, she felt more alive than ever, without shame.

They built a sad snowman that afternoon, with the ersatz white stuff that falls in the South, more ice rocks than easy fluffs. They played Scrabble Junior and fell asleep, all of them, in Allison's big bed watching a movie in the middle of the afternoon.

He would not have allowed it, would've raged at them, at their slovenly pizza box tossed aside on the floor and soda pops sweating on the hardwood.

She dreamed of Mike Shiller, of kissing him all during her presunset slumber. She had no idea the real danger he was in as he made fantasy love to her among her sighs.

She heard *Claire de Lune* and felt his flesh. In her dream and on her pillow, Allison smiled.

30

Monty was waiting inside Shiller's farmhouse.

He didn't wait like a cat watching a mouse; cats were too bored and made too much play of the kill. Neither did Monty wait like a cowboy poised on a cutting horse, eyeing which calf he would cut from the herd; that sport depended too much on the first move being made by the calf.

Monty waited like a killer. The worst kind, the human kind, whose only mission is to murder, not to tame or eat you, the eerie, powerful kind of killer who pursues you in dreams where you can neither scream nor move away.

He waited for darkness, which he knew would come within the hour. He had shut off Shiller's electricity, so the darkness would be a complete vacuum when Shiller stepped inside and shut the door behind himself. He waited for Shiller, whom he knew would come shortly after dark, to call in the horses from the pasture and put them in their heated stalls before the temperature plummeted and became deadly to them.

He wore only white cotton clothing. No threads of white cotton were traceable to the source, and Monty knew that. His light parka was white and stuffed with nothing—no down or foam or other insulation that could be identified as anything more than impossibly common. He had shaved his head bald, no hair for

DNA testing, and had taped his fingers with stark white plain medical tape. He wore two pairs of surgical gloves that anyone could buy at any drugstore. His shoes were covered with the same tape first and then cotton shoe covers, all of which he had bought at different drugstores before he had shaved his head and while he wore sunglasses and a business suit.

The sun began to slope on the horizon as if it were bending in to see him lurking there inside the windows. Shiller's farmhouse took on a murky luster, as if mist rose from the old throw rugs. It was only the air of a bachelor's accumulated dust in the slanting sunset.

He brought a shotgun. In a flash, from the distance between the front door and the chair where Monty sat, it would blast Mike Shiller in half instantaneously, cut him right between the rib bones and the belly. His brain would live longer than his lower half, the half-minute or so that it took his heart to drain all its blood out onto the floor where he would land on his back, blown there from the force of the shotgun shell expanding.

This farmhouse had the silence of another planet, a place where no life stirred at all, where foreign objects merely sat obliquely for eons. No cars honked from the country road a quarter of a mile down the gravel drive. No children's voices echoed from the schoolyard basketball courts. No church bells or helicopters.

Only silence. A funeral home at night, all that deathly silence compressed, the bodies having the appearance of human life but being only soundless relics. Shiller's big TV should have blared, his free weights might have sometimes clanked as he heaved them, maybe his microwave buzzed or his toilet flushed or his own deep voice growled as he commanded into the phone. But now, nothing. Just the hollow resonance of Monty's steady breathing. Night slowly began to drop a sinister cloth that would cover Shiller's eyes when he arrived home.

Monty's car was in back of Shiller's long one-story farmhouse. It couldn't be seen from the road. After he killed Shiller, he would drive his own car to the rural road and walk back, drive Shiller's truck over the tire tracks in the driveway, and leave it there, covering any prints that might be left in the icy residue. Cars on the well-traveled rural road would erase Monty's tire tracks before anyone found Shiller's body.

A floor heater clicked on, and a rush of warm air rustled some lace curtains that trickled daintily across the front windows. The mark of a woman. Nothing else in the place said so. The mark of a woman who was gone.

Car headlights angled into the driveway at the end by the road. Monty twitched, squinted. The car turned in and then backed out to travel the other way. He would know when it was Shiller for sure, because the gate would swing open when Shiller got out to open it.

He had made a topical search for the syringe. In the refrigerator, in a box of loose change on Shiller's bureau, through some of the pockets of his clothes in his closet, in the bathroom cabinet. Nothing. The man lived like a refugee, like Monty, he had thought to himself. Mustard, beer, ketchup, and a carton of Marlboros in the refrigerator. Dirty jeans and socks piled on the neatly made bed. A fossilized Big Mac and sadly melted milk shake beside a *Guns and Ammo* magazine on the bare kitchen table.

And yet, and yet . . . Monty kept thinking . . . he is not human, he gunned down my boy like an animal, and now he's got evidence . . . and I can't walk through here and feel any brotherhood with the son of a bitch because we neither of us own more than one kitchen pan and two bathroom towels.

He looked through drawers and found nothing

except boxes of bullets and condoms and toothpicks. In the living room he held a framed portrait of two boys who could both have been mirror images of Shiller. Without the moustache and muscles, of course, but dead ringers nonetheless.

The phone rang. Monty set the frame back calmly. An answering machine growled, "This is Shiller. Start talking, unless you want money. I ain't got any." Monty checked the shotgun. The caller hung up without a word.

In the hallway he inspected a college degree hanging crooked on the wall. Summa cum laude, it read. ". . . Has conferred upon Michael James Shiller the degree of bachelor's of science in Criminal Justice . . ."

A sigh came from Monty as he positioned himself behind the big recliner that faced the front door, his foxhole position from where he would take out this man he hated so much, this lonely, learned cowboy cop who had nothing but frames and lace to remind him daily of what he had lost in life.

Monty had only Shiller to remind himself of what was gone.

He said aloud, his first spoken words in hours, "I'm gonna kill you, you child-murdering son of a bitch. It ain't my fault if you're the first fucker I've popped who was worth a damn."

As in a play, when the orchestra starts and the crowd coos, all the lights from outside dimmed. The blackness was a cord that tied up the silence at Monty's feet and hands. There was no turning back.

31

They had the layout of the apartment on a map drawn from other apartments like Jasmine's. As night fell they had floodlights, giving the front of the evacuated old gray building a surreal, one-dimensional cast.

The city block was strangely abandoned and quiet, nothing like its usual teeming self. The boys with jam boxes on their shoulders, the old men congregating outside storefronts—groceries, liquor stores, pawnshops, psychic readers, an Army Navy surplus store, a record shop—were all gone, sent a safe distance back a few blocks during the hostage standoff. The women coming from city buses with bags of lettuce and soup were nowhere to be seen.

There were only cops. SWAT cops in paramilitary vests and boots. Bomb-squad cops in asbestos jumpers. Detectives in cheap sport coats and stained ties. Uniformed cops in black with gold buttons. Cops on horseback wearing cowboy hats and cowboy boots with their uniforms, ambling back and forth to keep away the curious or the dazed who wandered too close. The caravan of police cars, vans, wagons, and motorcycles made prisms of red and blue beams that gave the frigid air a kind of life, a dance of colored swords that penetrated the bleak white fluorescence of the floodlights shining on the building front.

Hadeesh and Shiller were inside, in the hallway of Jasmine's apartment level, pressing their backs firmly against the wall, waiting to move in. Hadeesh wore a black sniper's jumper. Shiller was in his standard black Stetson hat.

"Why aren't you scared?" Shiller asked.

Hadeesh joked. "Allah is with me."

"Yeah? I hope he brought a Katyusha rocket launcher with him. Hadeesh, I'm too damn old for this. One more year and I'm a lawyer, man. No more of the commando shit."

Hadeesh whispered, "You will miss the excitement."

Shiller grimaced. "The excitement of what? Going home every day amazed that I'm still alive and didn't get shot in the back?"

"A wise lawyer, Detective, should feel the same way. People in this country have a special loathing for two things, from what I have learned: attorneys and constipation. You can see it on the television advertisements over and over, they are selling laxatives and lawyers."

"Hadeesh, boy, don't sit around on your days off and watch TV. Get a woman. Go out and knock down some strange, you know. Tell 'em you're a cop. Women love cops. I once had a gal for a while who could have an orgasm just at the sound of me ripping the Velcro apart on my gun belt."

Hadeesh smeared black camouflage on his face from a can in his pocket. Shiller checked the clip on his .380 semiautomatic pistol. It was cold, but because of their bulletproof vests they were sweating.

Hadeesh was defensive. "At my junior college where I am studying, there is a redhead." He kissed his fingertips and then let it go in the air. "Beautiful. I asked her would she go bike riding with me, and she said, 'I heard that men in your country don't bathe.' And she made this kind of face like I had pinched her. I told her that my father owns a dry cleaners and my mother is a mathematics professor and that they taught me not only to bathe but also to never leave toenail clippings in ashtrays like American men do. She said to me, 'Well, my daddy's a marine, and I don't think he'd like me dating a terrorist.'" He sighed. "The most terroristic act I have committed is once when I called up an airline and asked for a prearranged vegetarian meal on a flight to see my sister at school in Chicago."

They instinctively slid to sit crouched on the floor when a doorway opened at the far end of the deserted hallway. Two uniformed officers were swaggering toward them.

"Look," Shiller offered, slapping the brim of Hadeesh's cap which read SWAT in big gold letters across the front, "they're going to bang on that apartment door one last time, then we go in. Whoever's in there has the drop on us, that's for sure, so—" He pointed a finger. "—You keep this in mind. If we make it out of there, I have the perfect girl for you. Long legs. Blond hair. No brains."

Hadeesh's eyes had a flinty thrill in them. "Ah, the perfect woman. And from the description I take it she is an American."

One uniformed cop spoke seriously through Shiller's and Hadeesh's muffled laughs.

"There's no lights on in there. We're going in blind. The phone's off the hook. Not a word in three hours from inside. You got the apartment layout, Hadeesh? Good. We don't know where the woman is. The perp could've gotten out of the building before we got here. Then again . . . he could be in there setting up on us. Detective, her boy ran off from the squad car. Jerry walked away for a minute to help unload surveillance stuff, and the kid took off from the dog. All the neighbors say the kid knows his turf like the back of his hand, goes around here by himself all the time, some kind of little mole or something. We're all-points on him already. But the theory is he'll come back."

Shiller stood. His heart was thudding dully in his throat, as always when he had to back up a sharpshooter or go into a room where someone was sure to try and kill him. He wanted it to be Monday, to see himself squarely in his desk in one of his law classes. He wanted to see Allison Robbins. He wanted a hot shower, a beer, a kiss, anything to prove that he had survived this ordeal. Going blindfolded by darkness into a room with a killer was not what he wanted, but it was happening again.

The uniform was telling them crisply, "Shiller knocks, then goes in first, out of your way, Hadeesh, so you can have front stage. The SWAT guys are on their way up. Take your positions. Here's a picture of the woman from her church directory." He cleared his throat, uncomfortable that what he said might be taken as a joke, which it was not. "Don't shoot her."

Rodney was crying big tears and feeling sick to his stomach. He had been in the darkened tunnels of his apartment building a hundred times, so that wasn't what he was feeling scared of—not the dark. He and Hoyle Roberts and Nicholas Kingsmill had traveled every inch of the tunnels every summer day of their lives except, as he recalled, not when they wore diapers.

Some places along the way you could sit up but never stand. Nicholas said that a long time ago the tunnels had been used for gangsters to hide in when liquor was illegal and bank robbers needed a place to hide their loot.

But Rodney's mom had made her oh-please face when Rodney told her about the gangster tunnels, and she had said that the tunnels were supposed to be for air-conditioning, but the government ran out of money for central air and had to put window unit air conditioners in all the apartments. And she had told him to quit crawling around in there. But he had not quit.

He had played cards in there by flashlight with his buddies, and they pretended they were a million things. Pirates. Spacemen. The best was when they pretended they were in a dinosaur's belly and had to get out before the dinosaur woke up and started drinking tons of seawater and drowned them.

At every opening to every apartment, where he looked in through the mesh so that the empty dark rooms appeared to be drawn on a piece of graph paper, he had called out, but no one answered.

Then, without even wanting to or thinking he was going to, he started crying. First his throat hurt and then his eyes exploded with hot water and he lay in one spot for a few minutes and cried like when he was a baby. He whimpered over and over, "Mama . . . Mama . . ." but she didn't call out his name as usual. Always when he said "Mama," her voice came instantly, but not this time.

And he cried because he knew she was dead. He crawled faster, lugging the gun under his belly, looking for the familiar shoestring that was tied to the grate through which he could crawl right down into his own bedroom after popping the mesh off the vent. Long ago he had taken the screws out, like Nick and Hoyle did to the grates that led into their bedrooms. The tears made his vision blur. But with the flashlight he had taken when he picked up the gun from the store, he could see when he blinked hard enough and wiped the moisture away with his coat sleeve. He could see for a minute or so. Then the tears came again. Then he cried, "Mama," again, and she would recognize him even though his voice was cracked and sounded like a tiny kid. She would recognize him. But he was so scared she'd never answer anymore.

He dropped softly onto his bed. Tried the light switch but nothing happened. He knew from television shows that he needed to be very quiet. He knew that he needed to find the bad guy before the bad guy found him. The room was very bright from some odd kind of white shower of light from outside. He saw his Texas Ranger baseball cap and put it on. He turned off his flashlight.

His bedroom door was open to the hallway. If he stepped upright into the hall, his shadow would stretch before him. He figured that out after his shadow scared him almost to death and made him bite his tongue to keep from screaming. So he crawled, dragging himself on one elbow and keeping the gun pointed upward.

There was something . . . lumpy on the bathroom floor. Laundry? Please, Jesus. Let it be my mama's slips and sweaters that she hangs there to dry, her white nurse's hose and her smooth pajamas. He had to stop and lie flat for a moment because a wave of horrible fear got hold of him. He felt as if he was choking on fear, wanting so bad for his mom to reach out and take his hand and put his head next to her shoulder and say, "Shhh, now boy, everything's all right."

She was there. She was the lump on the bathroom floor. Rodney made an animal sound. He put his fingers in her hair and begged her to wake up, but he wasn't using words. Only sounds came, garbled sounds. He crawled onto her, smashed his face into hers, and found the tape on her mouth. The moments were flying like lightning bugs around his head, so fast. The tape wouldn't come off; he didn't have a fingernail with which to get the edge. He couldn't see and he was soaking wet with sweat and so scared of the dark that his body was paralyzed. He lay down beside her, and he sobbed.

The front door opened and it sounded as if someone let in about fifty big dogs that all bounced in different directions at one time. Someone yelled, "Police!"

But he didn't look like a policeman. He had a mechanic's suit on, a thing that zipped up the front like the guy who worked on cars at the garage down the street, and his face was painted black, and he was crouching as he came down the hall toward Rodney, toward Rodney's mama.

So Rodney stepped into the hallway just as the bad guy hit the white light streaming from the open bedroom door. Rodney was in the dark. Now was the time. He shot the crouching guy who wore black face paint and a ball cap. He shot the big man stalking toward his poor mama in the dark with a gun in his hands. Hadeesh caught the shot in the gut and spun in pain, howling like a coyote in a cartoon. He fell back off his haunches onto his spine, gripping himself in the middle like a big self-hug, kicking his legs. A flashlight beam hit Rodney in the face and blinded him. Over the screaming of the bad guy with the ball cap, another man in a big cowboy hat said, "Rodney, drop that gun right now. I'm a policeman, you remember me, we shared that Butterfinger."

"Y'all get on out of here away from my mama."

The cowboy sounded as if he was going to cry. The other man had stopped making noise.

"Rodney, don't point that gun at me. Lower your arm now and let the gun drop onto the floor."

Rodney cocked the hammer and aimed at the light.

"Jesus, boy!" The light went sideways. The cowboy had stepped around the corner of the hallway. He was yelling, "Where's your mama?"

"In the bathroom. Dead."

A low moan came from the cowboy cop. "Put the gun down, Rodney. I've got Striker up here. I'm sending him down the hall to protect you."

The dog? The beautiful dog? He heard muffled talking, the dog panting, then a bark, and then a German word. And then in the angle of silver at the end of the hallway, he saw the awesome form of the dog.

Rodney knelt, let the gun drop, and wiped his eyes with his coat sleeve again, though it did no good because the tears came so fast.

The dog came toward him and sat dutifully at his side, whimpering each time Rodney sobbed again. Then the cop in the cowboy hat came down the hall and held out his hand. People ran by them. Ambulances began to howl in the distance. Rodney's mom moaned when they pulled the tape from her mouth and her wrists. "Got a pulse," a woman cop shouted, but he didn't know if she meant his mom or the cop in the ball cap. He couldn't see anything because of the tears and the fact that he had his face buried in the dog's fur.

The cop picked him up effortlessly and carried him like a baby, which was okay, because that's how Rodney knew he was crying. Like a baby. Striker followed.

The cowboy cop said as they stepped into the cold, falsely lit air, "Shhh, boy. Everything's going to be all right." He handed Rodney over to the arms of another policeman, and he said, "Take care of him. I got to go back up there and be with my partner."

32

Monty wasn't ready for what happened. Nothing had showed. No car lights along the driveway. The gate didn't swing open under the halogen light at the road. It had grown darker than he was used to in the city. He had sunk into a pudding of darkness that he could stir with his hand as he sat waiting behind the big recliner that faced the front door.

Then from nowhere the front door shattered inward. Shiller loomed larger than life in the door frame, a .44 clutched at the side of his leg like a hot steel torch.

"Jones, just how fucking stupid do you think I am?" Shiller had screamed from the shattered frame, moonlight outlining him from behind so he had a golden aura. He stepped inside like a gunslinger into a saloon.

"Show your fucking ass, Jones. You've come to kill me, but I know that first you got something to say to me. So stand up and say it, goddamn it."

Monty stood from behind the chair. He pumped the shotgun. Shiller stepped forward, crunching glass beneath his cowboy boots. A cold wind blew in behind him and made a whistling noise like a tenebrious cello note. Monty aimed. So did Shiller, arm straight, .44 steady, finger itching.

"How'd you get in here, Shiller?"

The anger poured like lava. "I fucking live here, you

numbnuts thug. Come on, Jones, get your piece of me. Fire. And when you do, I'll pull off a shot reflexively. Let's kill each other and let God sort us out, as they say. You ready?"

"You killed my boy."

"How old was your boy, Jones, when you told him how cool it was to point guns at cops? Was he five when you taught him that cops suck? Was he ten when you ingrained in him that killing people and doing drugs was his right, in fact his destiny? Was he fourteen when you said that he didn't ever have to do anything the fucking police told him to do? Like drop the gun and turn around and don't move. How'd you make him so stupid, Jones? Just by giving him your goddamned no-good loser philosophy on life?"

"I'm gonna shoot you, you motherfucker."

Shiller was alive, aflame with hate. "Good. I'm gonna shoot you, too, and drag you right into hell with me. Come on, hot-rod gangster." He took another step forward, crunched more glass; the wind blew shut the splintered door frame.

Monty set the butt of the shotgun on his shoulder. "I want the syringe."

"Kiss my ass."

"You're going to hold it up to her to get her testimony on me. You know she popped him. She knows what I did. And I—" He said it with oozing wrath. "—I know, Detective Shiller, that you have the evidence she's so scared of. I want it. Or I'll make sure you're dead and can't use it."

Monty stepped from behind the chair. The shotgun was leveled no more than three feet from Shiller's chest. Shiller's .44 barrel was close enough to separate Monty's head from his shoulders with one twitch of the finger.

"They cremated the DA today, genius," Shiller spat. "I fucking released his body yesterday. His eardrums are ashes."

"Then give me the syringe."

"No."

"Then I'll kill you."

"So you keep saying. What's wrong, Jones, tired of the food on death row?"

"If I killed your boys, those kids in that picture over there, would you let me live?"

Shiller's arm relaxed to his side. The .44 hung as limp as his head. "If I were you, Monty, I'd figure that I had it coming."

"Fuck you." Monty lifted his strength from the butt of the shotgun on his shoulder and eyed Shiller.

"What do you think, Jones, that God isn't watching you? You think you're going to walk through life selling drugs and murdering people and that no price for that will be exacted by a higher power?"

Monty chuckled menacingly. "So you hope there's a God, Shiller, is that it?"

"No, Monty, for men like you and me, I hope there's not a God."

Monty put the shotgun down by his hip and took one step back. Shiller crossed to the kitchen, so close Monty could smell the cigarette smoke drenching Shiller's trench coat.

"If God wants to punish me, Shiller, why didn't He kill me instead of my Othel?"

"Too easy." His voice echoed from the dark kitchen. Monty heard a beer bottle spew. "He's the expert of exacting. Hell's not as bad as living on earth after one of your kids has been taken. Is it, Jones?"

Something in Monty wanted to scream and cry, to fall on his knees and curse God and keep killing cops until the pain stopped. He pointed the shotgun past Shiller and fired once. Wood cabinets and a cheap chandelier rained as the fire crushed them. Shiller didn't jump. He just leaned on the counter and sipped.

"Goddamn you, Shiller! You killed my son!"

"Monty, nothing good will ever come of what you do or what you are. Kill me. You're still going to wish you'd been there for him, taught him better, taken him out of that violent life. You're always going to wonder whether I killed him or whether God took him from you because you had it coming. Nobody disregards human life as much as God does. So He used me to teach you how valuable it is." Then he slammed down the beer bottle. He balled his fists and came forward, and Monty felt a surge of fear.

Shiller screamed like a man in horrendous physical pain. "I had a line on a man who kidnaped and raped and stabbed to death a schoolgirl walking home, Monty! I was . . . pumped! He knew I was coming for him. I knew . . . Jesus, I knew I had him. What was your fucking kid doing in the alley with a toy gun acting like a fucking idiot badass?"

He lunged into the living room where Monty stood, and Monty knew that Shiller was out of control. The .44 waved as Shiller raged like a charging bull.

"I . . . AM . . . SORRY, MONTY!"

Monty sat in the recliner. "He was a good boy."

Shiller's voice broke. "I know. Were you a good father?"

"No. His mama ran off when he was just, you know, a baby, so I took him to my mama. She raised him. Do you know that he died never knowing I was his daddy?"

Shiller sprawled himself on the ratty sofa. The phone rang. The answering machine picked up, and then a voice spoke.

"Shiller, this is Al. The woman is going to be okay, and the boy's fine. He's with his grandma while Jasmine spends the night in the hospital for observation. Hadeesh is still in surgical recovery. You can see him in the morning.

"Listen, Shiller, we all appreciate you talking that

little kid Rodney out of the gun he was holding. You're a good cop. We haven't picked up the perp, but we figure his message to Jones was, 'Hey, I can get in anywhere I want and kill anybody you love.' It's Solomon's drug and racketeering guys for sure. We've got Monty's mother under protection for a few days. She's cooking for all our guys and telling their fortunes. Good work tonight, my man. The next Bud's for you. On me. See you."

Monty stood. "What happened?"

"Solomon's boys think you're talking to us. They slapped around your girl Jasmine today. Her kid took a gun hidden by a store owner and went in to save her. He was scared and shot my partner. Pointed the thing at me. But I didn't shoot him, you see, because I'm too scared to shoot anybody anymore. Which means that someday if I don't quit, I'll get some hard-working cop shot dead because I hesitate. All in a day's work, Monty. And how was your day, honey?"

"So I don't forgive you, Shiller. I can still make you a deal."

"So. Deal."

"I know about Solomon's whole operation. Names. Dates. Times. Murders. Robberies. I know who the cartel buys from and who it sells to. When. Where. How. You get Jasmine and the boy and my mother and me into witness protection. Out of the country."

"And you do what for me, Jones?"

"I let you live. You never look over your shoulder again."

"So, Jones, you know Alvord Samuelson, the acting DA?"

"He's a brother. I grew up with him. Shiller, I don't want anybody else to die because of me. You go on to law school and be content knowing that my mama burned that syringe Allison used. We'll take it to

Marie together. Nobody has nothing on anybody else."

"I'm forgiven?"

All of Monty's muscles flexed. The anger was gone, but the regret was acute. "No. Not forgiven. It's just a business deal. The score is even."

Shiller stood. "And again, you give me what?"

Monty stood erect, a mammoth black monument. "I gave Othel that toy gun. You didn't throw it down on him. That's what I'll tell Alvord if you get us out of the country."

"You scared, Jones?"

"I ain't scared of you or the law or time or prison. But God? Yeah. I'm scared of God. I'm a bad son of a bitch, Shiller, but I don't want no more trouble with God Almighty."

"Meet me in Alvord's office tomorrow afternoon at four."

Monty left as he had come, fading into the shadows. Shiller called the hospital, got a report that Hadeesh was holding fine in recovery. Then he took his beer onto the porch, sat in the porch swing. He was too cold inside to feel the cruel winter cold lambasting him from the outside.

33

She came into his office with the simplest beauty, like someone setting a candle in a dark, cold window. He stood.

"Hello, Mizz Robbins."

"Hello, Detective."

She wore a blue cashmere dress that stopped just below her knees, but when she sat it lifted so Shiller could sigh at her lovely legs. He pictured those black spike heels digging into his chest as she straddled him in bed.

He wore blue jeans and a crisp white shirt under a black wool sport coat, and in the ensemble he felt like her yardman come to the door for his wages. His Stetson sat unglamorously on the file cabinet behind him. He wanted to put it on over his mess of black hair, but he was afraid that if he moved she would disappear. He remained standing.

She said flatly, "My children are with Marshall's mother for the Thanksgiving break. I thought this was the best time to come and tell you what I have to say."

Her hair was smooth in front, but when she turned to set aside her plain black overcoat he saw that in back her hair rose into a perfect French twist. No pins showing. He had never known a woman whose French twist didn't have pins showing.

"And what is it that you'd like to tell me, ma'am?"

"Oh." She said it as if he had startled her. Her face was slightly lined around the eyes, but they were large and very kind eyes. He wanted to touch the flawless red lipstick she wore.

She said again, "Oh," and then, "I want to tell you that I killed my husband."

With his supremely unfettered facade, Shiller asked, "Would you like some coffee?"

She had not blinked or hung her head. This was a deed of pride more than remorse, and he knew it. "No. But I suppose after I talk to you I will need a lawyer. Nobody in this county will do it, of course, so you'll have to get a special prosecutor, no doubt."

"Mizz Robbins—"

"You were right, Detective, I did use a syringe. I injected water into his ear and it caused what appeared in pathology to be an aneurysm—"

"Mizz Robbins, you need—"

She looked at him, defiant, not furtive. "I won't make excuses, but I will tell you that I never knew until I started therapy that I was a battered wife. A girl like me, rich, smart, all that stuff, you'd think I'd have known. But I didn't know, or if I did then I denied it. I was ashamed. He was hitting me and threatening me and holding me hostage every day, and I was the one who was embarrassed. I can't expect you to understand. But when he started on the children—little bruises and episodes of humiliation—I did what I thought I had to do."

Shiller pulled a file from his desk and slapped it down. "Mizz Robbins, you'll have to get in line to go to prison for this one. I got four other signed confessions, plus I got one woman who keeps calling me to say that she killed your husband by mental telepathy."

Allison frowned just a touch at the eyes and mouth. Shiller opened the file and read from it.

"This one here did it, he says, by injecting your

husband with a new lethal drug he invented in his laboratory on Neptune, and this guy sneaked into your house and blew your husband's brain apart by blowing into his penis. This lady won't say how she did it, she just wanted to confess that she did it, then she wanted the phone number to the *National Enquirer*. This nice lady killed him from her attic with a voodoo doll, she says, because Satan told her to. You with me?"

"Detective, I'm trying to get myself right with God."

"Oh, yeah, God called, too, and confessed, which He had to do by phone because it was lockup time at the asylum."

She smiled drearily through the first sheen of tears. "What will I tell my children about what I did?"

Shiller shrugged. "Tell them that when they grew up they'd have hated him anyway. He was an asshole. Everybody hated him."

"I had the motive."

"So did I, ma'am, and a half million other people."

The tear fell. She caught it with a long fingernail which he noticed was neither painted nor bedecked with a diamond anymore. "But I had the opportunity."

"Okay, give me the evidence."

"You've got it." She stood.

He gnawed an unlit cigarette. "Prove it."

She sat back, sighed greatly. He offered his handkerchief. "So, Detective Shiller, how can you just disregard what I'm telling you?"

He rose to his feet, kept a hand on her slender shoulder. "Coming through all this misery of yours, Allison, honey, I assume you don't have a bubble, so I'll assume you don't have a bubble for me to burst when I say this. Cops look the other way all the time. We know when doing nothing is the right thing to do."

She dabbed at the tiny tear. "Won't you get fired?"

He smiled, a snapshot of rugged heroics. "With any luck."

She hugged him. He smelled flowers, something floral on her skin, but couldn't bring himself to touch the bouquet. If he put his arms around her, he knew, in ten seconds he would have his hands on her nice ass and his tongue down her throat. So he stood stoically, eyes closed so he couldn't see her skin next to his lips.

"I killed him."

"I know." He risked putting one hand gently on her back. "I am firmly of the opinion, sweetheart, that he needed killing." He suddenly had puppy eyes, regarding her with an emotion she recognized as a sheen of his long-lost innocence.

"It's my conscience, Detective Shiller. It hurts, you know? I'm not a murderer. Am I a murderer? Sometimes I hardly can believe I did it, like someone else did it, like it wasn't me." She was twittering, plucking at her fancy purse.

He sat on the desk, took her soft arm, and pulled her to himself. Whisper-close, but not kissing-close. "Allison, I have interrogated hundreds of murderers. And guess what I've learned? There really, truly are reasons to kill somebody, and cops understand that better than anyone else."

"And when you decide that, you just let killers walk out of here? Shouldn't you arrest me?"

He reached, conked the Stetson onto his head, and said while pulling on his leather bomber jacket, "No, we don't let them walk very often. We just say we'll look into it and then we don't look into it. That's it. And, yes, I should arrest you, but I'm not going to. It's my call, and I absolve you. If you go over my head and confess, it won't end so chummy. With me, you've cleared the tower."

She regarded him tenderly, and his heart felt weary of wanting to see that look every morning and again every night.

"Why are you letting me go, Detective Shiller?"

"It's not a winnable case for a prosecutor. And besides—" The eyes under the hat brim were as tough and worn as a wrangler's favorite saddle, and then a seductive playfulness came across them. "—Letting you walk is the honorable thing to do. That's my middle name—Honorable."

She was too gloomy to smile, but she wanted to. "I thought your middle name was Danger."

He laughed. "Yes, ma'am. When it comes to catching bad guys, Danger's the name. When it comes to you, I'm afraid that my honor is all I got to offer."

She pulled back. Her breath was minty, her eyes sad. "Why did Marshall hate me so much?"

"He was sick. And he loved another woman maybe, and he didn't have the class to just leave you for her. He had to make you think you didn't deserve him. Stay in therapy, will you? Call if you ever need me."

She slid her coat on, said dryly, "So there's a hit man who's going to shoot me, you say?"

"No. Monty killed him."

"How do you know?"

"Trust me. He took care of it."

She made a girlishly puzzled expression. "Why would Monty do that for me? He hardly knows me."

"Your old man was everything Monty Jones ever hated about white guys, Allison. Besides, Monty doesn't like bullies."

She turned from the door as an afterthought. "You're alone for Thanksgiving?"

"My sons are coming over that day."

She lingered. He added nothing to the statement. When she was far enough down the hallway so she couldn't hear him, he stepped out the door, calling, "I'd ask you to join us, but then I'd fall in love with you, and we'd have constant sex, and I'd beg you to be mine and start shooting everyone who even looked at you twice. It's not like I need inspiration to become a lunatic, you see. 'Bye, Allison, honey."

She stopped in the bustling hallway, pulled on her black gloves slowly. A glance back would be another chance for him, the kindhearted cop, to reconsider her vague flirt. He knows I'm alone at Thanksgiving, she thought as she waded away slowly on the granite floor. She did glance back at him in a flutter of romantic angst.

Like a handsome, crusty Federal alone at his remote desert outpost, Mike Shiller waved good-bye with a finger to the brim of his Stetson.

The elegant blond French twist disappeared into the gloomy afternoon swirl of gray clouds. Shiller felt the candle go out and the window grow cold and empty.

34

The sun was very bright, making sharp glints off all the mismatched garage-sale glass objects in Marie's tiny living room. Outside the picture window the slum row houses looked like a ghost town buried in white sand. The sand was really a fine dusting of ice forming after the morning warm-up melted it, and now the dusk chill was freezing it again.

Marie had fussed over Shiller when he arrived—

taken his leather jacket, put his overstuffed antique chair by the small space heater, brought him a cup of coffee. She hugged and kissed Monty and wanted to read his fortune from the lumps on his bald head, but he declined and now sat pouting on the couch.

When Marie had blown out of the room like a talking whirlwind, Shiller asked, "Why is she so nice to me?"

Monty leveled him with a look of contempt. "She's nice to everybody."

"Does she know who I am?"

"She knows you shot Othel, if that's what you mean. But she's forgiven you." He said the word the way an asp hisses, as a symbol of inner poison. "She says that forgiving people makes her feel good."

Shiller shifted in the chair that nearly swallowed him into its cushions, the way he shifted every time someone said Othel's name, like a man whose back itched. He cautioned Monty, "Look, whatever you remember about Alvord Samuelson, I want you to forget it. He may be your soul brother, but he isn't your friend. He's the meanest son-of-a-bitch prosecutor who ever drew air. For eight years he's been the best at what he does. He doesn't lose often. Don't screw around or call him homeboy or try to bullshit him."

With no emotion, Monty replied, "I know the man. He's put numerous of my . . . friends I guess you'd call them . . . in for time, more time than they'd have gotten with anybody other than Alvie. I respect the brother."

"You need a lawyer, Jones."

"I just need Alvie to give me his word, is all. When we were boys and played pickup basketball almost every afternoon at the recreation center, Alvie always was picked to keep score because he didn't do any lying. He won't lie to me today."

"You'll have to go inside the Watson Organization,

convince them that you want to work for them, find out who's heading the racketeering and prostitution and who they're buying the drugs from out of the country. If they find out, they'll kill you."

Monty rose to stand at the window. The panorama of poverty beyond him through the glass looked stark against his expensive pinstriped suit. He had sunglasses on as he gazed, and he made Shiller think of a kingpin looking down on his factory of crime.

Monty told him, "Hey, asshole, tell me something I don't know. I can do it, get the information, and be in the Bahamas by Christmas Day." He turned to Shiller. "I heard you quit the police department. Allison told me."

Shiller's coffee cup slammed. "You talk to Allison?"

Monty's smile came slowly but with sinister force. "Hoo, Lord, Shiller. I just say her name and you get a hard-on. Why don't you make out with the lady?"

"Why don't you?"

Monty laughed loudly, crudely. "Shit, son, I already got me enough woman troubles to cripple Hercules."

Shiller hung his head. "I haven't got anything to offer a woman like Allison." He put down the coffee cup and saucer and went to stand by Monty. "I gave thirty days notice to the PD. After Othel I kinda lost my trigger nerve. Damn lucky for little Rodney that I did, I guess, but if he'd been somebody else and wanted to shoot again, my partner would be dead while I stood by and choked and watched."

Monty was as steely and quiet as a black secret-service man guarding his window post.

Shiller lamented, "I wouldn't know where to begin with Allison. She's so—" he groped.

Monty offered. "Nice."

"Yeah," Shiller sighed, "that's the word. I guess I'm used to girls who make me want to duck and cover. They're either mean bitches who expect you to adore them and follow orders or they're saps who cry 'cause you don't love their cat. I don't know. Allison is very kind and gentle, but sassy, you know. She seems to play fair, to want her own life, to need only as much love as she's willing to give."

Then Monty laughed louder. "Goddamn, boy, you about to break into a love ballad on me? Do you know what I had to do to get Jasmine to let me back in that big bed of hers? I promised first to buy her a color TV and then to accept Jesus Christ as my personal savior immediately after our wedding if not sooner. Shit. I had to give that bitch my balls on a necklace she can wear."

Shiller remarked dully, "I'd like to see that."

"Yeah, me, Monty Jones in church."

"No, I mean you buying a television instead of hijacking a truckload."

They almost laughed together, but then caught themselves and slid back into reserved tolerance.

Monty spoke first. "So in a month you're not a cop anymore and I'm not a dope-dealing hitman. You won't be the good guy and I won't be the bad guy."

Marie flounced in, flailing her huge arms, the colorful silk robes vertiginous around her like a pastel cloud. "Done!" she sang out. "Your syringe, my sons, is smoke. Now let's thank the Lord God that He loves us enough to give us each other. Then I'm going to have a Jack Daniels."

She fell to her knees and prayed so loud Shiller thought the ceiling would fall. Then she poured two fingers of whiskey in small glasses for herself and Shiller and asked him to come sit with her on the couch. He had the notion she was going to insist that he sit in her lap.

Her face was round as the moon and dark as cocoa. On the cocoa canvas she had painted her features in vivid, beautiful colors like a sunset on a deep red desert. Gold eyelids. Purple cheeks. Searing red lips. She had three chins that burbled when she talked, which she did fast and furiously like a record on the wrong fast speed. But her voice was deep and her penetrating eyes sparkled. In the way she looked and smelled and sounded, like a black sea flecked with rainbow hues, Marie was Mother Nature. She was Mother Earth in her love of all creatures. And in the way she was looking at Shiller, with kindness and calmness, he could see in her face the Mother of God and the mother all people would have wished for.

"Now, Mike," she began, rubbing his hands between hers, "I see around you your aura. Such a fine man you are, mmm-hmm, yes. You are showered in orange because you are a witty man, in green because you are honest and very dependable. Oooh, now, there's red; yes, you have much passion to share. But look here, darlin', at this black mass, this black sword that slices through your heart, well, honey, this will not do! All your goodness oozes right out of your soul through this wound, angel. We cannot have this, now, can we? Do you know, sweetness, that the Lord God has forgiven you? You do not need to get up every morning, honey, and stab yourself in the heart again and bleed out all your goodness in order to atone. Naw, baby! Listen here."

She placed her giant, strong hand over Shiller's pounding heart, saying, with her forehead almost touching his, "Our mistakes do not prove that time stands still. If we go on living and go on loving, our mistakes prove that time goes on. Life goes on. It curves and it bends, and sometimes, baby, it's decades before we ever know why things happen to us, if we ever do get to know at all. For a long time, honey, I did not think that I should taste the rain or touch the sunshine if my baby Othel could not. But I prayed, and I was told that the only way my Othel's short life would ever be celebrated was if I went on and celebrated my very own existence. He would want me to love. He would want me to laugh. When I weep, Othel weeps, and I will not have that, no sir, darlin'. I will honor Othel in Heaven with my joy on earth."

The silence was long. Monty was a sphinx by the window.

Shiller could only say, "I guess I don't have much faith in God, Mizz Jones."

She effused, "Oh, baby, everybody thinks that faith is this big damned rush of something that goes through you like a big orgasm. It ain't that, honey! Naw! Faith is when you don't feel anything inside, just emptiness and hollowness, but you go on and whisper up a little something to the Lord. Talking to God when you don't feel anything at all, that's faith, sweetheart. Believing when you don't even feel like you believe in anything. That's when God knows that you love and believe in Him the most, for sure. Now you heal up that black wound in your heart. You forgive yourself, baby."

Crusty old Mike Shiller muttered, "Thank you, Mizz Jones. You're a wonderful woman."

From across the room Monty snarled, "Alvie's here."

Marie pushed herself up, singing out, "Sweet little Alvie. He used to stay all night with us when they were boys, Mr. Shiller, when they were about eight or so years old, and Alvie used to wet that bed. Did you know that? Alvord Samuelson. What a fine human being. Answer the door, Monty. Mr. Shiller and I are going on the back porch to have us a swig or maybe two. Come on, Mr. Shiller. I'll read your palm out here."

35

Alvord Samuelson had the formidable stature of a matador. He was narrower than Monty because his muscles were more defined and less padded. He appeared to have no body fat, as if, had he struck a pose, he could have been a sculptor's black Adonis. In height they were eye to eye, but since boyhood they had never seen things mind to mind. Alvord was a West Point and Georgetown University Law School graduate, and after two decades as a military counsel, had come back to his hometown to become a prosecutor.

Word was that Alvord was too good for the shoddy ranks of the district attorney's office, which was commonly a springboard for youngsters on their way to becoming midgrade defense attorneys. But Alvord stayed and earned a reputation as both a scholar and a dramatic showman—he knew the law and he knew how to persuade juries, a rare and unstoppable combination among his peers. His pious composure in the courtroom often gave way to ravishes of emotion and disgust on behalf of victims of violence. Defense lawyers shriveled when he led the opposing team.

"Mojo," he said somberly in the quiet living room, "this is the first time in twenty years I've seen you without handcuffs."

"Want a beer, Alvie?"

"If you've got a cold glass."

They ended up talking over the cluttered kitchen counter, surrounded by cookie packages and second-hand curtains. In his bright purple flannel shirt and blue jeans, Alvord looked casual, but his demeanor was not.

"Shiller told you why we couldn't meet yesterday in my office?"

Monty removed his sunglasses. "He said it's being painted. I figure you just didn't want anybody to see you talking to me."

A jaundiced, deciphering gaze, then Alvord shook his head. "Old Mojo, always thinking everybody's got an angle. Shiller's here?"

"On the porch with Mama. She wants to speak to you when we're done with business."

Alvord labored not to smile. "How is Marie? Is she still a house always burning to the ground?"

"She's the same. She's good."

Alvord drew in the shadow of frost on his glass, thinking, then he said, "Tell me what kind of deal you want. I can't make any promises."

"I can bring down the Watson Organization. I can get inside. In a month I can bring you tapes, enough for plenty of indictments. I know who runs the whores, who collects for protection from which businesses, and I know who keeps the books and where they keep them. For that you wipe me clean and send me away in witness protection, with my family—Jasmine, Mama, and Rodney."

Alvord leaned, folded his arms across his flat belly, and said in a low voice, "What about the drugs?"

"I know that, too."

"Why would they let you in? They already think you're talking to us. Shiller put that word out so somebody would snitch you out on some murders we think you did."

"I'll get in, Alvie. I got money and I got favors due

on the street, and the Watson boys would like to tap it. I'll get inside because those motherfuckers are more greedy than they are smart."

"You know they'll check you constantly for a body wire."

Monty did something he hardly ever did. He opened himself a bottle of beer and took a long swig. They heard Marie's pealing laughter from outside. It calmed Monty, reminded him why he was selling out to the police.

He said sternly, "Not every time. It'll be random. I'll take the chance."

Alvord stood quiet a long few moments, then said with immense dread, "Solomon ran Watson's cartel like a Nazi commandant. Some of those boys are glad he's dead. Maybe you can get some of them to work with you."

"No," Monty said contemplatively. "I do this alone."

"And I walk you for the murders Shiller has on you?"

"Or you go into court with Shiller's suspicion, my alibi, and a fucking cigar band."

"You know, Mojo, if I don't deal with you, all I have to do is wait. You'll pop somebody else here in town. You'll screw up. You're a habitual. Eventually I'd get you."

Monty grinned insolently. "Meanwhile, Watson appoints a new gang leader and the crime rate here goes higher. With you in charge. More dope shipped in, more killings, more hookers, more young kids recruited to slaughter other young kids, more businesses going down because they can't pay Watson for protection, so he's robbing and killing them every day. I'll help you stop all that. Otherwise, Alvie, you can walk out right now with the hope that I don't change."

Alvord turned and took the fighter's stance, and Monty braced for the punch. But Alvord only said,

"You get down there to the Bahamas and so much as cheat at cards, I'll know it. It won't be a matter of extradition because your butt will be in my witness program and thereby you will be my property."

"Brother, why you going off on me like this?"

Then Alvord came, but not with a punch, though he wanted to and could have. He bunched Monty's dress shirt into a fist, clutched so hard he broke a sweat, and held Monty so close Monty could smell that sweat.

"You, Montgomery Jones, are the kind of no-good black man who causes people to cross the street at night when they see me coming. You and your kind give all decent people—especially other black people—a bad name. You could've made something. No social services failed you. No white people whipped you in the cotton fields. You had a good mama and a warm bed and you knew how to throw that breaking stuff over home plate like no sixteen-year-old kid ever dreamed of. But you stood up and pissed on it all 'cause you wanted to be a gangster. Well, you're a gangster now, and coming to me to bail your ass out of the rotten, stinking life that you chose. I'm going to let you go now, and I want you to back up real fast out of my face."

Monty seethed in the kitchen, feeling his face flush with hot blood. Alvord commanded from the living room where he was putting on his coat.

"You got thirty days. I want solid indictments on the top five, including Watson and his sons. We bought a bar in the Bahamas West End for Alex Johnson; you can run it. In about a year you'll be called back here to testify. Meanwhile everything you do and say in the islands will be watched. Don't ever relax, just keep yourself alive until I get you back here on a witness stand. Pick an assumed name. I suggest Uncle Tom. He also was a slave to his own stupidity and fear. We'll do the body wire when you're in."

Alvord stood still. Monty could feel from the cold

draft of air that his boyhood friend was standing with the front door open.

Alvord said with his operatic righteousness, "I lived in the same neighborhood as you. The same white people shoved me out the same doors. Just like you, I wanted to be free. I wanted to walk out in the open and be just as tough and good as I had the right to be. You learned to steal and kill. I worked my ass off in school. Which one of us is free now, huh, Mojo? Which one of us is walking out the door with his head up? I don't get shoved around anymore. But you. You come see me soon, and I'll tell you how and where you're going to live the rest of your crummy life . . . brother."

The door slammed. Monty took Alvord's half-empty beer glass and hurled it against the wall so hard that it shattered.

36

Monty was drifting. The sounds of the night outside his car were a familiar lullaby. Jazz so sleazy you could feel the sweat on the saxophone player's forehead. Cars backfiring or idling in various stages of collapse, as they slowed to buy girls or sped up to avoid cops.

There were sirens. Ambulances warbled in the distance. Cops hit one whoop on the dash to make someone move or to pull them over to the curb. A collection of old men on the corner was talking loud jive, shucking around each other and pointing their cigarettes, passing a bottle, ignoring the cold through their old clothes and rotted shoes.

It was all as comforting and lulling to him as the rhythm of seashore waves to a rich man napping on his beachfront patio.

He smelled exhaust fumes from outside, marijuana smoke, burned cooking grease, the scent of pungent barbecue sauce. And then another familiar smell.

He opened his eyes, studied the rearview mirror, closed his eyes again, feeling his throat tighten and his stomach drop.

He asked, "What are you? A fucking Cherokee? Were you born to sneak up on a man, Allison?"

"You must have narcolepsy. I could've cut your throat. And don't you ever lock your car doors?"

He rubbed his eyes. Maybe she'd disappear. "No need. The boys I run with don't bother to open the door before they blow your ass away. Allison, get the fuck out of my car."

Her cigarette smoke from the backseat assailed him. "Don't worry. This time I brought a cab; it's waiting."

He fixed the mirror where he could see her face caught in a circle of silver streetlamp light. "How'd you find me this time?" He made a growling, desperate sound. "Goddamn it, Allison. Go away."

"Shiller told me where to look. I called him."

Monty chuckled. "You called Shiller on the phone? Did he puke or pass out or piss his pants when he heard your voice?"

"He's wonderful, you know."

Monty grimaced. "I wouldn't know about that. Anyway, if he gets mixed up with you, I hope he sleeps with earplugs in—just in case he pisses you off and you bring a syringe to bed with you."

"Not funny, Monty. I feel guilty for what I did. I've been having nightmares and trouble eating."

He put his face closer to the mirror, hoping that talking to her reflection would make the scene seem less real. "So chew on this thought, sugar tits, were it your ass down there pushing up daisies, your sorry husband wouldn't be feeling guilty. No, sir. He'd be jogging at the club and lunching at the club, fucking the babes. He'd be damned proud of himself. You know I'm right."

She smiled, very pretty and soft. "I told Shiller I did it."

Monty laughed surprisingly loudly. "Hoo, man! That must've queered his plan. See, Shiller already knew it and had decided that if he put you in prison he'd never get to fuck you. Old Shiller. That boy has played too many games with his helmet off." His laughter played longer and died slowly.

"Monty, I came to thank you for not killing me. I know I can't ever see you again. I wanted to say good-bye."

He cleared his throat, checked his watch, touched his designer necktie, the language of his discomfort with her tenderness.

He said bravely and clearly, looking at her in the mirror with the eyes of an outlaw, "There wouldn't have been any justice in killing you."

She looked war torn and pale. He could tell she was wrestling with the fatigue of grief and guilt.

She said, "Murder is not the first action a battered wife should take, Monty."

He chuckled. "Sure it is. And the second thing she should do is reload the gun, even the odds, sucker punch the chickenshit fucker with a three fifty-seven. I pity the fool who beats on his wife, 'cause he's got to go to sleep someday."

She said listlessly, "When I got into your car that night, I thought Marshall battered me physically and emotionally because I wasn't good enough. Like if I had been better, he wouldn't have done it. That's such a destructive myth. I've learned so much in recovery therapy. It was never me at all; it was his illness. He would never have stopped until he killed me. I've also learned that I did have options. Rich and smart as I am, I was just too sick to know it. Battered women and kids need someone to stand up for us, you know."

Monty's frown was slightly, comically wounded. "I stood up for you. And Shiller, he stood up for you. You're alive. You've got your kids. Most of all, they've got you. That's the way it ought to be. The good guys should win."

She put a hand on his shoulder and met his eyes in the mirror. In that oval of shimmery light he could see that she had grown stronger. Her gaze was no longer a flinching supplication. She could raise her chin.

Monty joked, "Yo, Allison, give Shiller a piece of ass for his chivalry, will you?"

They laughed. She squeezed his shoulder and felt that it was brick. "And you, Montgomery Jones, what can I give you?"

He studied her and then said, "Nothing. You were my alibi. We did the wrong things for the right reasons, and the score is cool. That's my profession."

Allison patted him. "You be careful. I know that what you're doing for Shiller is dangerous. I better go. I'm glad we met."

"Me, too. But then, hell, I'm glad I already had the measles and mumps so I won't get them again."

She laughed lightly. "Be nice. You might want to see me again someday."

He snarled at her, teasing, "I might want to see you again, sure, when I need to be reminded how glad I am to be rid of your skinny white ass."

She opened the car door. Monty stopped her.

"Hey, Allison, what'd you say, that thing about real friends knowing your middle name?" He looked around nervously as if someone might see the tough guy cracking. "My middle name is Ray."

She popped off for his pure amusement. "I know. I saw it on your wanted poster at the post office."

They shared a bond of lingering laughter. There was more to tell between them, but there was nothing left to say. They looked at each other a long, quiet minute as darkness thickened and the ribald jungle sounds of night heightened.

She waved at Monty from the back window of the cab like a girl going off to camp. Monty was lost in the winsome, confounding thought of her when his Watson contact approached.

37

One Month Later

For Christmas Day, the temperatures were unseasonably mild. The lavish sun made the forty-degree weather feel almost like sixty degrees.

Hadeesh was in a bright red jogging suit and high tops next to Shiller in the front seat, eating an apple. Shiller was watching Allison through binoculars as she played around the yard with her children.

"It is your last evening as a police officer," Hadeesh reminded him, "and you want to spend it like this? I do not think this is good, Detective. I think there is a law against it perhaps."

"I'm trying to figure out something," Shiller answered, keeping the binoculars pressed to his eyes. "Anyway, I'm not on duty yet."

Hadeesh crunched. Allison knelt in the lens beside a petite blond girl straddling a new red bike, a bike that was practically a miniature. The blond girl was riveted to her mother's face, and Allison was ardent in whatever she was saying. The girl braced her feet on the pedals. Allison ran, pushing the girl and the bike, and laughing so hard that she had to put her face skyward.

She wore black leggings and a bulky black sweater, and she looked like a glamorous, slinky showgirl dancer. She had curled her hair so it strung down in kinked ribbons and flew graciously as she ran. Her lips and cheeks were flushed pink from the cool air. She shoved the tiny bike as she ran, and the tiny girl began to pedal, and then freedom happened before Shiller's eyes. The girl was alone, upright, moving forward, amazement glittering from her face in the magnified images he could see. He went back to Allison, delicate hands covering her mouth. Did he see a tinge of regret go through her pride? Her baby, her four-year-old angel, was going a distance without her mommy for the first time, propelled by that daunting but inevitable spirit of growing up.

A bigger girl who was a time-warped younger version of Allison, came into view to stand in front of her mother. They were applauding and smiling, and instinctively Allison began to braid the older girl's long blond hair. Her fingers weaved, they talked, the young girl laughed, and Allison bent around and kissed the child's rosy cheek.

They were moments of interminable sensuality for

Shiller, watching this beautiful woman love others so much and seeing the love they had for her. He could almost taste it in his mouth, and it tasted like fresh bread, cool strawberries, sweet chocolate. It tasted like childhood pleasures.

A lanky boy with a burr haircut sauntered over while the tiny girl kept rounding the circular drive again and again. She had it down now. She would never be back. The girl with the braid mounted her own bike, which also looked new, and sped off standing on the pedals, showing the tiny girl how the pros could do it. Allison reached for the boy and squinted disapproval of his too-long tee-shirt and too-baggy pants and untied tennis shoes.

Shiller smiled when she put on the baseball glove the boy shoved at her.

"Hey," Hadeesh sat upright, "she throws pretty good."

She rammed the pitches into the kid's glove without mercy, not at all like a doting mom or even a girl. Shiller chuckled. Allison missed one that sailed over her head, and the boy ran past her to retrieve it. A good boy, knowing that Mom shouldn't have to run for the ball. A budding gentleman who understood how far he should go to take care of her.

Shiller watched, knowing he would never get over her. That she had ruined his life. That even if she was skinny and had telling lines on her eyes and she couldn't field grounders, she would always be the only girl he could ever love. The thought of her would always take his breath. The sight of her would wet his palms.

"I'm an idiot," he said.

"Yes. I know. Is there some reason you don't go up there and speak to her?"

Shiller ignored the question and asked his own. "You hurting?"

"No. I am almost healed. That boy Rodney was a

good shot. He missed every major organ and artery in my right side. I go back to work in a month."

Shiller lowered the binoculars. "How you doing with Nina?"

Hadeesh's face blushed. "She is a remarkable girl."

Shiller grinned. "Don't let her give you a blow job. She's so good at it you'll never want to do it with her any other way." He poked Hadeesh's shoulder. "I knew she would be right for you. No need to thank me."

Hadeesh beamed. "Since the day you brought her to my hospital bed, Detective, I have wanted for nothing. Did you know that she has no gag reflex?"

Shiller burst out laughter. Hadeesh reached for a handshake, which Shiller returned.

He watched Allison a few moments more. She was on her back in the grass, the children splayed around her like puppies. And he knew what they were doing.

Hadeesh said it for him, "They are talking about what shapes the clouds have. That cloud is an alligator. This one is a bunny rabbit . . ."

He was right, and Shiller knew it.

"I thought I had lost everything," he said solemnly to Hadeesh. "I thought I would never feel anything again. And here this gorgeous soft-spoken babe floats into my vision like one of those damn clouds. At my age. Finding out your insides aren't dead. I guess if clouds can look like bunnies, then this woman who's a stranger to me can look like love. You know, pal?"

Hadeesh said gently. "Yes, Detective. I know. Second chances are quite wonderful."

Allison sat up, leaves in her hair. The little one fell onto her for a hug. It was an embrace that Shiller could feel, as if his own arms were around them all.

"She's beautiful, Hadeesh."

"Mrs. Robbins? Oh, indeed she is, sir."

"No." Shiller was hushed. "No. That little girl. Look at her. Look at that boy and that pretty girl with the braid."

They all stood and dusted themselves off to head into the house. To build a fire and mess with their Christmas presents and eat leftovers. To be together, and to share love.

"She asked me why I did it, Hadeesh, and I didn't have an answer, only I think I always knew."

"Yes, sir." He said it with great respect. "You did it for the reason so many police officers do our jobs. You did it for the children."

They drove away. Hadeesh had dinner plans, and Shiller had an empty farmhouse to light up and try to make warm. But first he had two sons to call and say, "I love you."

38

Dewey Watson squinted, and the wrinkles around his eyes deepened to crevices. In fifteen seconds, after a wave of Dewey's hand in the air, Monty Jones standing before him could live as a friend or be dead, shot by the two gigantic thugs flanking him in Watson's office.

Watson would either wave his hand toward Monty, silently signaling to frisk Monty and finding the body wire he was wearing. Or he would wave Monty to the chair at his desk, gesturing that the mistrust was finished and Monty was in. Monty had drawn a breath, hoping Old Man Dewey didn't see the telltale throbs of Monty's crashing heart in his neck. Monty had gambled, had whispered to Shiller in the darkness of a police interrogation room, "They've patted me down at all three of our meetings. This time they won't. Old Man Dewey knows that if he keeps shaking me down, then he looks stupid for working with a man he don't trust."

Shiller and he had stared at each other like men about to arm wrestle, a steely kind of exchange of fear and courage. They had not spoken as Monty removed his shirt and Shiller began taping the wires that snaked to the recorder under Monty's belt.

Dressed again, standing with Shiller before a two-way mirror, examining his image, Monty had intoned, "This is the last time, right? Then I bring you the tape and give Alvie my deposition, right? Then I'm out of the country, okay?"

Shiller had leaned casually on a table, arms folded, Stetson cranked back. "You're sweating, Mojo. They'll smell it, sense the wire. Just relax. I'll be right outside in the van. If you're queered I'll bust in."

They were alone in the dimness, but speaking conspiratorially. "You can't get in before they pop me in the head."

"Then take the damn thing off and let Alvie go totally on your deposition. He knows now from you where all the evidence is, the books, the warehouses, the numbers—that'll all be seized before the arrest warrants hit the streets."

"No." Monty was resolute. "I want the mother-fucking Watsons on tape. I want them to draw hundred-and-ten-year sentences so I can know where the bastards are every day for the rest of my life. Shit. I am sweating. Shit!"

Shiller had lit a cigarette, and his exhale fogged the

tiny cubicle in a rancid silver cloud. He had taken off his Stetson, combed his fingers through his thick hair, let out a great sigh. "It's time, Jones. Don't hug anybody, and don't ask any of 'em to slow dance with you."

They walked, their footfalls in tandem and somber on the granite floor of the deserted basement. Monty felt every sound, the way a convict must as they trudge him to the electric chair, when he knows that these moments are his last and suddenly every earthly banality glitters and glows with regretful excitement.

He felt the metallic swiping of Shiller's trench coat, the low buzz of exposed lightbulbs over their heads, the scratchy crackle of a uniformed cop's hip radio in a distant room, the film of smoke that trailed Shiller's cigarette clamped in his teeth. A door slammed and echoed. The elevator pinged and sounded civilized, calling to his mind the expensive hotels he had stayed in when he was on top, when he was The Man.

Shiller disobediently stubbed the cigarette out on the elevator's tile floor. "You sure they aren't watching you?"

"They were until today. That's why I came here, because they're off of me. Hey, Shiller, you ever use the word 'nigger'?"

Shiller grinned. Cold light streamed through a glass door that led outside, into the flaky snow, into what could be Monty's last winter morning alive.

"Shit, Jones, this ain't LA." His grin was cocky.

" 'Cause see, Shiller, maybe you're out there in that van listening, and maybe you don't care if another 'nigger' gets taken out."

They had been in a deserted cubbyhole, a door that opened only outward to an alley between the PD and the jail.

"Oh," Shiller joked, "like my blow for racism is to sit and listen while they tie you and gag you and stuff you in the trunk and then kinda get around back too late to follow you and . . . that kind of thing? Because I secretly have it in for all black people?" He stared at the smudged glass door as if it were a museum painting and caused him to think and wonder. Then he looked squarely at Monty. "Jones, in twenty years I've never hit anybody who was handcuffed or made a hooker blow me before I hauled her in. Maybe the good thing about me is that I don't hate a particular race or gender or creed: I hate all the bad guys equal, like all good cops should.

"And yes, I guess I have used the word 'nigger.' See how easy it is for a real cop to admit his mistakes? Besides, Jones, I haven't used that word since I grew up and my brain finally got bigger than my cock. I'll bust in if you need me, period."

Freezing air had slapped Monty. Shiller was holding open the door.

"I ain't scared, Shiller."

"Then you ain't human, Jones."

"Did you ever have a moment when you really, truly thought you were going to die, man? And all of a sudden you wish you could go back to just before that moment and change what you did, to fix it so death isn't coming at you?"

Shiller's watery, fatigued eyes had glinted. He did not smile when he said, "Yeah, about a million of those moments, every time I ran into a dark house after guys like you."

"Then why'd you do it, asshole?"

"Oh, didn't you know? People become cops for the big bucks and the beautiful babes. And, of course, for the doughnuts."

And now Dewey Watson was squinting, his decision of whether to frisk his newest boy Monty or not swinging in the air like a hungry vulture as one slowly suffocates in the desert.

The tape was spinning against Monty's hard, rippled belly muscles. A trickle of sweat leaked from his hairline down his left temple, a pearl of death that he could not move to wipe away. The three-piece-suited thug on his left sniffed.

Old Man Watson said, "Sit down, Monty," and let his hand fall in the direction of the wingback chair facing his desk.

In the surveillance van, with its snow-banked windows and its panel of electronic equipment all lighted and grinding, Shiller unclenched his fists at last. He had been ready to call for SWAT and fly inside like a cowboy firing from both barrels in a saloon brawl.

Watson's youngest son, Joey Bob, stepped right up and dunked himself into the prison piss pool. He said to Monty, who could barely suppress a jubilant laugh, "Here's the list."

Monty perused. "I go in and get the money every day for you?"

Joey Bob's waxy red scar ran the length of his face on the right and continued angrily down his neck. It had been a sharp knife years ago. Someone had not expected him to survive. "No. They pay us weekly. If not, you notify me, and I go to their business and remind them how much they really do need our protection. You know?" When he smiled the right side of his mouth drooped under the weight of the scar.

Monty said dryly, "All right," and slipped the papers into his breast pocket. "How did Solomon handle the whores? You want me to do it the same way?"

Dewey had an enviable mane of silver hair and a deep suntan. His front was as a concrete manufacturer. He told Monty plainly, "Wild Child Lopez is our man on the border. He picks girls coming across, gives them Champ Royal's number to call if they want work cleaning or babysitting. He picks them young, you know, kids, because who wants to fuck a twenty-year-old hag?"

They all laughed in a grisly bout of amusement.

"And Royal brings them to me?"

"No. He runs them and brings you the take. You keep the book on that . . . uh . . . get the book for him, Joey Bob . . . and you handle our take. The ones who go sweet on somebody or get greedy go to the movies."

It was a huge risk, but Monty asked blandly. "Yeah. Where?"

Dewey said so nonchalantly that Monty almost whooped for joy. "Rex keeps a lake house at Whitney."

"And pays taxes on it, I'm sure," Monty laughed.

And they all laughed as Dewey's other son, Rex, blushed from where he stood in the background at a small office bar, nursing a nicely scented Scotch.

Dewey continued, all the while fussing with snipping and lighting a Honduran cigar, "You don't handle the snuff-film money. Rex does that."

And then it happened, so fast and so easily that Monty almost barked like a yapping, excited hound dog.

Rex said from behind him, "Did you bring the money for the drugs?"

The giddiness overtook Monty and he had to pulse a beat to regain straight-faced composure. "Yeah, sure, for twelve kilos, right, Rex? And I get half the . . . you know . . . proceeds or I ain't in for selling them."

Dewey growled, "Calm down. Buddy took a third."

"Buddy was a fool. You want me to sell your stuff . . . I'm going to increase your business, so to speak, by about two hundred and fifty motherfucker customers that I bring with me—"

"So we don't lose," Joey Bob pointed out.

"Not by my math—"

"Okay, Jones, okay, half, then," Dewey commanded. "Now everybody get the fuck out. I got a lunch date." Then to Monty, "You know why it'll be good having you do our books, Jones? Because you're a nigger and niggers are best at one thing in the world, aren't they? Multiplying."

They all laughed. Joey Bob like a nervous Peeping Tom. Rex like a silly girl. Dewey until his face was red and his lungs made wet, crusty sounds.

Shiller sat back. It was done. Stellar. Dewey Watson had admitted racketeering, prostitution, murder, and drug trafficking. He had implicated his own sons and two of his top henchmen. They were all done for.

"That," Shiller muttered as he blew out smoke and shivered in the van, "is a wrap, boys and girls."

He watched Monty out the window of the van through a sheet of frosty ice. At the busy corner as cars and pedestrians milled around him, Monty stood erect in the bitter wind. He was a giant who dwarfed the others around him. They were bundled. Monty was upright as a ship's majestic mast. He shifted the brown folder Dewey had given him—names of young girls, how much they made having sex with old men, and, Shiller suspected, a clear trail to how many of them had been murdered for the pleasure of the sickos who wanted to watch it on videos the Watsons sold around the country. Monty lit a cigar, Honduran this time, given him appreciably by his new boss Dewey Watson, and he waited for the Walk signal before he crossed to his car.

Shiller began pulling away slowly from the curb, laughing to himself aloud, "Jesus. The son of a bitch won't even jaywalk anymore."

39

Sitting at Shiller's kitchen table, Monty looked like a man in a Ralph Lauren suit ducking in to use the phone at a diner. The lights were off except for a lame circle of yellow from the bulb over the kitchen sink. Monty blew into the steam from his coffee cup.

He grumbled, "I wish they'd call, damn it."

Shiller sat sprawled in a chair across the table from him. His boots were off and his feet in white socks were propped and crossed on the table. He had his sport coat off, too, and his shoulder holster made a black line across his blue chambray shirt. His blue jeans were crisply pressed and made a crinkling sound when he moved.

He told Monty, "Any minute now. They've had time to get on the ground; they're probably on their way to your new Bahamian palatial beach house, complete with a German shepherd puppy I special-ordered for Rodney. You want something to eat?"

Monty fidgeted. "Naw, man. I looked already in your refrigerator. There's enough moldy shit in there to cure polio."

Shiller lit a cigarette and said quietly, "When I took your mama and Jasmine and Rodney to that FBI plane tonight, Marie said for me to tell you that she loves you, that she'll be all right . . . and she said for me to tell you good-bye."

Monty glanced into the edgy silence. "Meaning what?"

"She didn't elaborate. She wept for a while in the car, before we got to the plane, but when we got there she seemed resolved to something. She hugged me real big and then asked me to give you the message. Tell him I love him, that I'll be all right, and tell him good-bye."

Monty stood. He felt rattled, antsy. Shiller rambled into the bathroom and then to the kitchen for a beer. From the kitchen he called out, "Your girl's a looker. She looks like a magazine model or something."

Monty answered only to quell the silence. "Yeah. With women as pretty as Jazz, you got to decide whether you're going to beat up all the comers or none of them. Long time ago I decided to whip the shit out of every one of them."

Shiller returned. His shirttail was out. He stopped when he saw Monty looking at a picture of Shiller's sons, holding it up to the window so the slants of moonlight could illuminate it.

"These your boys in their baseball uniforms?"

"Yeah."

"They any good?"

"They've got heart."

"Well, you need that or luck." The cast of the moon made Monty half in dark and half-lighted, like the opera's famous phantom. "I wonder," he said, "do people ever stop missing a child who has died?"

Shiller had held the swig a long moment; he swallowed finally. "I'd bring him back to you if I could."

"I should've killed you, Shiller."

"You tried."

They stood there, warped in forced togetherness for the evening. The shadowed half of Monty made the silver moonlit side look like half a man, like a monstrous mutated hologram with one eye, on one leg, having only a single arm. Then it occurred to

Shiller that he had not checked Monty for weapons, that the dark arm could be reaching for a gun.

"You shoot me," he warned, "and you'll miss out on all that great Bahamian fishing."

"You take care of these boys, Shiller. You treat them every day like you might never see them again."

He turned to face Shiller's window. "I see you fixed all the busting up you did last time I was here."

Shiller breathed easier. "I had the time finally. I'm on Christmas break from law school."

Monty chuckled rudely. "You want to be a fucking lawyer."

"It beats working. I'm going to need you to turn around and spread 'em on that wall there. Just one last time."

He saw Monty's jaw and fists tighten, but then submission came. Monty took the frisk stance, and Shiller patted him lightly but completely.

When they were face-to-face again, Monty said derisively, "Do you know that everybody in the whole fucking world, including little kids and poodles, hates lawyers?"

"Yeah, sure," Shiller grinned, "until you need one."

The phone rang. Shiller talked briskly, hung up.

"They're in the Bahamas, safe. You leave tomorrow night at midnight. We go alone to a private airstrip. You can take no bags, no nothing. When you're airborne, the warrants for the Watson Organization hit the streets."

A cloud passed over the moon. The room sank into opaqueness.

"Why do you live this way, Shiller? Why don't you want anything? You got no food in there, no bedspread, no books except those stupid law-school pieces of shit you read. You got no friends, no doodads around here like flower vases or candlesticks, no girl to see you come home. You got no windchimes or patio furniture or ferns hanging around. No dance records or scented soap. Are you Amish?"

"You're giving me a brain cramp, Jones. You be in the PD tunnel tomorrow night at eleven P.M. to meet me. I'm sneaking you home tonight, then tomorrow you go about your business as usual—poisoning people with drugs, busting heads, acting like Shaft. Do everything regular."

Monty was more curious than afraid. "You people are not going to hide me? I don't get a four-star hotel on the county's tab for all my heroics here?"

Shiller snapped at him. "If you drop out of sight, the Watsons will be tipped that something's up. And us 'people' is only me, Alvord and whoever on the force is being paid by Watson to watch for unusual department activity. For you to go underground tonight would definitely be unusual. The Watsons aren't following you, but they know you're still moving around. Keep doing it."

"When will the warrants go out?" Monty asked.

Shiller said ominously, "Just as your plane leaves the ground. As tight as we've kept it, there could be leaks. If it leaks, you're dead."

Monty knew the gloom, and he knew that talking about it wouldn't change the danger. He joked with Shiller. "Man, this macramé on the wall has to be from the late sixties. How about I give you a couple hundred thousand dollars and you buy an ashtray or two and quit dropping your butts down into beer cans everywhere."

"I can't believe I'm getting decorating tips from Super Fly. You know, pretty boy, I live the way I want. Anything you get in life, everything you own, can be just taken away. Someday some woman who says you did something wrong, but she won't say what, she just packs up all your pretty-boy shit and takes it to her new house with her newer, prettier boy. See?"

Monty shrugged. "So you get more pretty-boy shit, man. You don't have to wallow around in squalor because somebody with a bigger dick than you stole your girl."

Shiller hollered, "He doesn't have a bigger dick! He has a bigger brain! He knows how to keep her!"

And Monty hollered back, "You'd have kept her if you wanted her!"

Shiller sat, dejected. "Go home."

Monty put on his cashmere coat and black leather gloves. "Look, Shiller, you've got your boys. You got nothing to mourn about."

"They don't even know me."

Monty quipped, "Yeah, well, that's your own fucking fault. But when they do come here to this refugee encampment, maybe it just doesn't feel like a home to them, you know. Maybe it feels like a gas station bathroom. Cold and not too clean. Put some quilts on those two twin beds where they obviously sleep on their weekends. And buy some damn linen napkins. I saw you tonight eating that soup, wiping your mouth at the table with a sponge from the damn sink. Just because your boys don't live here doesn't mean that they shouldn't wish they did."

Shiller stood and came toward him. Monty asked, "What're you doing?"

At the door, Shiller smirked. "I'm covering you to your car, you dumb shit, so if somebody tries to take you out, they have to shoot me first. Got it? Stay behind me."

"You're a hero, Shiller. You going out there in your socks?"

"Yeah. They'll put it on my tombstone. 'He died with his socks on and he saved Super Fly.' Come on."

Monty stopped at the last step. "So what it is, Shiller, is that you'd rather fuck a bunch of nobodies than be with a somebody you love who might leave you after all."

Shiller pushed him. "What it is is none of your business. Give me the keys. I have to start your car for you. If it explodes, you can have my prized macramé."

It didn't explode. Nobody had rigged it while they

were inside. Monty said insolently as he slid behind the driver's seat, "If I'm not there tomorrow night, then I'm dead."

Shiller snapped, "Maybe in your will, you'll leave me all your doodads. Try not to get killed."

For good measure, Monty said, "Yes, dear," and then sped off down Shiller's winding driveway.

40

The problem with shopping, Shiller posed to himself the next morning as he shaved shirtless in a steamy bathroom mirror, is that you have to be looking for something that you want. Otherwise, like he did at the grocery store, you were just buying the same stuff you always bought, which is a constant reminder that you really don't want anything.

He couldn't remember the last time he had purchased anything that reached out and tugged at his want-to. He bought frozen pizza because he knew how to cook it, ice cream because his boys ate it when they visited, and toilet paper because he was human. He bought beer because it put him to sleep at night, new underwear because his mother had taught him to keep them fresh, and movie tickets because that's where girls always wanted to go after they heaved themselves into his truck while popping their chewing gum.

It was a sunny, frigidly repellant Saturday morning, New Year's Eve. The coffee water boiled while he showered. Willie Nelson sang "Blue Eyes Crying in the Rain" while he shaved. With coffee mug in hand and fifteen-year-old pink button-down on with his timeless black corduroys, he went to the phone, a rotary dial relic that he had brought with him since his first apartment after college.

Alvord Samuelson's wife Kitty answered on the third ring.

Shiller asked to speak with her husband.

Her voice was smoky, sexy. "Shiller, it's his day off, New Year's Eve."

"Hey, Sapphire, criminals don't take days off. Neither do cops or prosecutors."

"You've been reading too many Dick Tracy comic books."

He grinned. "When are you going to invite me back for more barbecued steaks?"

"Yeah, Shiller, I like having you over for dinner. It saves me having to bother putting out utensils. Hold on. I'll go get your hero."

Alvord's regal baritone took over. "I listened to the tapes. We got those Watson suckers, didn't we?"

Shiller sopped his hair with a towel. "Monty meets the FBI plane at midnight."

He could visualize Alvord turning away from where Kitty stood washing dishes or making the bed, lowering his voice. "I've told the plane just to slow down to thirty miles an hour on the runway, don't even stop. I mean, I don't want any loitering out there. Door opens, he's inside, they're airborne. Six A.M. tomorrow our warrants hit."

Shiller rolled up his sleeves, zipped his corduroys. "Ol' Monty made it look easy, didn't he?"

Alvord said it with a smile on his inflection. "Yeah,

it isn't like one of those Grisham novels, is it? Months of secret surveillance, wire tapping, stealing secret files, running through train stations, and jumping out windows onto trucks. We're doing something wrong out here."

"I like those books, though, where the bad guys are real sophisticated and powerful, and there's all those car chases and you get your house bugged. Don't you wish it was like that, Alvord, and you could unravel a bunch of crooked judges who'd been on the take from the Mafia for twenty years, and in the meantime the FBI puts five million in your bank account?"

Alvord laughed loudly. "Sure. Problem is, down here in the trenches, for five bucks and free beer at cocktail hour a real judge would blab about his criminal status just to impress his hired date for the evening."

"Well, when I'm a lawyer, you and me will uncover some great juicy conspiracy and write a book about it."

"Shoot, man, we don't have any criminals with the class to conspire. In real life the same ego that makes them think they can beat the law makes them bold and stupid enough to brag about who they are," Alvord said sourly.

"Alvie, they trusted him. He was their peer. And he brought hundreds of drug customers, plenty of businesses for laundering money, and, of course, his considerable cash flow, and all they had to do was tell him how it worked."

He could hear that Alvord had just gotten a kiss on the cheek in the background as he said to Shiller, "Those stupid, greedy, arrogant bastards. All Monty had to do was ask. That's how it is in real life. Lucky for us."

Shiller gazed out at the angled refractions of morning sun as winter storm clouds burrowed on the horizon. He said, "Lucky for Monty," and then he left Alvord to the pursuit of more warm kisses from his gorgeous wife.

41

There was one more score that Monty needed to settle before his exile, one enemy left to settle with. Russell Goff.

That was Monty's first idea on the morning he was to leave. As soon as he thought it, he thought better of it. If some dirty cop who was on the take from Watson had leaked the coming warrants and indictments, then the mere turn of his ignition key would splinter Monty into a million very dead pieces, or a sniper would shatter his skull with a rifle from half a block away as soon as he stepped outside.

By noontime as he sat counting stacks of hundred dollar bills he had withdrawn from a bank account, intending to tape them to himself under his clothes—he knew the feds were providing all expenses in the Bahamas, but twenty-five thousand dollars in spare change couldn't hurt until he finished testifying and got back into his bank accounts—by the time the money covered him like a green chest and belly mold, he had rationalized that he probably could get away with it. If the Watsons knew anything, they'd have come for him already.

Surely. He muttered it to himself as he lazed on his king-size elegant bedspread. In twelve hours he'd be rocking and bumping across the Gulf of Mexico, blasting toward the open sea.

He turned the wet cigar end in his mouth the way a safecracker spins the lock. Left, then right. Smoke billowed. Monty didn't blink.

He was watching a movie in his head, though it may have appeared that he was focused on the white fireflies of scarce snow twirling upward outside the cut-glass windows that slanted to the deserted lake. He wasn't. He saw inward.

Goff. A punk rapist and murderer who got twenty years and did eight. On one day of those eight Goff stepped up behind Monty in the prison yard and shanked Monty in the right side. He'd been aiming for Monty's kidney, but missed. The fight had been vicious. Monty bent Goff's knife arm so far back it snapped like a glass tube, and Goff had head-butted Monty hard enough to crack Monty's skull between his brows.

It was an Aryan attack, done by a prison white supremacist to a black, any black; just so happened Monty was bent under the basketball hoop catching his breath.

He remembered the breathtaking bomb of pain, numbed only by the rage that welled in him when he turned and saw Goff smiling, raising his arm to drive the shank in again.

He twirled the cigar, watched the listless snow caught in updrafts. The cigar rolled left, then right. Mental locks were tumbling.

It was four o'clock in the afternoon. Seven hours until he met Shiller. It would take thirty minutes to find Goff and less than a few seconds to shoot him in the face.

By 4:15 the thought of killing Goff had become the plan of a man who reasoned that by the time anybody found Goff's body, he would be in another country under police protection. He drove his car out of the driveway and skidded on a patch of ice that had refrozen in the linear afternoon shadow of the steeple of the small church at the end of his street.

The redheaded pit-faced bartender at a redneck bar called The Rig sniffed a fifty and told the gargantuan black man (whose fancy clothes smacked of an undercover cop's expense account limit) that Goff hauled trash and recycling paper out of the local newspaper building.

"He pushes this big gray bin on wheels all through the building all day, makes a big pile down on the loading dock, and then throws it all into a truck that somebody drives away the next day."

Monty asked, "How come you got such a fucking clear job description?"

Shaw shrugged, pulled at a scab in one of his pocks. "'Cause he talks about how someday he might put a dead body in the empty truck and have it filled up next day with papers. It all gets dumped into this thing that shreds it like real fine, and Goff thinks nobody would never find even a piece of the body. It's girls, he means. He has a taste for killing girls. You know. Reduce, reuse, recycle, but first rape." He smiled and his teeth were furry yellow and brown barnacles.

The newspaper's loading dock was a covered street-level area on a corner now deserted of afternoon workers and traffic. It had one wide entrance and a wide exit through which the wind howled as Monty skulked in the shadows. Towering above the dock area were the newspaper offices which now percolated with reporters and editors fevered by deadlines to get the next day's edition onto the streets by two A.M. But the docks were cavernous and shadowy, so deep and dark that Monty's footsteps echoed. When the big crate elevator settled and the grates lifted, the hull of a gray battleship rolled out, spilling newspapers like fish squirting away scared. Goff pushed it easily. He was strong, a prison boxer of mild acclaim for his speed and his biker tattoos. He wore a blue jumpsuit with a black turtleneck and some kind of military boots. Monty's right side cramped at the sight of him.

Goff sat down to smoke. He lit the match, tossed it, and reached to swat at the bug behind his ear. The bug had a familiar coldness to it and the shape of a gun barrel.

As they drove, Monty made Goff huddle on the front-seat floorboard. The wiry little guy fit just fine and couldn't jump out before Monty could shoot him in the brain. He was dismayed that Goff was crying, snorting snot, and shaking all over.

"Man, it wasn't me. They made me shank you, the Aryans did. I ain't no nigger hater." Sob. Sob. Monty rolled the steering wheel with his thumb, smiled at a cute black girl with a Buster Brown cut and a cigarette holder in the car next to his at the traffic light.

Goff whimpered. "They said if I shanked you they'd protect me from those other niggers, not from you, because you didn't give nobody no trouble, but from the others. They said if I didn't shank you, they'd drown'd me in the toilet but that about twenty of them would wife me first. . . ."

He deteriorated into spasms of sobs. Monty puffed, knocked a chunk of ash out the window. The downtown theater district was awash in strings of lights and people. They gyrated between the movies, the jazz club, the restaurants, the java houses. Fashionable people. People from safe neighborhoods.

"Mojo, listen to me." He was heaving now. "I got me a job. I got a clean room at the mission. I got two pairs of shoes, even. Mojo, Jesus . . ."

The panic had struck him like a karate chop to the heart. He wasn't ready to die. He wasn't ready to die.

Mojo's voice must have sounded like Satan. "So now you know, hot rod, how those girls feel while you choke the life out of them, when they know they won't see their mamas or babies anymore, while they choke on your mushy little cock and look at your skeleton-skin face. Now you know."

Goff cried like a baby abandoned alone in a crib.

"How many of 'em you done, Goff? Five? Six? People's daughters and sisters. Fuck you. You got to kill helpless girls or shank brothers with their backs to you to get any jollies in life. You're a cockroach. I'm . . ." He screamed it, ". . . RAID!"

They were in an alley, a furrow of trash and foul smells and slimy rivulets of water. Goff, his jumpsuit wet now to show the concave of his chest, was sweating even though when they talked their hot words were pillows of white air.

"Mojo, shit, I'm getting it back, I tell you. I'm getting a life. I got shoes. I can read now. Please. Goddamn. Please."

"I hear you got a plan to take out more women, got it all worked out. Recycle, reduce, reuse. But first rape."

A splinter of pain went through Goff's thin-skinned, bony face. "Shit. It's talk. It's fucking bull-shit talk."

Monty growled, "You cured of raping helpless girls and shanking black men with their backs to you? You cured, is that what you're telling me? I don't think you're cured at all. I think you're still a chickenshit squirrel who can't take anybody on face-to-face. That's why you're dangerous, because you don't give the other guy an even chance."

Monty yanked him, turned him, slammed his face into the ice cube of bricks. He heard a rib break.

Goff went hysterical. Hyena sounds.

"NOPLEASENOPLEASE! . . . GODNOPLEASE!"

Monty relaxed his gloved grip, let out a slow breath. Goff felt the tension ease.

It was the last thing he ever felt. The last thing he heard was, "Hey, Goff, rape this."

Monty backed up to avoid any spatters. Goff turned, crying, and put his hands across his face as if the sun were burning his eyes.

Monty shot him. The first bullet exploded through Goff's front teeth and blew out the back of his head like bloody graffiti on the brick wall. The second one Monty fired through Goff's groin, blasting the rapist's favorite weapon to a string of shredded, bloody flesh.

Monty checked himself. No backwash of grime. Another clean kill. The last one. He drove toward his car wash where the floor mats would be incinerated and the interior of the car would be wiped clean.

But this time, instead of looking for Goff's killer, the cops would be protecting him. Monty laughed, turned up Smokey Robinson, and crunched a Tic Tac.

42

At a half hour before midnight the private airstrip was deserted and steeped in a growing fog. The stars were phosphorescent pinholes overhead. Shiller and Monty stood at the end of the grassy runway, fog churning as if they were ankle deep in a smoky river.

They waited for the small FBI plane to appear as if one of the white pinholes had been hurled toward them.

Monty winced in anguish as Shiller held a spotlight on the papers they held. "Jesus, Shiller, my new name is Larry McShane? Man, there ain't any brothers named Larry, and do I look Irish to you? Bonehead feds. I ain't going to be no Larry McShane."

Shiller lifted his trench-coat collar against the grating breeze. "There are lots of black guys named Larry," he said, and then couldn't think of one.

Monty squawked. "See how dumb you are? Black guys are named Lawrence. And we got no Terrys either; we've got Terrences. There's Williams, no Bills. And I assure you there isn't a black McShane anywhere on this planet."

"There is now. You. Shit, I'm cold." He smoked nervously. Monty pressed the papers into his overcoat breast pocket as Shiller snarled at him, "I guess in the FBI computer there wasn't a dead guy with a clean social security number for you named Mohammed Abu Abdallah. Shucks, Larry."

"We got only James, no Jimmy, except J. J. Walker, but that's his name, not his cute little white calling card given to him by the white woman his mama cleaned for one day and it stuck. We got Robert, no Robbies; Daniel, not Danny—"

Shiller, up for the sobriquet races, challenged. "How about Bobby Brown and Danny Glover? Huh? See there?"

Monty blew white breaths of disgust. "Stage names. They don't count. Swishy artiste types. I'm talking about real men and outlaws and brothers of the crusade."

"Shut up or I'll shoot you and say you ran."

"You can't shoot me. You ain't a cop anymore."

Shiller searched the sheath of sky now being muddied by a flimsy tapestry of clouds. Behind them the wind rustled a grove of oaks that made a creaking sound, a boat rocking on cold, deep water. He reached into his coat and slipped the strap off his .44 without letting Monty see him do it.

"Okay, Larry, how about Tony Dorsett, Chuck Berry?"

"Ten to one their mamas call them Anthony and Charles. Notice if you will that basketball's greatest are respectfully not called Mike Jordan or Pat Ewing."

Shiller frowned. "Stop whining." He rocked back and forth on his heels, waiting for the moment, listening to the rustling of the scratchy branches behind them. It was too dark for shadows. They were bathed in nothingness.

He planted his feet, then turned to Monty and hit him squarely in the gut, a heave that would've lifted a punching bag into the air. When Monty slammed forward, Shiller planted a slam upward under his chin that sent Monty's feet off the ground. He landed on his back on the dusty turf with the sound of a wrestler crushing the mat.

For a moment, white puffs shot up like a chugging

steam engine as Monty grunted and panted for air. He rolled to his side and screamed through gritted teeth, "What the hell—"

Shiller's boots were inches from Monty's face. "That was for Goff. Nobody cares about Goff, of course; he's not enough of a kill to keep you here and jeopardize the Watson indictments. You son of a bitch." He took out his .44, cocked it, and kept it pointed at Monty's head as Monty groaned and began to taste the rusty warmth of blood from his split lip.

Monty grunted, "How'd you . . ."

Shiller straightened his gun arm so the barrel was only a foot from Monty's face. "Idiot. I put a bug in your car right after the deal was made with Alvord. No wonder you're not a cop. You're too damned stupid to pour piss out of your boot."

He uncocked the gun. Put it back in the holster. Turned his back on Monty. Monty lumbered to his feet holding a handkerchief splotched with blood to his lips. He hunched up his shoulders and turned a moment to watch the wind stir the treetops.

"You could've killed me with that kind of punch."

"I ain't that lucky." Shiller fired up a smoke.

"You could've just left town, Monty. Or maybe I could've just left town or any other normal Joe Blow could have and would have. But not you. You're a killer, a murderer. We can dress you up and take you out like some big fucking heroic star witness, and you're still just a barbarian whose first choice and favorite pastime is killing people. I hate your guts."

Monty said angrily, "You know, Shiller, I wasn't any chickenshit thug like you thought. I didn't drive by people's houses and shoot at rooms full of little innocent kids. I didn't jump couples in their driveways and kill them for the forty-five dollars they had in their wallets. I didn't drag convenience-store clerks from behind the counter and shoot them for a hundred bucks and some cigarettes. I didn't haul girls out of their cars at the mall and rape and strangle them."

He had the tone suddenly of a black evangelist, rabid and rife with conviction. "These little punk gang members and rapists like Goff, they don't give anything back to anybody. They just take. If I made two hundred thousand dollars selling dope, I did stuff with it. I gave big pieces of it to people who came to me and asked, who needed it bad to pay doctors and dentists. If I made half a million doing an arson job on warehouses that didn't warehouse nothing anymore but junkies, I used some of it to rebuild stores and fix up churches in my neighborhood. When I found out some dumb goddamned gang punk was forcing an old gas station owner or dry cleaners owner on my street to pay for protection from the gang, I went in and took the bastards for a ride and didn't bring them home. When my neighbors couldn't get justice from the fucking lame police, from you, I went and got justice for them. Rape my neighbor's little daughter? Fuck the court; let Monty be the judge and the executioner. Save the taxpayers the money.

"I wasn't what you thought, Shiller. I wasn't a coward. I gave back whenever I took. That's the code. That's what's missing today from these little shit-ass savages—respect for the innocent. Anybody can by accident shoot a little kid on a street corner while they hide behind a car door. But a real man, a real brother, faces down the motherfucker who has it coming, and he makes it right and nobody gets trouble who doesn't have it coming."

Shiller had been smoking calmly, half understanding what Monty said and half fuming at the arrogance of it. He said sarcastically, "You're breaking my heart, you know that? The Renaissance Gangster Monty Jones. 'The Black Al Capone Wears Robin Hood's Tights.' That's how they'll bill your act." He chuckled unkindly. "You know what makes those little brothers of yours tick today? Your dope. Meth, coke, horse. They buy it from you and load up on it and then they shoot little kids asleep on living-room couches. It isn't like you rebuilt churches and stores with money you got witnessing door to door with a Bible in your hand. You sold drugs. And the people you sold it to lost all their morals and sanity, and quickest of all with that rushing buzz your drugs put into their heads, they lost their respect for the innocent. You greased the gears of their brains, Jones, so please, please don't tell me that what you did had any reverence or was any form of justice."

Monty shouted, "It isn't my form of justice the people out there don't trust anymore, Shiller, it's yours!"

"Well, Jones, it's like they say. The American justice system is the worst one in the whole world until you look at all the other countries!"

Something cracked in the trees behind them. Monty shivered. Shiller took out the .44 and stood very still. The wind chafed on the oaks. He turned and saw in the flat board of night sky a plane. Green light on the right, red light on the left wing. It was coming toward them. He heard it when Monty did, puttering like a lawn mower as its propellors clipped the silence.

It was descending, then skittered onto the dirt airstrip behind them, propellors coughing, lights out.

Monty walked erect, shoulders back, head up, as the FBI agent popped the hatch of a door and began unfolding a ladder of stairs. Shiller did not follow, but stood back. With about ten feet between them Monty turned to say something, another barb yet to be thrown. But a shot rang out from the oak grove and Monty's chest exploded. Shiller heard the FBI guys bark, "Shit!" One of them leaped to the dirt and began firing into the forest blindly.

Shiller leaned over Monty. The blood gushing from Monty's chest wound was pink foam, thick with air from his lungs. He had no more than a minute to live. The gunfire going on beyond him was becoming slow motion, distant symbol clashes.

"I got to go after them, Monty. Some dirty cop must have told Watson. But you got him. You've left plenty behind you to do the job. You got them all."

Monty, from some fleeting blip of strength, clinched his teeth and whispered, "I got it, didn't I, tonight? I got what the jury would've given me anyway."

The foaming ceased. Shiller's hands were drenched in blood as he took up his gun and followed the airplane's floodlight into the abyss of tangled trees and deadly darkness.

43

In the bleak light of the next morning's inevitability, Shiller went for the only kind of therapy he truly trusted. No antidepressants or cathartic psycho-sessions. Along a horizon rimmed with thick, cascading clouds, he rode his favorite horse like the proverbial bat shot out of hell.

Finally he dismounted. He felt breathless, enervated in the blustery cold morning wind. The ride had been more than a release; it had been plain damned fun. His dusty riding boots hit the frozen ground, and he patted the snorting palomino. Her wild eyes showed that she had enjoyed the romp as much as he had. She stomped, gushed hot snorts that turned to white tufts in the air. With the bit out of her mouth she could take water from the trough, and so could Shiller. He scooped his mashed, trampled old felt cowboy hat into the water trough and guzzled from it beside his thirsty horse.

Allie Cat the horse nuzzled him. He laughed greatly. "Ready again already? Shit. You're too much woman for me, baby."

The pasture gate creaked. Allie Cat galloped to the bale of hay where her buddies malingered, probably to tell them all about Mike Shiller's prowess whenever he climbed on her back. How he could duck the dangling limbs like a pro, how when she jumped the river that ran along his property line he lifted just right to be up off his butt when she slammed down on her feet, how he was a hell of an ace bush pilot, an airborne acrobat atop her massive form and flaming speed.

He sat on his top wooden step, peeled off his long duster, and sat in shirtsleeves, still sweating. The headline in the newspaper he opened was too familiar and depressing: Monty's picture beside a grainy photo of Dewey Watson handcuffed beside a cowboy-hatted cop who was his scowling, muscular escort. Joey Bob and Rex were blurry images behind Dewey, their hands locked just as tightly and their faces just as cinched.

But Shiller closed it, didn't read it. He wanted to be baptized more by the sun and the air so crisp it almost crackled when he lay down in it. He drifted, sunbathing his face through a blanket of chilled breezes. His flannel shirt felt warm. His faded, ratty old jeans were creased in all the places a cowboy might want to bend.

The phone rang. He growled and swaggered inside to get it.

"Hello."

A chirpy, small-town twang hit him. "Mike, it's Trish."

"I guess after all these years I'd know that." He rubbed his eyes; his fingers smelled woody like rope and pungent like the hay he had hauled that morning at dawn.

No greeting from her. "Did little Mike leave his new baseball cleats at your house when he was with you last weekend?"

"Yeah. I already put them on your back porch. Tell him they're out there." In other words, ungrateful wench, I did it for him, not you.

"Good. Thanks."

"Trish?"

She made him feel as if his life was a bus ride and he carried nothing but an old leather suitcase, a vagabond on the curb watching fancy cars roll by while he chewed Red Man tobacco and itched bad in his crotch. She made him feel as if he had worn out before his time.

She asked with palpable diffidence, "What is it?"

He sat on the arm of the recliner. "Why did you leave me?"

A panicked twitter from her. "Oh, God, Mike, not again, not now. My house is a wreck and the clothes dryer is broken—"

He tried to sound soothing. "No, this isn't an emotional thing. I want a clinical perception of what happened. Was it my job or did I drink too much or was I ever mean to you—"

This was a conversation about fractures, so it could only be a fractured conversation. "No, Mike, Lord no, it was none of those things, but—"

"Then, that day I came home and your stuff was all packed, what was on your mind exactly?"

He could feel that she went from stiffened resistance to watery dread. He could see her fiddling with the curly phone wire. "I just thought, you know, Mike, I just thought that I could feel life passing me by when I was with you, I don't know."

He was neither angry nor sad. For the first time in

his life he was looking at his diseased organ through the safety of the formaldehyde jar where it had been stored after it was removed. He could not forget the pain of the disease or the agony of the operation, but now he knew he might live.

He pushed slightly. "Yes, you do know."

She, on the defensive: "Were you happy?"

He, in honesty: "No, but I loved you."

"Well, I wasn't happy. And I didn't love you."

"Ever?"

She gulped. "It was like I was so proud to have stayed married for the first twenty years. But I knew I wouldn't be proud if I stayed for another twenty. It was over. The right thing to do was to let it go."

His palms were strangely moist and his throat painfully dry. "So," he hesitated, "so if I were to go on now and love someone else, really love her and take care of her, be devoted to her, take her to bed, and make her mine—if I were to go and do that now, I wouldn't be cheating on you, would I?"

"No, Mike. You're cheating yourself if you don't."

As if he had extended his hand for a shake he told her, "You were a good mother to our boys. I should've thanked you for that."

She said without a waver of emotion, "You were a good cop. I should've gotten out of the way and let you be a great one. See you, Mike."

"See you, Trish."

He took a shower and sang while he lathered himself. The instinct while he dressed to reach for his gun and his badge was moot, and he had to laugh aloud at himself.

From a big shopping bag tossed on the kitchen table he took some stuff. Four flowered placemats and napkins coiled in wooden napkin holders. Two ornate brass candleholders fitted with bright white tapered candles. A cookie jar. It took him a long time to decide where to put the cookie jar. Kitchen cabinet? Living room by the TV trays? Breakfast table? And an ashtray. A crystal one. The potpourri thing gave him the most grief. He finally set it on the nightstand by his bed with the new spread.

He put on his Stetson and his new bomber jacket, smoothed his moustache, slid his sunglasses into place. As he passed to his truck, Allie Cat nodded over the fence. Shiller nodded back at her. An afternoon storm was driving in.

44

Allison took a long walk. She looked as jumbled as she felt, faded jeans and scuffed boots with a full-length sable, her hair piled loosely and elegantly but her face unadorned and clean, her jewelry priceless and the country road before her clumpy and cracked under snow patches.

She was crying, kicking loose rocks, and ignoring the flat fossils of horse manure beneath her boots as she trudged.

The mixture of anger and profound sadness had no other outlet but sobbing. She couldn't stop and didn't try. The sky floated over her like a boiling gray river as the clouds raced southward in a mass.

"Goddamn it, Marshall. We had it all. We had IT

ALL, do you see that?" She looked back at the hill on the chalky horizon where the giant white colonial mansion loomed like Tara. "Look at our beautiful kids. Our dream house."

She covered her face in agony at the sight of it. Through her fingers where she watched, and where hot tears squirted she could imagine the prison bars between the children and her. She cried louder, openly, and she could feel a huge threatening drumbeat closing in on her. "Oh, my God, Marshall, I didn't mean to kill you! But you wouldn't stop. You wouldn't stop. It was over, the marriage, but you couldn't be decent and fair. No. Not you. You monster. You wolf. Oh, God, you hit me in the face." She disintegrated to the cold ground.

"I wanted to leave; you said you'd kill me. I wanted a divorce; you said you'd kill me. I wanted at least the debauched happiness of separate lovers; you said you'd kill me."

She searched the churning sky. Her eyes were wet and weary. She screamed. "You had no reason to hate me!"

She stood, woozy from grief and hunger and fatigue, and she walked more. The visions of the beatings assailed her memory. Each cloud that joined the one before it overhead carried a gruesome scene for her to watch again. A cascade of horror. His wretched face jammed hotly into hers, screaming through gritted teeth that if she left him he would destroy her. His cold hands clenching her wrists and slinging her into walls while she cowered and pleaded.

His frigid, animalistic glares into her eyes as she whimpered while he rammed her with his penis. The bruises. The hot summer night she spent locked in a garage storage closet and he would not let her out. The crushing intimidation and humiliation, the threats.

You walk out on me, Allison, and I swear to God you'll never see these children again . . . I swear you'll be penniless . . . I swear I'll put you in a mental hospital for life . . . I swear I'll kill you . . . You walk out on me, Allison, I will destroy you and everything you ever hope for, because nobody, nobody walks out on me! Then he had lifted her over his head and thrown her into a huge wall of mirrors.

She screamed now as she had back then, covered her face, and cowered under the cloudy cascade of gore in the sky, the visions.

"No! No more, Marshall! Stop it! I'm . . . leaving you!"

She shook her fists at the clouds and began to walk with a terrible determination toward the mansion on the hill, grumbling through her tears.

"It's a home now, goddamn you, Marshall. It's not a prison anymore. It's my beautiful children's beautiful life. I'm sorry I killed you. But I'm not sorry you died."

She drove wildly, parked outside the courthouse where the district attorney's office was, and took the wide ramp of stone steps two at a time. On a Saturday the building was a deserted tomb, but she knew that Alvord Samuelson would be in his office. They were social acquaintances; he had worked for Marshall for years and had been in Allison's home many times for official functions. He would be there. She knew his doggedness about his work.

He looked up glumly when she flung open the door to his small office. He had not yet moved into Marshall's cavernous work suite. Alvord pushed his glasses onto his shaved head and set his jaw firmly. She had come unannounced and disturbed a massive, testy gorilla during his sacred ritual of curing crime.

He registered a spectrum of expressions. Anger at the interruption. Pleased to see his friend Allison, the mourning widow of his benefactor. Confusion that she looked so disheveled and pale and untamed.

Shiller's sweet face and words tangled in her

thoughts. "If you go over my head and confess, it won't end so chummy . . ."

"Alvord—"

"Allison, good heavens, are you all right?"

He stood. The textures of her last moments of freedom leaped out at her perceptions. His bittersweet, calculating black eyes. His stark white teeth. His smooth blue cardigan and black slacks, yes, a black golf pro. She could hear herself panting and feel herself beginning to choke on fear.

"Alvord." She knew she looked like an escaped mental patient in a stolen fur coat. "I—"

Mary's pink face came to her. "Mommy, I can write my name now." Ellen in her shiny basketball clothes, loping on the court, squealing with the other girls, ponytail flapping. Jason flowered in her mind, too, so precious up at the plate with his batting stance still so awkward, but the look from him when she yelled "Go Jason." Oh, that look, it said let me go, Mom, but please always be there.

Mary's tiny toenails. Ellen's first budding strawberries of tiny breasts. Jason's great big grin. Mary's spunk. Ellen's innate kindness. Jason's goofy jokes.

"I killed him, Alvord. I murdered Marshall."

Her old friend's big wide shoulders dropped. His gaze narrowed. "Sit down, Allison. Calm yourself, and tell me everything. When you're through, I'll read you your rights."

She confessed when and how and why. Alvord sat like a Sioux chief, abiding her without question. She did not mention Monty. She knew from the morning's newspaper that he had been slain by an unknown gunman as he waited to leave the country. She did not mention Shiller because she could not dream of causing anything bad to be said about such a good man.

Alvord was quiet a long time after she finished. She could see him at her dinner parties with his sophisticated, lovely wife. He had been smiling like chocolate that might melt in the extravagant candlelight across from her at the elaborate table setting. But now his visage was as bleak and grim as if he were about to drop the switch on the electric chair.

He walked to the windows and looked out on the gritty city streets where his enemies skulked. Killers. Like Allison.

"Allison." The edge in his voice was sharp enough to cut her throat. "Are you under psychiatric care?"

She said weakly, "Yes. For battered spouse syndrome."

Alvord drew in a long breath. "And your doctor has told you that in a murder trial, he would testify that at the time of the murder you were mentally incapacitated by this . . ." He said it with contempt of incredulity. ". . . This syndrome, hasn't he?"

"Yes. How did you know that?"

He turned at her coldly, an enraged warrior. "I've cross-examined a few hundred defense team psychiatrists in my days. I know their ability to defuse the killer's culpability. Where is the syringe?"

"Burned."

Alvord stood right at her knees. "And you have proof that Marshall had hired someone to kill you."

"Detective Shiller does. Alvord, I think I may vomit."

He found a towel in his exercise gym bag on the table and poured water on it from a pitcher on his desk. She put it to her hot, dry face. Then he paced, genius on its thinking feet. He had shown no sympathy, no emotion at all.

"Does Detective Shiller know what you have just told me?"

"No. Of course not."

"It is he who released Marshall's body for cremation? Based on the medical examiner's report of a natural death?"

"I don't know, Alvord. But Marshall was cremated."

He paced more, went behind her, and opened the hallway door, and then slammed it as hard as he could, just to get the feel of some release. "Okay," he said, "okay. I can go to the grand jury—and believe me, no matter how many tenderloins and chocolate mousses you fed me, lady, I would love to put you away—but the grand jury wouldn't indict. There's no evidence and the autopsy doesn't support your confession."

Allison slumped. "Isn't my confession evidence?"

"No. The defense would be too easy. You're under psychiatric care for some dire syndrome and now you're delusional that you killed your husband. Then Shiller would testify about the murder-for-hire plot and it would all get murky: maybe if you did it, it was self-defense."

"I want to get right with God."

He was a sphinx, no glint of sentimentality. "We could have a hearing and commit you, but your shrink would say that he's got you under control. Unless you're suicidal or homicidal we can't court-order hospitalization. Are you thinking of killing yourself or somebody else, Allison?"

She looked up at him plaintively. "No, Alvord. Please. I'm not a killer."

"The hell you're not."

Allison felt her way up from the chair on weak legs. "Have you ever been the victim of a tyrant, Alvord?"

He was unmoved. "I'll tell you what I know. Batterers can victimize anyone. I won't stand here and tell you that I don't care about the times and ways Marshall hurt you." For the first time his stony eyes averted hers. "It wasn't a secret, Allison. We saw. All of us who knew you. We saw it. And we looked the other way because of who he was, because of what he could do to our careers."

"I wasn't a very good wife, Alvord. I was expensive and ungrateful and unfaithful. I just didn't know how tragically all our sins—mine and his—would end up. I thought we were just like everyone else."

"He didn't abuse you because you were stupid. He abused you because he was cruel." He sat down, opened a file, seemed to dismiss her.

"Are you going to arrest me?"

Alvord's glare was one that could slice skin to the bone. "I don't pity you, Allison. If I felt pity for people I'd be a social worker or a preacher. I'm not doing you a favor or saying I'm scared to try and put you away. The ME and Detective Shiller and some slick defense lawyer would kill my case against you. You're free to go."

She sat slowly. Alvord looked up vexed.

"Does that make it right with God?"

He answered, icy and low. "You have atoned. There's no more a human can do."

She stood to leave. "Thank you, Alvord."

He sparked resentment. "No. Don't thank me. This isn't because I'm afraid to put some battered woman on the stand and make her account for murder. This is because on the technicalities alone, prosecuting you would be a waste of time and taxpayers' money. Nobody should ever thank me for being a nice guy. My heart beats about twice a minute, that's how cool I am to all this depravity. Thank me, Allison, for being too smart to play a losing game."

She went out. The clouds were gone. The afternoon was fresh and glittery. All she wanted in the whole world was her children. Soon they would rush at her as she opened the back door. Mary would gush, "Mommy!" Ellen: "Hello, Mother." Jason: "Hey, Mom."

The healing could start at last.

45

The children told Shiller where to find her. At the ornate double front doors after he rang the bell, they crowded each other, staring at him as if he wore a clown suit or was juggling oranges. They were curious, guileless.

The oldest, the blond girl with the gymnast's lithe build and the purple retainer on her teeth, said, "Mom likes to play the piano at the university in the concert hall. By herself. Kind of weird, don't you think?" But she was grinning.

The boy—shy, suspicious, protective—asked, "Are you here to ask if you can work in our yard? 'Cause we already have a yard guy."

Before Shiller could answer, the little one piped in, the curly-haired elf with flashy blue eyes, wearing a pink leotard and a lopsided rhinestone tiara. "You got any chewing gum?"

He did and doled it out. Then a woman behind them, a woman with a mortician frown, waving a chocolate-coated spatula, asked him like a royal palace butler, "Can I help you?"

"I'm looking for Allison. I'm Mike Shiller."

She upped and downed him coldly. He thought of picking his nose until she decided whether he was worthy. The little tiarad ballerina leaned at him, cupped her hand over her roses of lips, and whispered, "That's our nanny, Lallie. She has hair growing out of her ears, but she'll like you if you say how great you think Troy Aikman is."

Lallie with the hairy ears stepped forward. "I'll tell her you called on her. Come on, children, our cakes are ready."

The door closed. The little ballerina peeked at him through the curtains all the way down the long driveway to his car.

He found her just where they said she would be. The doors to the small auditorium in the university's performance hall leaked the sound of her playing the piano. He stepped inside.

She looked peaceful up there alone, plucking those keys. He sat in the back through a long piece, a grand sort of number that was romantic and tragic at the same time. Then he stood and walked the short aisle toward her.

She stopped abruptly, but she didn't seem surprised to see him. She just said, "Hello, Detective," as if she were concentrating on something else.

"No, not detective anymore. You play great. Is that a musical term? Great?"

She demurred. "It is now. Here. Sit down."

He was beside her on the bench. "The sun is shining finally," he reported, as he fidgeted. When he stopped fidgeting he said, "Monty was killed yesterday."

"I know. I saw it in the newspaper. What will happen to his family?"

"They stay in the Bahamas. After all the indictments come down, they still need anonymity and protection as much as Monty did."

Shiller poked a piano key that sounded kindergarten-clumsy at his touch. He looked around the stark auditorium. The chairs slanted upward and became muddled in the shadows at the back. The curtain behind them hid loops of ropes and scores of lights. The piano where they were was set to the side of the stage; she had turned on only one light that made a spot of soft white around them. She wore jeans, a sweater, some kind of soft suede slippers with socks, a braid in her hair. Wisps of hair fell forward onto her cheeks and forehead.

She asked softly, "Do you think Monty died a hero?"

"Monty didn't die. He was killed because he associated with evil people. To me his death seems rightful, just like your husband's. Live by the sword, die by the sword. I guess that's all I remember from the Bible . . . except when Jesus said that after you get married a woman's supposed to leave her mother. I could never get my ex to see that it meant I didn't have to barbecue for her ball-busting mom every weekend."

Under her fingers the piano keys lilted nicely. She smiled. He liked being in her presence.

He admitted it so she wouldn't have to. "I guess you need some time to get over your husband and all."

She took in air as if she had just come up for it after a long time under water. "I'm over him." Her fingers worked the keys like little white, red-tipped wings.

She told him as he sat hat in hand, "When someone does nothing but make you cry while you're with him, you don't tend to weep very much when he's gone. Mike, what's the difference in what Monty did and what I did?"

"You thought you had to do it. Monty enjoyed killing. That's a pretty song. What is it?"

She used both hands. The piece grew fussy and fluffy in places, but her fingers aced it.

"*Pavane for a Dead Princess* . . . which I almost was."

She played. He lapped it up like a big dumb hound dog licking up ice cream left in a bowl by the bed.

"Nice perfume, Allison."

She grinned playfully. "Nice bomber jacket."

He plugged his hat back onto his crown of black curls. "So, how about it? You and me, my house, mad love. Right now. I'll show you all my new doodads. We'll make passionate love, and if it's not good for you, then there's absolutely no charge. That's the kind of decent guy I am, you see."

She turned up her face and laughed. "And then you'll help me with my daughter's slumber party?"

He pressed himself against her on the bench. "Only if right now you'll play some country-western on this washtub." He patted the slick black baby grand irreverently.

"I know one," she said. "You think I don't know a sad country song, but I do."

And there it came, and it filled the room, and Shiller could only shake his head at his great good fortune which was, after all, a long time in coming but well worth the wait.

"Satin sheets to lie on. Satin pillows to cry on. Still I'm not happy, can't you see? Big long Cadillac. Tailor-mades upon my back. Still I want you to set me free . . ."

He sang. She blushed.

"How's my singing voice?"

Over the melody she said loudly, "I thought a cat had his paw stuck in the cabinet door!"

"Oh, that's good! I'm getting better!"